THE ACOLYTE

CLINT WESTGARD

ALSO BY CLINT WESTGARD

Unspeakable Rites: An Alkemya Novella

The Shadow Men:

> *Realm of Shadows*

> *Council of Shadows*

> *Dance of Shadows*

The Sojourners Cycle:

> *The Forgotten*

> *The Apostate*

> The Acolyte

> The Double (forthcoming)

> The Sojourner (forthcoming)

The Maleficio Chronicles

Trials of the Minotaur

The Farthest Reaches: A Collection

Published by Lost Quarter Books
www.lostquarterbooks.com

This edition 2017

The Acolyte by Clint Westgard is licensed under
the Creative Commons Attribution-NonCommercial-
ShareAlike 4.0 International License.

Cover image: © Agsandrew | Dreamstime.com

ISBN: 978-1-928035-36-7

For Mary Shelley

CONTENTS

PROLOGUE

I paced from one end of the kitchen to the other, circling the island at its center. The water surrounding downtown Vancouver glistened in the sunshine, an incredible view that any other day would have left me enraptured. Instead, I could not keep my thoughts from the meeting that awaited me. It was much more than that, of course. Everything rested upon it.

Lasinha strolled into the kitchen from downstairs, where he had been busy with the transfer equipment. He still did not entirely trust me enough to let me know how it all worked. The equipment here, at least what I had seen of it, was far superior to anything I had used before. It was capable of creating multiple channels, multiple transfers, or so Lasinha claimed.

"Nervous?" Lasinha said, as he pulled a can of ginger ale from the fridge. He turned and gave me the same easy smile he always did. Normally it set me at ease, but not today.

"Shouldn't I be?" I said.

Lasinha shrugged as he opened the can. "It will be as it will be. The Grand Regent is a fair and just man. He will recognize that you are a fine vessel for the faith."

"I hope so," I said.

Lasinha smiled and looked out at the incredible view. "It will be over soon enough anyway. And then we can get back to our task. The Church needs us."

I nodded. So he had told me every day since he had come to me again after two years' absence. He had come again into my life and announced himself my savior.

"There will be hard days ahead. For all of us. I will ask more of you than I did before. You will have to make choices that you don't particularly like. Sacrifices."

He was talking about Ana, I realized. She was the reason he had come back, not me. In spite of what he told me. "I will," I said, following his gaze to look down the mountain.

"Good."

I broke away from the seductive vista outside the window to look at Lasinha. "What made you choose me?"

"You chose yourself when you became a Regent. When you joined the true faith."

"No," I said. "This is different now. This Order is... I don't know what it is, but you chose me for a reason. You had dozens of people on this world you could trust." And hundreds more in other universes, for all I knew, willing to do whatever he asked. "But you chose me."

Lasinha appeared to study me, considering what exactly he wanted to tell me. He seemed to realize his usual platitudes would not suffice this time. "I didn't choose you. The Acolyte's Eye did."

I winced at the memory of the floating orb that had been used as part of my Protocols upon Lasinha's return to this world. Its strange rasping breath had been deeply unsettling, as had the sensation of it studying me. Almost as unsettling as the terrible visage of the Acolyte manipulating the Eye. His face seemed broken and disjointed, as though it had been taken apart and put back together at odd angles.

"What do you mean?"

"The Acolytes don't just use it for the Protocols, though that is, of course, its main purpose. It doesn't just reveal your connections to your other selves, to the other universes, which you will begin to understand more fully once you experience the Protocols more. Soon you will be able to do the Protocols on yourself.

"But the Eye isn't just that. It also tells us about your other capabilities. Or at least gives us some sense. I don't pretend to know too much about all this—this is the Acolytes' purview, you understand. They indicated to me that you would be well suited to this particular task. I thought so as well, of course. That's why I came to you, after all. But the Acolytes—with the Eye—they see you for what you are."

And what was that? I wanted to ask, but did not have the courage too.

Lasinha would not say anything more, appearing to contemplate the horizon beyond the room. He finished his ginger ale and glanced at the ornate watch on his wrist. "Come. They'll be coming across soon. Then we can begin."

ONE:

OSAHI'S OUTPOST

1

It is some time after the channel vanishes—the ferry and the tiny room where Morris Loverne has just been overwhelmed gone with it —before I can find it in myself to move again. I feel adrift. Events have conspired again to leave me alone, with no one I can turn to.

Though I can no longer trust Morris—he is a creature of the Seeker and a Society agent, after all—his familiarity, our shared history, was a comfort to me. There was something like trust there, no matter how illusory it might have been. He was a friend once, however false he proved to be. Those are the only kind I have.

How pitiful it all seems now. The illusion of trust. That is all I have—illusions and lies. Even my body is not my own. My mind seems less and less so with each passing day.

Especially now, as I am reeling from the aftereffects of the transfer. My hands are shaking and my legs are trembling. It takes all my effort to keep my feet under me. I have to close my eyes against the sun, painfully vivid against the cloudless blue sky. My head aches. Everything hurts, actually, and, as I take a first tentative step, I collapse onto the rocks.

A swirl of thoughts and colors assaults me. I try to blink them back, to no avail. Somewhere, lurking behind this internal cacophony, lies Aeida, waiting for his chance to take control. He is still so dangerous. No matter that he is not what he was, this is still his body.

A terrible coughing fit assaults me, bruising my lungs. I don't know if I can survive another crossing, not in my current state. It was never like this before. But I was never like this before either. This remade mind, stolen and tamped, was not intended to be sent across the channels. It was supposed to stay lost in a universe known only to the Watchers' Order and myself.

If I am to restore myself to my body, I will have to attempt another crossing, especially now that I am here in another lost universe. It is inevitable. The thought terrifies me. Will entropy work further upon me each time, until there is nothing left of me and Aeida but a twitching mass of limbs?

That thought is almost as disturbing as those I have about what has become of my body. I imagine it, hidden somewhere in the endless universes, suffering under whatever tortures Molijc can devise. He will not win, I tell myself, as I work to steady my breathing and still my body. I will not allow it.

The Seeker has asked me to become his agent for the Society, or whatever faction of the Travelers he serves, and foment revolt within the ranks of the Regents. I have no doubt I will have to account for my failure to do so someday, but hopefully when I next stand before him, it will by my own eyes that meet his terrible ones.

I do not have the luxury of worrying about him. My time is short; I can see that clearly now. It is only a matter of time before Aeida gains command or this constructed mind collapses in on itself and neither of us survives in any form. I must restore myself before that happens. I must destroy Molijc and end the tyranny of his faith before that comes to pass.

My urgency brings me to my feet. There is no time to linger. As I rise, the colors grow brighter and brighter, at their center a pulsating orb that penetrates deep into my brain, lancing it like some doctor removing a tumor. Darkness is ascendant, and I feel my legs go from beneath me again.

I do not know how much time passes before I awake again. Looking up at the sky, I see that the sun has gone across the sky and is on its way to setting. I have no sense of how much time I have before darkness arrives, but a chill has already stolen into the air and I find myself shivering. I will need to find shelter soon and assess my options from there.

My first attempt to stand fails, and I end up on the ground, dizzy and nauseated, but my second succeeds. I look around to reacquaint myself with my surroundings. The waterfall is before me, the thunderous roar of its descent swallowing all other sound. Beside the fall is a cliff of rock that looks, to my untrained eyes, impassable. To my left the river passes, curling like a snake ready to strike. On every other side I am surrounded by forest.

There is no sign of habitation anywhere, no evidence that humans have ever passed this way. I have no sense of where Osahi and his people might be hiding themselves in this apparently vast wilderness and no idea of where to even begin in my search. A thought occurs to me as I ponder this conundrum: what happened to Nicola?

She came with me across the channel, but I did not see her after I came across, and there is no sign of her now. Given the injury she was suffering from, she cannot have gone far, and a quick search of the immediate vicinity reveals her prone form, hidden behind some rocks closer to the waterfall from where we had come through the channel.

I rush to her side, putting a finger to her neck. There is a pulse, though it is faint. I lift up her shirt and see that her wound has bled through the bandages Morris put on her. There is nothing I can do for her in that regard. I do not, I realize, a tremor running my hands, have food or even proper clothing for where we are. The chill in the air will only get worse once the sun sets.

I wonder how close we are to Osahi's refuge. We cannot be far, I reason. Nicola would have been well aware of how precarious her health was and that she was in no condition to begin an arduous journey. Surely she would have set the channels so that we crossed somewhere near our final destination. Yet that does not appear to be the case.

Is that the result of an abundance of caution? Or was she intentionally leading us astray? I cannot trust her—I cannot trust anyone, not entirely. Not even myself.

For a time I am paralyzed by indecision, unsure how to proceed in this new world. Finally I decide I will have to attempt some kind of search, and I leave Nicola where she is, judging her to be safe enough for the moment, and start to reconnoiter the area. The only trace I can find of any human activity is a thin trail leading toward the rock face alongside the waterfall. I follow it along to the base of the cliff, where it comes to an abrupt end. As I look at the cliff, I can make out what might be a path to its summit.

"Motherfucker," I say to myself, the sound of my voice startling me and bringing me from a reverie I was not even aware I was in.

Along the base of the cliff wall I see a place where a small crevice has formed, and I go to investigate it. It is near the waterfall, the mist dampening my face when the wind gusts. The noise is incredible as well, a ceaseless roar. The crevice is large enough to shelter two or three people, and the ground in it is lined with leaves and grass. There is a small depression at its edge where a fire had once burned.

I retrace my steps to where I left Nicola, finding her awake and trying to stand up.

"Don't," I say. "I've found a place we can camp in. I'll carry you there."

She looks as though she will argue with me, her dark eyes fierce, but relents in the end. I pick her up and carry her to the crevice, letting her settle herself there while I go in search of firewood. There is plenty of deadwood nearby, and when I have collected what I think will be enough to last us for the night, I return to the crevice. Nicola is asleep again, a slightly pained expression on her face, though her breathing remains steady.

Aeida knows how to light a fire without matches or tools from his youth in the Pacific Northwest. It is strange that he can remember this, when everything else from that time is vague and unrealized. His mother and father, all of that, has apparently been removed to allow space for me, though a few things seem able to bleed through to now.

How I long to scream at the Acolytes, to stand before them and ask why they obliterated two people's beings. For what purpose? How do they justify this to Molijc and themselves? I cannot fathom it. Whatever their reasons, I will see them answer for what they have done. They are as much to blame as Molijc. He may have held the gun, but they fashioned it and gave it to him to use.

Nicola is awake by the time I get the fire going. She raises herself to a sitting position as I kneel over the flames, feeding branches in until the blaze is glowing healthily.

"I'm impressed," she says, her voice sounding weaker than before.

"Just a trick I picked up over the years," I say. "How's your stomach?"

She shrugs, wincing as she does so.

I nod. "We don't have any food. Is there some nearby that I can scavenge? I didn't see any, but this place has clearly been used for camping before."

"I don't know," she says. "I expect most people go on to the citadel. If they do camp here, they probably have supplies with them."

"The citadel," I say, hesitating over the word. "Osahi is there? It's up this rock?"

After a moment's hesitation, she nods. "Climb the cliff and find the trail heading north. It's less than an hour's walk through the forest."

"You can't make it up the cliff, can you?"

A longer hesitation, before she shakes her head. "No," she says, with great reluctance.

"I'll go up at first light tomorrow," I say. "Osahi should be able to send someone down to get you back up here before the end of the day. Will you be all right?"

"I'll be fine," she says.

I nod, and we both fall silent, staring at the fire as darkness begins to envelop us. The air turns cold with nightfall, and I can see Nicola beginning to shiver from the cold. I give her my jacket and add some more branches to the fire. She lies back down and falls into a fitful sleep, while I stay by the fire, keeping it stoked, my mind still racing from the events of the day.

What will happen to Morris, I wonder? The agents who came to intercept us were Travelers, I thought, from the brief glimpse I got of them. They were not dressed as Black Robes, but they had that military bearing to them that was unmistakable. I have grown skilled at picking those sorts out of a crowd.

But I well knew that the fact that they were Black Robes did not mean they were not ultimately answerable to Molijc. He has insinuated his agents within their infrastructure. I should know—I helped him do it. And the Society does not have any reason to pursue Morris— surely the Seeker would act to protect him even if they did—whereas the Grand Regent most certainly does.

I know what Molijc will do to him. He will have the Acolytes perform their terrible work to extract whatever information they can and render him another of the half-things that wander about the campus or Order transfer point, blindly doing whatever the Grand Regent or Lasinha bids. A terrible fate for anyone.

Will the Seeker act to spare Morris that, or will he decide that it is better to keep his involvement secret, provided he can trust Morris not to reveal it under the Acolytes' extraction procedures? I think I know the answer to the question, based on the final expression on Morris' face before the channel closed.

It is a long time before I can get that image from my mind and I am able to lie down beside Nicola, stealing a bit of her warmth, and sleep.

2

When I wake, it is still dark out and I am shivering from the cold. The fire is out, gone down to just embers, and I work for a time to bring it to life. Nicola stirs beside me but does not wake. I stay by the fire until the warmth has returned to my body, but when I lie beside Nicola again, I am unable to fall asleep, my mind focused on my thirst and hunger and the arduous journey that lies before me.

When there is enough light that I can see, I abandon any attempt at sleep and walk down to the river. Though I know it will likely end with me becoming ill, I drink my fill of the water, hoping that I will not begin to feel the effects until after I reach the citadel. Feeling refreshed, I return to the crevice, where Nicola is awake and has gotten to her feet.

"I thought you had gone," she says, sitting back down in obvious pain.

"I just went to get some water," I say. "It's not far to the river, if you can manage it. I would try not to. You're likely to get sick from it, which is the last thing you need in your condition."

She nods, though she doesn't appear to be listening to what I say, her expression distant. I crouch across from her and take her hands in mine. "Listen," I say, "I'm going to go get some more firewood for you. Keep the fire going just in case you get stuck here another night. Try to wait out on the water, but if it's afternoon and no one has come, you'll need to chance it."

Nicola takes this all in with a dim stare. I put a hand to her forehead. It is hot to the touch. I do not linger—time is of the essence now—and gather as much firewood as I can and bring it to the crevice. I am sweating even though the sun is not yet in the sky.

"That should last you through the day and the night if you're careful," I say. "Now, I'm going to go. I'll make sure Osahi sends someone for you, no matter what."

Nicola does not acknowledge that I have said anything. It is as though I have already left. Though I am worried about her state, I decide staying with her will only worsen her condition in the long run, and I head out to where the trail ends at the cliff and begin the climb to the top.

I move at a painstaking pace, but still my arms are soon screaming in agony at my efforts, while my legs tremble with exhaustion. Sweat pours off me, running into my eyes. My palms are damp with perspiration as well, making each new handhold precarious. It seems impossible to imagine I will be able to make it all the way to the top. Still, I push on. There is little else I can do.

Though most of the climb is hand over hand up the face of the rock, every now again there is a small switchback where something like a trail forms and I can proceed on foot. It is at these junctions that I pause to gather my breath and steady my mind, which, between the vertigo and the lack of sustenance, is becoming destabilized. I am losing all sense of myself and where I am in the universe.

But I forge on, knowing there is no turning back and not thinking about the cost of a misstep. By midday, judging by the position of the sun in the sky—having lost all sense of time myself—I reach the top. I fall to the ground, my whole body shaking, my lungs burning and my head pulsing with a migraine. I lie there, listening to the rasps of my breath, letting my sweat cool on my body.

Eventually I force myself to my feet and walk on from the cliff, not daring to turn around and witness the full scale of my ascent. A forest lies not far away from the cliff's edge, the river emerging from it, and I make my unsteady way toward it, pausing only to drink my fill of the water again. It takes some time for me to discover the path heading north that Nicola spoke of. It is barely visible among the tangle of the trees, thin and hardly worn, with undergrowth encroaching all around so that I find myself wandering off it without even realizing.

I pick my way through the forest as best I can. It is difficult to see more than a few feet in front of me, and I find myself stumbling on low-hanging branches or having to come to an abrupt stop in the face of some limb that I fail to notice until it is nearly touching me. With the canopy of the forest not allowing the sun to penetrate, it is quite cool along the path, made more so by the elevation, and I find myself shivering from the cold. Or perhaps it is whatever bacteria I have consumed in the river visiting its ruin upon me.

I walk for what seems like hours, my steps growing slower and more plodding, and my fear that I have somehow wandered off the trail and missed the citadel entirely growing. The thought of Nicola, lying alone in the crevice, makes me fight through my own exhaustion and despair to see this to its end. I have already lost Morris to a fate as terrible as death. I will not let Nicola perish. Her death will not be on my hands as well.

It seems everything I touch inevitably leads to ruin, even as I somehow persist and survive in spite of all that Molijc, the Seeker, and the Society have done to stop me. Mere survival is not enough, though. I must restore myself and set right some of the wrong I have done to all those who fell under the heel of the Protectors and then the

Watchers' Order. Can such a thing even be attempted? My sins seem to multiply as I try to set them right.

It is with the weight of these thoughts heavy in my mind that I emerge from the forest to see another hill standing tall upon the landscape. Atop it, the land has been cleared and a series of buildings have been constructed. I can see what looks like crops planted in fields that have been terraced along the hillside. The tallest building, standing high above the rest, has the appearance of a watchtower, and as I leave the forest behind to climb the hill, I can hear whistling and shouts echoing from above.

I am met by three people when I have ascended about halfway up the hill. One of them is the woman who was involved in my capture in the other world when I was still unsure of my identity. She stands open-mouthed, staring at me, while the other two look confused.

"I don't believe it," she says.

"I am here to see Osahi," I say. "One of your people brought me here. Nicola. From the Society. She's at the bottom of the cliff. She's hurt. You'll need to send someone to her as soon as possible."

The woman sends one of the others ahead to pass on word of who I am while she and the other escort me to the citadel. None of us speak. As we pass through the structures, I marvel at the village Osahi has constructed. There are few people on the streets and they all stare at me as we pass by. The woman leads me into one of the central buildings and gestures for me to wait with the other escort while she passes into one of the back rooms.

I can hear her conversing with someone, without being able to identify the speaker or what is being said. Finally, she returns with Osahi, grim-faced and exhausted. He looks me over with a doubtful eye.

"Joseph Aurellano, I presume. Or is it David Aeida? So many names, and yet you do not seem to exist."

"I am David Aeida," I say. "Formerly of the Watchers' Order. I worked with Lasinha from the beginning. I'm here to help you save the Church."

His face betrays no expression, but I can feel him studying me again with renewed interest. At last he nods, a decision reached, and waves for me to follow him.

3

"How did you find me?" Osahi says as he leads me down one of the streets of his village.

Almost all the buildings are simple and single-storied, with none of the gestures toward ostentation that I associate with my rival in the Church. Most seem to be dwellings, except for the half-dozen or so at the center of the village, which are obviously built for some official sort of purpose. One will be a place of worship, for Protocols and prayers and the other rituals of the faith. How long has it been since I observed them?

"Nicola brought me here. Morris Loverne found her." I hesitate, considering my words.

Osahi stops and glares at me, knowing what I am doing. "You can be truthful with me or you can die. The choice is yours."

"You would kill a Regent?" I say. I try not to think of my own murder of Osahi's people in Lasinha's compound, hoping he will not ask me.

"The people in charge of the faith have shown no compunction in doing so. The Society as well. Why should I be any different? I cannot afford to. The stakes are too high now. Besides, there are fates worse than death."

"Yes, there are," I say.

"You would know, I suppose," Osahi says, leading me to the smallest of the central buildings. "And you remember everything now?"

I hesitate again, drawing another look. "Yes," I say.

Osahi pulls open the door and gestures for me to enter the building, which I do, feeling as though I am being drawn toward my doom. My unease is confirmed as I step into a large room and see in one corner the Acolyte's Eye and a table. De Vroes sits at a table in another corner busy at a screen. He looks up at me in surprise.

"I'm amazed you're alive," he says, looking at Osahi.

Toma nods grimly. "Too good to be true. We'll see if this is a miracle. Or what the truth of the matter is."

He gestures for me to go to the table and submit myself to the Eye. I am paralyzed by fear at the thought. Will the Eye be able to determine if I am within Aeida, now that the Acolyte's tamps and other constructions have been released? If I lie about who I am and why I am here, it will know. But I must lie. Osahi cannot know who I really am, or he will use me as a pawn in his battle with Molijc. He may still anyway.

De Vroes takes a half step toward me, as if to guide me to the table. I strive vainly to find a reason to refuse their request, but I know Osahi will not let me wriggle free of this.

"I don't have all day," Osahi says, gesturing again toward the table.

"You'll have to forgive me," I say, struggling to find the words. "The last time I sat on this table with you two was not so pleasant."

"Let's hope this time is not a repeat of that then," Osahi says.

I resist a smile, in spite of myself. He has not changed at all, which reassures me for some reason. I lie on the table, allowing De Vroes to strap me in, trying not to think about what the Eye might reveal, or how my fragile mind might respond under its ministrations. When I am firmly strapped in, De Vroes injects me with the Acolyte's serum, the liquid shifting from blue to green in color as I watch the syringe descend. With that done, De Vroes rotates the table until I am lying perpendicular to the ground, facing the two of them.

De Vroes glances at Osahi, who nods, and the Acolyte goes to the table and activates the Eye. It begins to float toward me, spinning gently, its rasping breath causing me to shudder. When it is right before my eyes, so that I am unable to look away, it halts and exhales. The darkness of the orb, that unfathomable material that seems to absorb all light, pulls at me as surely as a Seeker's gaze.

"Who are you?" Osahi says.

I try to look in his direction, but the straps will not allow it. The Eye floats before me, encompassing all my vision. "David Aeida. sub-Regent of the Watchers' Order. As I told you."

There is a pause, where I can sense Osahi looking to De Vroes, as if to confirm whether my response is the truth or a lie. I close my eyes, feeling ill, hoping against hope that the Eye will see the truth in what I said and nothing more.

"How did you find Nicola and compel her to bring you here?"

I force myself to take a breath to relax myself. "Morris Loverne found her. He knew she was a possible connection to you. We found her just when the Watchers did. They shot her. And then they found us. She didn't have a choice; we had to get away, and she needed help. You were her only chance."

"Where is Morris?"

"With the Watchers."

I can sense the concern from Osahi. "Does he know where we are?"

"No," I say. "I don't either. Nicola created the channels. I assume she obscured the destination or had the equipment erase it, so that they won't be able to track us. You'll have to talk to her about that."

"I will."

There is another pause as Osahi and De Vroes confer silently. I hear the door open and hear someone's footsteps down the steps outside.

"How've you been, De Vroes?" I say, affecting a gallant tone. "Survived the Seeker, I see."

"As did you," he says. "I'm very curious about that."

"It's quite the tale."

The door opens again and footsteps follow. "Now," Osahi says, "you say you were Lasinha's pet and now you're with Loverne. He's Laila's. Are you with her people now?"

"I am with whoever can bring down Molijc and Lasinha and restore the Church."

Osahi lets out a bark of a laugh. There is no mirth in it. "What do you know of the Church? You're a sub-Regent, stuck in another universe. All you know is what Lasinha told you."

"That's not true," I say. "Ana was the Adjudicator in that world after Lasinha left."

"A Society agent and Molijc's hatchet. I will certainly not be asking you to do the Protocols for the faithful here."

"I wouldn't presume to do so anyway," I say, keeping my voice even, not wanting to betray the emotion I feel for Ana, although the Eye may sense it anyway. In the end, it doesn't matter. David Aeida is still in love with her. I can feel his anger at Osahi's accusation coursing through me.

"Everybody always loved Ana," Osahi says. I can almost see him shaking his head. "Where is Laila?"

"The Grand Regent has her," I manage to say. It is the truth—in a manner of speaking. Certainly I believe it so. This thing strapped to this table is not me. I cannot allow it to be me.

"Are you certain?"

"Morris thought so. He didn't know, though. No one seems to." I say the last as a kind of question, hoping Osahi will reveal what he knows to me.

He ignores me, whispering something to De Vroes that I cannot make out. "And how did you come to be with Morris Loverne? I had assumed the Grand Regent swept him in one of his purges."

"He is now," I say. "He'll join the living dead. After I escaped you guys and the Seeker, I manage to get across to the Church's universe using the Watchers' compound."

"How did you get past the Watchers?" Osahi says, immediately suspicious.

"They abandoned it. I don't know why. The Society was watching it, though. So I had to avoid them."

"Yes, they were. I sent an extraction team after you there, you know. Do you know what happened to them?" His eyes are intent upon mine.

I swallow. "The Society happened," I say. "I escaped. Barely."

Osahi frowns, glancing over at De Vroes again, who does not raise his eyes from the screen. "Who was helping you there?"

"An Order member," I say.

"And where is this person now?"

"I assume the Society swept her up. I lost her during your fuck-up of a raid."

Osahi looks as though he wants to strangle me, but he restrains himself. "You're very resourceful, no doubt. Tell me now, why was the Seeker after you? Why had the Watchers done all that they did to you? Not that they need any reason."

"They don't," I say. I hesitate, collecting my thoughts, knowing that this is the difficult moment. I cannot reveal the truth. I cannot let them know who I am. And I can't mention Meredith, or Osahi will begin to suspect. More than he does already.

"I don't know exactly why they did it to me," I say,

hoping that a half-truth will be as good as the truth for the Eye. It is true for Aeida, after all. "They suspected me. Lasinha knew I wasn't his man anymore, that I didn't believe in the Order. And like I said, I know about it all. I was there at the beginning."

"You know where the bodies are kept, is that it?"

I close my eyes. "Mostly," I say. "Enough to be dangerous, I guess. And you know the Grand Regent. He wants to punish people."

"That he does. Now tell me how you came to find Morris in my world."

Another trouble spot. The last thing I want to reveal is that the Seeker sent me to him. That Morris is a Traveler agent. "Laila found me. Before Molijc found her. And her people helped me. They tried to get me across the first time. That's what started all this mess. And then they got me across this time. Got me to Morris."

They will know it is not the whole truth, but it is near enough that they may accept it. For the time being, anyway. That is all I can hope for.

"So now you've found me. What do you propose?" Osahi says. By his tone, I can tell that I have passed the Eye's test, and I feel a surge of triumph.

"I want to destroy Molijc and Lasinha for what they have done to me," I say, with a vehemence that both Aeida and I share. It is the truest thing I have said.

"Let's begin, then," Osahi says.

4

De Vroes unstraps me from the table and Osahi takes me outside. I am unsteady on my feet, though I try not to show it, exhausted from the climb and the ordeal of the Eye. The woman I met outside the citadel, who was one of my captors when I was last in Osahi's clutches, is waiting.

"Aeida," Osahi says, gesturing to the woman, "you're familiar with Suon, I believe."

I nod, and she offers a thin smile.

"She'll show you around, let you know the rules, and get you set up in a room. Aeida is a *guest*, and should be treated as such."

His emphasis on the word, and the quick nod from Suon, tell me that I am not so much a guest as a prisoner, to be watched and treated with caution. It is the best I can hope for at this point, I realize. I will have to prove myself to them, and I can only hope I will have enough time to do so.

"Come along with me," Suon says, taking me by the arm. "I'll give you the lay of the land."

She leads me back down the street Osahi brought me, to the central building of the village. "This is the administrative center," she says, taking me within.

"Anything you need—clothes, food, information—you come here. You want to do anything, leave, or something like that, you need permission from the people here."

I nod. "I can't imagine I'll be going anywhere for a while. Doesn't seem like there's much around here to see, anyway."

"Depends what you're interested in," Suon says. "There's a lot of amazing hikes, if that's your thing. There's the falls, of course, but you would have seen them. The rainforest to the north is amazing. It's a cloud forest. I'd be happy to take you, if you're interested."

"Want to make sure I have an escort, do you?" I say, immediately regretting the hardness in my tone.

She smiles. "Well, there is that. Also, I don't know if you've noticed, but there's only a couple hundred of us here in not a lot of space. With not a lot to do. Getting out into the jungle qualifies as fun in my books. Better than sitting here and watching the mold grow up the walls."

"Fair enough," I say. "I'll keep it in mind. Where do you guys get your power from?" I am fishing for details about their location on this earth. From the little I have seen there is no grid they can be connecting to.

"Solar cells mostly," she says in a flat voice, not taking my bait. "We have a few generators as back-up."

Suon leads me into the administrative building, the same place she first brought me to Osahi, and into one of the side offices. A woman and man look up at our entrance. "This is David Aeida," she says, with a wave of her hand. "He's a guest and he needs a room."

The woman squints at her computer. "There's empty quarters in the Frederik dormitory. He can have that. Gust can get you sheets and towels. I'll get everything set up here."

Gust leads me out of the room into the back of the building to a supply room, where he pulls sheets, a blanket, pillows, and a towel and stacks them in my arms. He tells me the washing procedure, which I immediately forget. I am having difficulty focusing after being subjected to the Eye. It is just the aftereffects of my crossing over, and that I need something to eat and drink, I tell myself. I've had nothing to eat in over a day.

By the time we return to the office, the woman and Suon have made the necessary arrangements and Suon takes me to my quarters, identifying buildings as we pass by them. Most are dormitories, as I suspected. She points out the church, a square, innocuous building with none of the usual flourishes of the faith.

"We have daily observances," she says, "though they aren't required."

I nod, but do not speak. She is trying to probe me for information, I know, for I have played this game so many times before. As soon as we are done here, she will go scurrying back to Osahi. But I will give her as little as possible to tell him. I don't want to risk getting trapped in some sort of lie.

There are four buildings she does not tell me about. One is the Acolyte building where Osahi interrogated me. The second, which is beside the Acolyte structure, is twice the size. Suon, when I ask her about it, says it is off-limits, a Hierarchy building. Which tells me that it will have the transfer equipment, and perhaps an armory as well, given the weapons Osahi was able to bring into the other universe. The third is the watchtower—the citadel overlooking the habitation and the surrounding forest. I do not bother to ask Suon about it, for its purpose seems obvious enough.

The final mysterious building is one of the few two-story structures in the habitation. It looks like a suburban house, not so different from the ones Aeida and I grew up in. There are windows, but blinds are drawn across them. Suon sees me looking at the house and shakes her head. "That place is off-limits," she says.

"Why? What's in there?" I ask.

She shrugs. "I don't know. Only Osahi and De Vroes

go in there."

I cannot disguise my curiosity, and a shadow falls across her face. "We're not going to have trouble with you, are we?"

I laugh. "Like I told Osahi, we're on the same side."

She looks doubtful, but doesn't say any more, motioning for me to follow her. We go to the village's far end, where the habitation gives way to the forest, a lone path extending beyond into the trees. Suon turns away from the jungle and leads me to one of a row of three long dormitories that form a wall between the jungle and the village.

"This is the Frederik dormitory," she says, entering the middle of the three.

There is a large common area with a rudimentary kitchen and scattered chairs and couches. The place is empty now, everyone seemingly at work. Beyond the central common area are two long hallways, lined with small quarters on either side, with a bathroom at each end. We go to the left until we reach an open doorway.

"Here it is," Suon says, entering the room and flipping on a light, revealing a simple room with a bed in one corner, an uncomfortable chair in the other, and a window at its center. "There's a closet for clothes. Not that you have any with you now. But we can arrange that later. What do you think?"

I resist the urge to say it reminds me of the dormitories on the Church campus where I lived as an Initiate to the faith. I cannot say that, for Aeida did not live there. He was in the other universe. Instead, I nod and say, "It'll do fine."

"Good," Suon says. "I'll let you get settled. You can go to the cafeteria for food now if you like. I'll check in later this afternoon."

Once she leaves, I do as she suggests, making my bed and hanging the towel up on the rack in the closet. My hands are shaking violently again from the effort. Though

I need food badly, I force myself to search the entire room, going over every inch of it to see what of interest I can find.

There is a microphone in the light bulb hanging from the ceiling, but nothing else, which surprises me. I expected a camera, but I am certain I did not miss it in my search. I leave it there, untouched. In the closet I find a loose board in the floor that I can jimmy loose to hide something small. It will be good to remember that as well.

When I am done with my investigation, I leave my room and go the dining hall to eat. The food is largely vegetables, fresh from the gardens, and rice. I eat ravenously, and when I am done, I go back to my room and fall immediately into a deep sleep.

I awake groggily hours later to find Suon staring down at me in the room's growing shadows, and give a start of surprise.

"Sorry," she says. "I didn't want to wake you just yet. You looked so peaceful. There are no locks on the door."

"I noticed," I say. "It's getting dark."

"Yes," she says. "It's almost seven. It'll be dark in an hour."

"I don't suppose you'll tell me where we are?" I smile.

Suon smiles as well, giving her face a lovely glow. "I'm afraid not. Truth be told, I'm not entirely sure myself. A safe, secluded corner of a universe far, far away."

"Fair enough. I'm impressed with what you've all accomplished here. All without the Watchers finding you." Not surprised, though—I know how careful Osahi is, and how capable he is of planning. He was probably building this place back when I was throwing my life and body away in vain attempt to overthrow Molijc. He is far more patient than I.

"Well, some have found us," she says, looking past me into the shadows.

"They were guests too, I suppose."

Suon gives a half nod. "Yes. I hope that you're not like

them, coming here to betray the faith."

"Certainly not. I'll prove it to all of you."

"Good. We don't get many new people here. It's nice to get to know someone new." Suon squeezes my arm and smiles. I smile in return and hide the shaking in my hands.

5

My first week in Osahi's village passes without incident, and I find myself gradually integrating into its particular rhythms. I do not see much of Toma, which is a relief. Though I have recovered from the worst and most visible of the aftereffects of the crossing—the tremors and headaches—there are other symptoms, subtle and insidious, that I am slow to overcome. This is much worse than the last time. Given how little time passed between both crossings, maybe I had simply yet to recover from the first instance.

I spend a great deal of time at the church in prayer here. Partly to hide the fact that I am not myself, my thoughts not entirely my own. Though perhaps that is not quite correct. They are my own, and I am many squabbling parts. Aeida grows bolder and bolder, trying to seize command. Often, when I am distracted and bored, letting my mind wander where it will, I find that it is Aeida's thoughts I am thinking. I have managed to catch him before he ensnares me entirely, but I shall have to stay on guard or he will banish me to the depths again.

My other reason for spending time in the church is to observe those living in the village here to see if there is anyone I know. Anyone I can turn to my advantage. Thus far the only familiar faces are Suon, De Vroes, and Osahi, and the last two I have barely seen since they interrogated me. Everyone I encounter is friendly though a little wary, as if they have been warned about me. No doubt they have.

I have spent some time wandering the village, getting the lay of the land, but I have been careful not to go anywhere that might draw attention or suspicion. As I never fail to notice, there is always someone trailing behind me, watching to see what I will do. They do not even bother to disguise what they are doing. What would be the point?

While I take care not to go near the four buildings that are off-limits to me, I do make sure to keep them in view as much as possible when I am about. I want to see who can enter and who cannot. The citadel and Hierarchy building seem to have the same people entering them day after day, which makes sense, given, what I guess are, their purposes. Only those in the Hierarchy would be charged with manning the watchtower and protecting the faithful.

I have only seen De Vroes enter the Acolyte building in the days since my interrogation, which tells me that he is the only Acolyte here. That makes sense as well, for the Acolytes have always been aligned with Molijc, from the moment De Gofroy fell ill. It does not surprise me that Osahi managed to get his fingers into the guild and find a few agents there, though something must have happened for De Vroes to leave and join him here. He would be far more valuable to Osahi within than without. I will have to see what I can find out about his past.

Of the suburban house, I have discovered nothing. No one enters and no one leaves. I have yet to see anyone go near it and I have no sense of what secrets it holds. It is a mystery, but one that doesn't yet intrigue me, for it is unlikely it holds what I require. The Hierarchy building is the most promising in that regard, and I will have to find a means of entry sooner rather than later.

Suon is a constant presence in addition to whoever is shadowing me. Always friendly, always smiling, forever finding reasons to touch me, to make clear her interest. I understand this game, for I played it and watched others do the same. It is no surprise that Osahi would return to his old playbook—he was the first to send Meredith to me, after all—for it is a proven tactic. Especially in my case, though he cannot know that.

The constant observation, the provided companion, and the care with which everyone acts around me actually serves to set me at ease. They suspect me and have doubts about my story, but they have no sense of who I really am. Of how valuable a piece I might be. Osahi will have his people elsewhere investigating David Aeida to find out whatever he can, which will be little. Lasinha was careful to keep him hidden away after he returned to recruit him into the Watchers.

Ultimately, I am biding my time, for as long as I dare, and letting Osahi come to me. When he is satisfied I am not a threat, or at least one that is properly contained, he will.

My daily visits to the church and my rituals there—prayer and meditation—have not gone unnoticed. As I hoped. Twice I have seen the same person taking the measure of me from the corner of his eye as he kneels in prayer. Soon enough, he will find the courage to approach me and say what is on his mind.

It is a strange thing to be in the church so often. I was never one for daily prayer, even when I had the faith. Many would say that I never had any to begin with, only the veneer of belief, with no depth. But that was never the case. I believed.

Can I still? That is a question I ask myself as I kneel in contemplation. I remember all that De Gofroy told me about the Protocols, about the nature of the universes, about the titanic struggle for the fate of it all that we were a part of. A few years before finding one of his books in the remainder bin of a bookstore, I would have called talk like that complete nonsense. It was not what the Society told us about the universes, about our infinitely multiple selves.

And the Society lies. That I know only too well. Their tale of pristine universes untouched by anything is as much a lie as our tale of an ancient struggle for the fate of our true and whole selves. What is the truth, then?

Have I ever felt my other regent parts, the pieces of me, in the other universes? The Protocols are supposed to provide me with the ability to do so, and there was a time when I was certain that I did feel those others. Could feel the boundaries between us, the fundamental tissue of being made plain. Now I wonder. It cannot have all been in my head. It was something. But what?

None of this matters, I tell myself. All that matters is that I restore myself to my body and destroy Molijc. If the Church is ruined in the process, if the faith is left destitute and the Society of Travelers triumphant, I am willing to live with that. So I tell myself. But do I believe that as well?

I don't know what I believe anymore. I don't even know who I am. The longer I remain in this body, the less sense I make—the less sense anything makes. If I return—when I return—what will be left of me? I do not like the answer that my inner self provides.

When I leave the church, riven by even more doubt—in myself, in my quest, in the universes themselves—than when I entered, the man I noticed staring sidelong at me is waiting. He falls in beside me as I make my way back to the Frederik dorms, trying to make it appear as though chance has brought us together. I grimace, wanting to yell at him that Osahi's watchers will not be fooled by such obvious tactics.

"My name is Ibrahem," he says with a nod. "You must

be new here."

"You know I am," I say, staring straight ahead.

He laughs. "Yes, it's true, it's hard to escape notice around here. But I'm different. I know who you really are."

"Is that so?" I say, and come to an abrupt halt to give him a hard stare. Over his shoulder I can see my watcher stop as well, idling in front of one of the other dormitories.

"Yes, David Aeida. I know you're Lasinha's pet. And I know what really happened to you."

I smile as venomously as I am able. "Please, do enlighten me."

Ibrahem shakes his head. "You misunderstand me, Aeida. I'm not here to threaten you."

"You could've fooled me."

"No, I'm on your side. We're after the same thing here."

I shake my head, still looking past him at my watcher, who is observing us very closely while giving every appearance of not doing so. "I very much doubt that."

"Oh, but I am."

Ibrahem seems unconcerned or unaware that we are being observed. I decide it must be the former; no one could be so oblivious of my escort. But why isn't he concerned?

"What side is that, then? I'm not sure I know."

Ibrahem smiles. "You're worried about your little minder." He jerks his head a little in her direction. "You don't need to waste any time worrying about her. She trusts me. Everyone here trusts me. But I'm like you. I know what Osahi is. And I know who you are David Aeida."

I flinch at his words in spite of myself. *Does he know?* But of course he doesn't. He couldn't. The only people who do are Meredith and Molijc, and possibly Lasinha. Morris too, I amend, but he will not know himself by now.

"You've said that," I say, my expression under control

again. "But I don't know what you mean. I take it you're with the Grand Regent, then? Or is it someone else you're backing?"

"I stand with De Gofroy's true heir," Ibrahem says, lowering his voice to a whisper. "Laila Johar."

6

Osahi awaits me in my room. He is sitting in my only chair, so I sit across from him on the bed. His expression is, as always, arrogant and unreadable, but his appearance, so soon after my odd conversation with Ibrahem, seems a little too neat. It makes me think my suspicions are correct, that Ibrahem is an Osahi plant to see where my loyalty truly lies.

If he hadn't been so clumsy in his attempt, I would have no doubts whatsoever. As it is, that awkwardness gives me pause. There can be no doubt that he is not one of my agents, for I had none with Osahi's people. Not at the end, anyway, and certainly not this fool. He could be one of Lasinha's. An agent, claiming to be working for a rival, has his fingerprints upon it.

Oh, how devious we all are. How we twist and turn and lie and pretend, until we don't even know what we are anymore.

"Are you enjoying your stay here?" Osahi says, his tone suggesting that the wrong answer could end my time here.

"It's an idyllic setting, no doubt," I say. "Well out of the way. I'm curious, though. Morris thought the other High Regents were with you. But I don't think I've seen any of them."

Osahi studies me through narrowed eyes, as though considering what to say. "They are with me, but not here. For their own safety—and our own here—they are in other locations. I don't want to give the Grand Regent an opportunity to take us down in one raid. He will have to work to bring down this revolt."

I stifle a grimace at his words. He is thinking of my own failed insurrection, learning from my mistakes. "A wise policy. How many know all the locations?"

"No one," Osahi says. "Not even me."

I'm not certain I believe him. He was the sort to never surrender that much control, but circumstances may have forced his hand. "That's prudent. Molijc's Acolytes are not so kind as yours."

"He has his claws as well. You just haven't felt them yet. If you betray us, you will feel them. Have no doubt."

I smile and shake my head. "I have no doubt. I've played this game long enough to know that it is paid in blood. But as I think I've made clear, I'm here to end it. Just as you are. Let me know how I can help."

Toma sighs and leans forward on his chair, resting an elbow on his knee and his chin upon his hand. "For the moment, things remain as they are. You are free to enjoy our hospitality here. We have some other things underway that I must attend to before I can turn my attention to you and how we might work together."

I frown, not attempting to hide my frustration. I do not have time for delays, for Osahi to attend to things—or, more accurately, to find the holes in my story and the real reason for my being here.

Osahi laughs. "You could tell me what you're really doing here and we could be done with this nonsense now."

"I've told you the truth," I say.

"Some of it, anyway," he says, still smiling. "You can be useful, I've no doubt, and you will be in due time. But right now I have other matters I need to attend to. I suggest you take advantage of this enforced idleness. Suon is always looking for an excuse to go on hikes into the cloud forest."

I purse my lips, stopping myself from rejecting the idea outright. He wants to push me into Suon's arms. Or get rid of me for a few days. Possibly both. My instinct is to say no, to stay here and complicate things for him, and to continue to see what I can learn about this place and what he is trying to hide from me. But I know he will not allow me that. If I stay, he may confine me to my rooms, or worse.

"Patience, Aeida. All in due time. Meanwhile, enjoy yourself. You look like you could use it."

He smiles again, that disingenuous smile I know so well. It makes me want to insist I remain here, to demand that we begin our work now. Instead, I smile as well. "I'll talk to Suon," I say.

He nods, satisfied. Another thing accomplished. "She'll be expecting you."

Of course she will, I think, feeling a surge of rage. I press my hands against the sheets on my bed to stop them from trembling.

I stay in my room for the rest of the day, stewing over my interaction with Osahi, Ibrahem forgotten for the moment. Though I know I have to find Suon and make arrangements to go on the hike Osahi wants us to take, I do not, out of spite for him. I will do as he wants of me, but I will not do it quickly. It is petty, but it is all the agency I have at the moment.

Finally, I quell my anger enough that I am able to leave the room and go to find Suon. I am almost able to convince myself that this will not be an utter waste of my time. Osahi trusts Suon, that much seems obvious, which means she will possess knowledge that is useful to me. I have no doubt that I will be more skilled than she at manipulation, given that both Aeida and I have endless experience on that front.

And she is pretty enough, though her beauty leaves me cold. Aeida, on the other hand... It is confusing enough dealing with conflicting thoughts, but conflicting desires—and reactions to those desires—are quite another problem altogether. That is one entanglement I will have to avoid.

I find Suon in the cafeteria, having a snack with some other Regents, all of whom excuse themselves at the sight of me. Without mentioning Osahi, I tell her that I would like to take her up on her offer of a hiking trip.

Her eyes glimmer with excitement, her happiness palpable. "There's a wonderful trail with some great views we can take to the north. It takes three or four days, depending on how fast you travel. I can't wait. I'll arrange all the gear and food. You should go to the administration building and have them give you some clothes. We can leave first thing tomorrow."

Suon's enthusiasm is infectious, and, after our conversation, I am almost looking forward to my brief exile from Osahi's village. It may be worthwhile to spend a few days not constantly on guard—though I will still have to be careful with Suon—simply enjoying a majestic part of this world. It may even help in what seems to be an interminably long recovery from the transfers.

And Suon may have answers to the questions I need answered. We shall see if I can extract them from her.

We are off at first light, after I meet Suon, bleary-eyed and in need of caffeine, outside my dormitory. I have the clothes the administrators gave me folded in my arms, and we pack them into one of the enormous backpacks Suon is carrying. When I heave one of them over my shoulders, I nearly topple under the weight.

"What is in this?" I say.

"Everything we need for the next four days," she says, already enjoying herself immensely.

Fog shrouds the forest surrounding the village, emerging from the trees in ghostly clouds as we make our way along the trail. The fog is heavy with moisture, which quickly leaves us drenched and me cursing myself for ever agreeing to come along. Confinement in my dormitory would be preferable to this. Suon seems unaffected by it, whistling to herself as she leads me along the trail.

The sun soon rises, dissipating the fog and slowly drying us off. It is a warm day, though the forest canopy protects us from the worst of the heat. We say little throughout the morning, even when we stop to rest, aside from Suon pointing out whatever she finds of particular interest about the forest.

Toward the end of the day, the trail we were on begins to incline and soon we are winding our way up a hill, or perhaps even a mountain. I cannot see through the foliage of the trees to be able to tell. After a day of walking, even if it was at a relatively leisurely pace, a difficult climb to end our journey is not at all what I am looking for. Soon I am drenched in sweat, gasping for breath, even as Suon carries on beside me, apparently unaffected by the climb.

As we go higher, the trees begin to thin, and we emerge from the forest and find ourselves on the side of a mountain. Unlike the mountains I am used to, with rock faces and snow-covered peaks, this one is green to its very top, with grass and a scattering of trees in places. The view, I am forced to admit when I have my breath again, is absolutely stunning. We can see the whole forest that we just finished traversing. There is a spire in the distance that appears man-made, which I assume must be Osahi's citadel.

"Worth it, isn't it?" Suon says in the satisfied voice of someone whose every muscle isn't aching.

I have a brief vision of strangling her in her sleep tonight and returning tomorrow to the village. It makes me want to giggle, and I just catch it in my throat, snorting and choking ridiculously. Suon looks at me, unsure whether she should be concerned for my well-being before bursting out laughing. A moment later, I join her.

It feels good. Everything does, actually. I am elated by the moment, by the sweep of the view, by the dull, somehow satisfying ache of my muscles. Tomorrow will be agony, but today is a triumph of sorts.

"Just a bit farther," Suon says, putting a reassuring hand on my shoulder. Its warmth feels good there. "We don't want to camp out here in the open."

"Why's that?" I say, as we begin another grueling climb. "Restless natives?"

She smiles. "Weather, actually. The wind can get bad out here in the open. I made the mistake of camping here once before."

"What about the locals, though?" I say, declining to let her evade my inquiry. "This trail is pretty well developed."

She makes a show of studying the contours of the mountain above us, and the one behind it. "We fixed it up a bit, but yeah. Obviously people have been using this for a while. Same thing with the climb up the cliff."

"What happened to those people? Or are they still around?"

Suon shrugs. "I don't know. I've never seen anyone else but us out here. There's no signs of settlement or anything that I've come across. They were here once, but I think that was a long time ago. Probably why Osahi chose it."

As we curve around the mountain, still climbing upward, we come to a stream that winds its way below. Somehow it must connect to the river that led to the waterfall where Nicola and I crossed over. There are exposed stones littered across the waterway, and Suon leads me across, hopping from one to the other.

On the other side, a short and steep walk up from the trail against the face of the mountain, there are a few half-formed caves that offer some shelter. Given their shared symmetry, I assume these are man-made, though I cannot guess their original purpose. They might have been homes carved from the rock of the mountain.

I offer to take care of the fire and leave Suon to set up our tent and sleeping bags. By the time I return, the tent is up, the sleeping bags spread out on air mattresses, and she is sorting through the food in her bag. She watches as I get the fire started, much more easily than the last time, with the matches, and nods, impressed.

"Here's your reward for a day's hard work," she says, digging into her pack and pulling out two cans of beer. I look at the labels—they are written in Spanish—and she laughs. "They're from another universe. We get supplies from outside when we can. Which isn't often. I've had these in my room for a while. They're worth a mint here."

I laugh. "I bet. I'm surprised someone hasn't started making moonshine."

"Oh, we have. They make some pretty good stuff, actually. Even beer. But it doesn't transport as easily as these cans."

She takes them down to the river and sets them in the water to cool, and we eat a supper of preserved meat and bread, with some fresh fruit for dessert. When it is done, we drink the now cold beer and watch the sun descend along the mountain, listening to the cries of the birds in the trees below.

When the sun is gone and darkness has taken hold, we look at the stars above in wonder. I am filled with a euphoria I cannot understand. I have not felt this way in so long. Suon puts some more wood on the fire and sits closer to me, which should give me pause, but I ignore those misgivings. For one night, let me be free of all this.

"It is hard to imagine all the same stars in all the other universes," Suon says. "It just seems impossible that they could all be the same."

"They aren't and they are," I say, recalling for some reason my conversation with the Seeker on the multitude of worlds and what he saw as our destruction of so many of them. "How long have you been in the Church?"

"Just about four years. And you?"

She joined the faith around the same time we began crossing over, which means Osahi may have recruited her from one of the universes he cultivated. Just as Lasinha did with Aeida. And I did with others. We all had our hidden universes where only we, and those we trusted, could go and where we evangelized for the faith. How many did we draw along this path to their doom? Too many to count.

And all for what? The Seeker is correct. We have left only wreckage behind us.

"I joined about the same time, I guess. That seems like a different lifetime now."

"Yeah," she says, shaking her head. "I can't believe I'm here. My parents... Well, they don't know I'm here. They don't know anything about this."

"It's hard," I say. "The uninitiated don't understand this. They hate us, because of the lies the Travelers tell. They don't understand how the Society has perverted every single institution in every universe it has entered. Were they in your universe?"

"Yes," she says. "They came much earlier than in the Church's universe, so their hold is even stronger there, if that's possible. They control everything, without even having to run the governments or anything. They have the technology and things that everyone wants and needs, so they always get what they want."

"They weren't in my universe," I say, remembering I am supposed to be Aeida. "But I saw a lot of what they did while I was in the Order. It's incredible to me. Guilds in a modern day society."

"And yet if you talk to the uninitiated they wouldn't see anything unusual in it. They just think we're fucking insane. And if you tell them that you have this secret understanding of the universe, it does sound kind of crazy. Even if it is true."

I nod, thinking of all the conversations I had with the

uninitiated over my years in the Church. Now I share their doubt, but not their obedience the laws the Society enforces. All that De Gofroy taught me may have been lies or delusions, but the Society is unmistakably a poison corroding every universe it touches, destroying the fabric of everyone's lives. And now I am their agent, however unwillingly.

Suon is looking at me, and I wonder about the expression on my face as these thoughts pass through my mind. "It must be easier for the ones who go back to the world, at least I imagine. You just live your life, just like any other believer. But once you get inducted into the Hierarchy…"

"There's no going back," she says, real sorrow in her voice. Our eyes meet, shadows dancing across our faces from the fire, and a charge of emotion runs through us both. I can feel it and I can see her feel it. I want to touch her, but I don't.

"It doesn't seem so," I say. "I dreamed of leaving, more times than I cared to admit. But…" I let the word hang there.

"I know," she says, taking my hand in hers. "I know. If it hadn't been for all this, having to go into exile. Fighting the Grand Regent. I probably would have left. At least, that's what I tell myself. I know so many who did."

"Me too," I say, leaning toward her. "But it's hard. The fate of the universes. Of our selves. If we don't fight for it, who will? Nothing could matter more, and when you're with people like Osahi and Lasinha, it really does seem like nothing else could possibly matter. They've dedicated their entire existences to this. They don't allow for other things."

"No," Suon says.

She looks away. I think she might be weeping. As I put an arm around her to comfort her and draw her close to me, a part of me tells me not to, but I push that voice aside. It is not me, or not a part that matters, anyway.

"Let's forget all about that," I say. Suon looks at me, as though I said something strange. "For this trip, let's just put all that aside and just let this be all that matters."

Suon studies me for a moment, as though weighing her choices, before tilting her head. It is a welcome, and I take it, leaning in to seize her lips with mine.

TWO:

FREDERIK

7

I stood beside Lasinha, feeling uneasy as the airship descended onto a vast, empty plain. There was grass and rolling hills as far as the eye could see in any direction, interrupted only by the odd gravel road and dotted intermittently by drops of blue that I knew were lakes, or more likely sloughs and dugouts. I could make out only one other farmyard, far along the edge of the horizon before us, aside from the one we were setting down beside. The nearest town, which we passed more than half an hour before, was called Eatonia. It looked like a tiny outpost of a few houses, some appearing in disrepair even from our high vantage, clinging desperately for survival amidst this unforgiving landscape.

I could not say what it was that left me uneasy. The correct answer was probably: *everything*.

Any descent in an airship could only remind me of the horrendous one I witnessed over a year ago where the cabin, so similar to the one I was now standing in, was consumed by flames. It was my guilt, of course, that brought these memories forth, for the role, however inadvertent, I had played in killing the three High Regents and the other Regents onboard. The man standing beside me, the author of that destruction, felt no such qualms.

Another factor to my disquiet was certainly that I was, in some sense, returning home. Eatonia was not so far from Medicine Hat, and these rolling, endless prairies were the familiar vista of my childhood. My grandparents had ranched north of Medicine Hat, and I spent many summer days there, helping with the cattle and wandering aimlessly through the pastures around their house. Those were the happy memories of my childhood; most of the rest I chose to forget.

The final reason, the main one, if truth be told, for my unease was the reason for our coming here. Frederik.

I had seen little of him since Lasinha and I had secured his release from the Montreal prison, only to turn him over to the Acolyte. He was in a pitiful state, heartbroken by Arajuano's betrayal and terrified at what we would do to him for his betrayal of the Church. I felt little sympathy for him. He had given most of the Church's funds over to an agent of our enemy.

But I feared what would happen to him all the same. I knew what Lasinha was capable of and I suspected Molijc was no different. But this was De Gofroy's son. That wouldn't matter to them, though—they would see that he paid in full for all he had done to the faith.

Several figures emerged from the complex of buildings that made up the yard. There were two ranch-style houses, long and single-storied, with verandas wrapping around their length, and several other quonset-shaped buildings of indeterminate use. They were large enough to store an immense amount of equipment or people. I bristled with sudden anger at the sight of them, yet more proof of all that Lasinha and Molijc had kept from me these last two years.

Dejian's betrayal cut the closest. We loved each other, though that well of feeling had long since begun to run dry, once his ambitions had begun to assert themselves. And once I had let Meredith into my life. He would blame her, if I chose to confront him about it. I could hear what he would say already. She was Osahi's agent and not to be trusted. He was still organizing against us, after all. Lasinha would say the same thing. He was probably the one to tell Dejian about her.

I could argue with him about it. Deny that Meredith was still Osahi's. She loved me and I her, and that trumped any hold Toma might still have over her. Or so I believed. But I knew that part of what drew me to her, and held me to her still, was the thrill of the unknown. The possibility that she might still be Osahi's in some way, even as I knew her feelings for me were real.

As the figures below tied the airship down, I saw that they were all Acolytes, for they were all dressed in what I considered to be their uniform, dark khakis and dark button-up shirts, as though they were anonymous drones working in the downtown office of some corporate entity. I wondered what all this rigorous banality said about what they did. It did not disguise them in any way, at least not within the Church itself. If anything, it made them stand out even more, which was perhaps the point.

"How long have the Acolytes had this place?" I said, looking at Lasinha.

"Since De Gofroy's time," he said. "Not many ever knew about it. Molijc did, obviously, and he told me. Aside from him, and the people on this ship, only the Acolytes are aware of its existence."

"What are they doing here?"

Lasinha gave me a shrug and a smile. "Projects. The Eye is part of it, as I understand."

The mention of the Acolyte's Eye only increased my disquiet. "Why are we leaving Frederik here?"

He had told me this was the plan before, of course, but now we were here and I could see that we were not just exiling Frederik, but putting him in the hands of the Acolytes, to do with as they pleased, my doubts began to grow.

"It's Dejian's plan," Lasinha said, which wasn't an answer. A moment later, as if conceding that, he said, "There are too many people among the Hierarchy, and especially the Protectors, who are Osahi's—or other factions who aren't with us—who might try to use Frederik against us. Dejian has the Acolytes. There is no doubt about where their loyalty is."

I pursed my lips. The unnamed other factions that he spoke of were my people. There were no other factions in the Church, unless one considered the possibility of infiltration by the Travelers. Which we always had to.

"Why do the Acolytes want him?" I said, at last realizing I had things turned around. Molijc and Lasinha didn't necessarily want Frederik here, but the Acolytes did.

Lasinha shrugged and smiled again. I wasn't sure I believed him. He might just be unwilling to tell me. I could guess, though, and the answers did nothing to quell my worries. The Acolytes were doing experiments here, and they would need a subject. Lasinha raised an eyebrow slightly, as if he could guess my train of thought, and I felt nauseated.

Whatever was going to happen to Frederik here was wrong; I could feel it with a cold certainty. Lasinha had no qualms about this, but then, he had no qualms about murder, either. The same was probably true of Dejian. They had shut me out of the decisions surrounding Frederik's fate, as well as the sorry state of the Church's finances. Who knew what else they had kept from me?

I needed to do something; that much was clear. Molijc and Lasinha needed a voice to counteract their worst inclinations. That could only be me. If I was to be a part of the Church's future, to help guide it as De Gofroy had wanted, I would have to regain their trust. I would have to speak to Dejian about all that had come between us. It would be a difficult conversation, but I saw now there was no other choice.

We did not leave the airship once the vessel was tied

down. The ramp was lowered and we watched from the pilot deck as the Acolyte led Frederik down the stairs. One of the figures below joined him in escorting De Gofroy's son toward one of the two ranch houses. The others busied themselves with untying the vessel, once our own crew had raised the ramp. We were soon aloft and heading west, returning to Calgary, the complex vanishing in the distance, leaving Frederik to his fate. The Church of the Regents was now ours.

8

We returned to Calgary and a broken Church and a shattered faith. The campus seemed lifeless and empty, as though all the Initiates and Regents had abandoned it, leaving only a skeleton of the once vibrant organism De Gofroy had built. Those who remained watched Lasinha and I with guarded expressions, no doubt having heard any number of incredible rumors. Some of which were true.

It was a desperate time. Though we were now the undisputed leaders of the faith—and De Gofroy's chosen—what was left to lead? Since De Gofroy's death, the faithful had fled the Church, and with these latest events, even more figured to. His books, once commonly read by those outside the faith, no longer sold, and the Protocol Centers that had been set up across the world were empty, costing only money. With the money Frederik had lost to Arajuano—to the Society—the Church had no funds left to proselytize, let alone to see to its other functions: the protection of the faith from the Society of Travelers and the search for the one true universe.

It was in this atmosphere of despair, where further calamity seemed somehow inevitable, that I met with Dejian. He had already ensconced himself in the Grand

Regent's chambers atop the tallest tower, with views overlooking the old university campus. Though nothing official had been said or done—and there was still the problem that Frederik was alive and had not formally stepped down from his position—there was really no other choice for the Church but to accept Molijc as the Grand Regent. The only question was if he could manage to save the faith.

In spite of the gloomy air that seemed to envelop everyone around him, Dejian was filled with energy. He was almost transformed from the man I had known when I left only a few short days before. His dream had been realized. He commanded the faith. When he spoke to me, it was not as to an old friend and lover, but as if to an imaginary audience that was recording his every word for posterity.

He received me in De Gofroy's study, where I had once stolen the files the Grand Regent collected on every Regent, containing information from informants and Protocols. They had been returned there now, I knew, though not without my having deleted certain files. My own in particular, as well Lasinha's, Molijc's, Ana's, and a few others I felt were relevant. I had removed the files from the hard drive in the terrible days before De Gofroy died, when it was still unclear whether or not we would emerge triumphant.

If Lasinha and Molijc had noticed these deletions, they had said nothing. I neglected to mention the deletions, or the fact that I had made copies of all the files, which I kept in a safe place. We all had our secrets, after all, and we all had our reasons for keeping things from each other. I was no different than them in that regard.

Dejian sat and motioned for me to speak, a self-conscious gesture, a king beckoning a courtier to deliver her message. I did not bother to hide my annoyance.

"Practicing for your new role, are you?"

Dejian smiled, not betraying any emotion. "Much has

changed in these last months, as you are becoming aware. Among them is that this faithful vessel has received a revelation."

I raised an eyebrow. "A revelation?"

"Yes. The lieutenant was my guide."

De Gofroy had once been a lieutenant in the Canadian army, as every Regent knew, and had fought in several major engagements of what had since become known as the Society Wars. These wars, which had taken place before I was born, had been initiated following the arrival of the Society in our world, along with the realization that the planet's oil reserves would be exhausted within the next decades.

Both had resulted in seismic shocks across the geopolitical landscape, shattering the political order of the day. The great powers of the time—the U.S. and China—had found themselves suddenly obsolete, and the Society had begun its slow integration into the fabric of all our lives. By the time I was born, they were already the final arbiter on the planet, even if they ruled nowhere. No government would stand against them, though we in the Church had tried many times to find some state amenable to a rebellion.

It had proved an impossible task. The Society was ostensibly independent and apart from politics—a necessity, given the importance of what they controlled—and yet the reality was their influence was felt everywhere. People did not see it anymore; the Travelers were like the color of the sky. But we in the Church knew. And for it we were dismissed as a lunatic fringe, as apostles of a cult that followed beliefs that went against all accepted understandings of the way the universes functioned.

Never mind that the laws of the universes had been written by the Society only a few decades earlier and accepted by everyone only because the Travelers had a monopoly on the facts under discussion. They shaped them to their end.

All this came to mind as Dejian began a soliloquy on the faith, his revelation, how De Gofroy had chosen him to guide all Regents and the Church, and how we were vessels for our greater, true selves. He expected me to accept all he said, just as the Society expected us all to accept what they said about the functioning of the universes just because they controlled the passages between them.

"De Gofroy asked all three of us to guide the faith. To protect it," I said. "He also wanted Frederik to act as Grand Regent."

"That was his sub-carcass speaking. He has come to me again. His true self, or an aspect of it. He has found a way to reach across the fabric connecting the universes and speak to me. To guide me and to ask that I guide us all," Molijc said, with a certainty that I found disconcerting.

"And his appearance just happened to correspond with Frederik fucking off and absconding with all the Church's money? That's useful, I suppose."

"You have never believed as I have, Laila."

I flinched, my whole body going taut with rage. "Don't you even. I have given everything to this Church. I have done everything that De Gofroy asked of me. I've done everything that was asked of me."

For the first time since I entered the room, Molijc seemed to look at me. "You've done a creditable job for the faith, of that there is no doubt. De Gofroy asked us all to see to the fate of the Church and we have done that, in spite of certain betrayals."

"It's that I want to speak about," I said, before he could launch into another speech. "The future of the Church is precarious now. Once it gets out about what Frederik did—and it will, in some form or another—more people will leave. There can't be any secrets among us three anymore. We can't afford to work at opposing ends. Not now. You and Lasinha need to trust me."

"Trust. Trust." Dejian frowned, as though the word

had some hidden significance he was not aware of. "I am surprised to hear you speak of that. You of all people."

I swallowed, knowing what was coming next. What would be said. I had spent the last days on the airship preparing myself for this moment. To no use, it seemed. "I know that I share as much blame in this as you or Lasinha. We both know what I have done."

Dejian went still, his lips curled into a failed attempt at a smile. He would not look at me. "I loved you, Laila," he said, and there was genuine hurt in his voice.

My instinct was to throw something back in his face. To say that he loved being Grand Regent more than me. That power was his true desire. That his pettiness in the face of my betrayal had nearly cost us the Church. But I forced myself not to. I knew that doing so would only result in my being cast from the inner circle of the Church, if not the faith itself.

"I know," I said, swallowing. "I love you too. I understand if you don't share those feelings for me anymore. I don't deserve them for what I've done to you. But I hope you know you can trust me. I will never betray the faith. Or you again. I swear it."

Dejian considered this before taking a long, ragged breath. I could feel the emotion overwhelming me as well. "I will always love you," he finally said. "Always. But I don't know if I can trust you again."

"What do I need to do?" I said. But I knew the answer to that question.

"Leave her. Return to me." He stared at me, his eyes hard.

I wanted to weep, to beg him to ask anything else of me but that. Did I still love Dejian? Perhaps. But there could be no doubt about my feelings for Meredith. I had not gone to her upon my return because I knew I would be coming here to speak to Dejian. I knew what he would ask of me, and I could not risk weakening my resolve.

I choked back my feeling. "Of course. If that is what it

will take."

"It is."

I nodded, unable to say any more. We talked some more about matters of the Church and what must be done now that Frederik had been deposed, but I heard none of it, and it was gone from my mind by the time I left the room. All I could think of was Meredith. How could I tell her? How could I explain it?

I knew what I would say. That it had nothing to do with my feelings for her or for Dejian. This was a sacrifice I was making for the sake of the Church. I must remain beside Molijc, especially now that he would become Grand Regent, so that I might have his ear as well as Lasinha. It was necessary. The faith needed me, and I had promised De Gofroy I would protect it.

There was some truth in that—Lasinha and Molijc's worst instincts, if left unchecked, could consume the entire Church. But vanity played its part too. I needed the faith. I needed, just as much Molijc needed, to be one of the ones who was necessary for the its survival. To be the one De Gofroy had chosen, at the center of it all.

Without the faith, without my role in the Hierarchy, I was nothing. I was that same stupid Laila Johar from Medicine Hat—the fuck-up who had bungled away her life for no purpose. If maintaining this place meant pushing aside the woman I loved, then I would do so. Even if it meant tearing myself apart.

9

Meredith did not say anything when I told her what Dejian had asked of me and what I had agreed to do. Her face betrayed nothing, beyond a slight tightening of her lips, and her eyes, which seemed to grow darker somehow. She offered no judgment, no comment. Her lack of display of any sort of feeling—not anger, not hurt, not surprise—broke me. I was barely able to stop the flow of tears, and by the end I felt as though I had survived a beating.

"I would like to return to Osahi," Meredith said—the only thing she said after I spent interminable minutes trying and failing to find the words to explain and justify what I was doing. There were none, at least none that would make a difference, and we both knew it.

"Of course," I said, flinching a little. I wanted to tell her that doing so would only confirm Lasinha and Dejian's suspicions of her and our relationship, but I knew I was in no position to do so. "If he will have you."

"He will," she said, with a fierceness that stung.

I could only nod and watch as she left our quarters. By the end of the day, I'd moved out of those quarters and into the palatial Grand Regent quarters with Molijc, under the watchful gaze of a few Protectors I did not recognize.

They were Lasinha's people, and I would quickly grow used to being under constant observation in those rooms, my every move and word scrutinized. I had been let back into the inner circle of the Hierarchy, but I was not yet trusted.

The next weeks we spent in a frenzied kind of damage control, trying to find a plausible reason for Frederik's continued disappearance. Dejian fulfilled his obligations as Grand Regent, and spent time going to Protocol Centers across North America, giving speeches and rallying the faithful. At his insistence, I was at his side, smiling, a piece of scenery upon his stage. How we could afford such a grand tour, with the Church's airship, I did not know, nor did I ask. If the Church had funds hidden somewhere, Lasinha and Molijc would certainly have been the ones to find it.

When questions came about Frederik and what had become of him, Dejian would smile and say that Frederik had gone to a secret location to dedicate himself to meditation and Protocols, to try to better connect with his far-flung other selves. His own revelation he did not mention. That, I knew, would come eventually, when he ascended to the Grand Regent's title.

Our story about Frederik was feeble and couldn't withstand any scrutiny. There were stories in the media about his arrest in Montreal and subsequent release, heavy with the implication that we had paid bribes to ensure no charges were brought for the supposedly heinous crimes he had committed. These were Society plants, and though we tried to counteract them with our own favored journalists, it did little to stem the rumors and stories that resulted.

Of course, most Regents paid little mind to the press. They knew that most stories about the Church were the result of Traveler propaganda, and gave them little credence as a result. Within the Church there were endless stories, however, many spread by those who felt we had too much influence in the Hierarchy.

When we returned from our grand tour, which I realized was to help prepare the way for Molijc to assume the title of Grand Regent, by demonstrating his ability to the faithful, Osahi demanded a meeting with us. He was furious, for he had no doubt ferreted out some of the truth of what had happened, with his agents in the Society. It confirmed all his suspicions of Frederik and proved he had been right all along.

The three of us—Molijc, Lasinha, and I—met with him in the main room of the Grand Regent's quarters where De Gofroy used to receive his supplicants. We sat, the three of us, in matching chairs arrayed close together, giving the appearance of unity. I was there for appearances only, for Molijc and Lasinha still would not share with me what their plans were or what they had done.

Osahi brought Meredith with him—of course he did— and she stood behind him, expressionless, as he sat across from us. He was wearing another of his elaborate costumes, playing the part of a buccaneer come to raid our vessels, it seemed, with an azure jacket, a ruffled white shirt, and formfitting breeches. The color of the jacket, and the way light played off it, was reminiscent of the Acolyte's Eye, or the garb of a Seeker. I found it disconcerting, though not as distressing as the fact that Meredith would not so much as glance in my direction.

Molijc began the meeting by standing to welcome Osahi. "Welcome, Toma. So gracious of you to join us. The glorious faith—"

Before he could continue with whatever spiel he intended, Osahi cut him off. "Let's get to it. I don't know what in the hell you three are up to, but quit your pissing around. Frederik should never have been Grand Regent. I only returned because you agreed to remove him. Now, here we are, a year later, and all you've managed to orchestrate is this disaster. It's unfathomable to me that De Gofroy trusted you to run a Protocol, let alone run the

Church."

It was an unfair thing to say, and even Osahi would know it. He had been as instrumental in Lasinha and I joining the Protectors as De Gofroy. His comments seemed more aimed at Molijc, and Dejian certainly took them that way. He was apoplectic, practically spitting at Osahi.

"You dare to speak to us that way, after all that you have done in defiance of De Gofroy's express wishes."

"The wishes that you whispered in his ear," Osahi said, offering no reaction to Molijc's outburst.

"Toma, it went against my better judgment to allow you back into the faith after your conspiracy against it. But Laila is a better person than I in many ways. She told me that forgiveness is the correct path. I have forgiven you your trespasses, but, make no mistake, we have not forgotten. We will not forget what you have done, and we will see that the price of your betrayal is paid in full."

I looked at Molijc, horrified at what he was suggesting. It was beyond brazen. Lasinha seemed unperturbed by it, his perpetual smile still present. Osahi, too, was unconcerned. He did not even look at Molijc, turning instead to Lasinha.

"If we are talking about betrayal, then let us be plain. No Regents have died at my hands. No one at all, for that matter. Not everyone in this room can say the same. So if you won't forgive or forget, rest assured that I will do the same."

Lasinha raised a hand to forestall either man from saying anything further. "We've all done things we regret, but no one's faith can be doubted. We did what we did because we knew the faith and De Gofroy's project was at stake. We are here now because it is still at stake. If we do not have peace here between us, it will fail."

Osahi's lips curled into a snarl. "Very well," he said. "What about Frederik?"

"He no longer has authority in this Church," Lasinha

said.

"He is a name, nothing more," Molijc said.

"That is what you claimed before, and look what he managed to do."

Molijc was about to reply when I looked at him. "The situation is in hand now," I said.

"Yes," Lasinha said. "No denying, he played us for fools. But that's over now. He's secured, and we won't be seeing him anytime soon. What remains is to ensure that we can transfer the Grand Regency to Dejian, as we all agreed, without incurring any more damage to the Church."

Osahi looked as though he were about to say something, but changed his mind and stopped himself. "Let us say I agree. What do you propose?"

Lasinha looked at Molijc, who nodded. "We've already begun to spread word that Frederik has secluded himself for study and contemplation. We plan to say that he has decided to step down and pass the Grand Regency on to Dejian."

Osahi shook his head. "That won't work," he said. "It will just feed the rumors that are already out there. People need to see him and hear it from him, or there will be questions. So long as he is out there, people will question your legitimacy."

"That will happen regardless," I said. "But I think you're right. People do need to see Frederik. To know that he is still part of the faith. And that he is all right."

I looked at Lasinha and Molijc as I said it, a challenge in my eyes. Molijc looked uncomfortable, while Lasinha smiled. I could think of only one instance when I had truly seen him sweat, and Osahi had been the author of that moment. Even then, it had only been for a moment. That night was another I would have liked to banish from my memories if I could.

Where was Arajuano now, I wondered? Had he always been a Traveler agent, or had we simply pushed him to it with his exile? Whatever the case, the results had been the same. He had nearly singlehandedly destroyed the Church. Now I wondered if we had done the same with Ana, pushing her to the Society, ostensibly to save her, only to have her disappear without a word or trace.

"I agree," Lasinha said. "When Dejian is ready to officially take the Grand Regency, we will bring Frederik back and have him step down. The faithful need to see in order to believe."

"They will believe," Molijc said, waving a dismissive hand. "I have been granted a revelation by De Gofroy. He has chosen me as his vessel to guide the faith. Everyone will soon understand. As faithful vessels, they will follow me, for I have been chosen."

There was a long silence after Molijc spoke. Osahi stared at him with something approaching derision on his face. I could not blame him. All the talk of revelations was something outside of the faith. De Gofroy had never claimed to receive guidance from his other selves. His belief had been rigorous, a matter of uncovering a true understanding of the universe. This talk of revelation was something else, nearly contradicting De Gofroy's own teachings.

Meredith, I saw, was looking at Molijc in disbelief too. Only Lasinha seemed unperturbed, but that was to be expected. I never knew what he was thinking.

"I hope what you say is true," Osahi said at last, though it was clear by his tone that he did not put much faith in it. "There are dark days ahead for the faith and for this Church. It needs De Gofroy's guidance; it needs his insight. I just hope you know half as much as you think you do."

Molijc smiled, a cruel and invincible smile. "I know what is necessary for the faith. Everyone will see soon."

Those last words sounded like a proclamation of doom. Osahi just laughed and got up to leave. Lasinha's smile broadened, and he stood to escort him to the door.

Meredith followed, after allowing herself a small glance in my direction. I saw my fears and doubts mirrored in her eyes, which only increased my unease. The room felt stifling and claustrophobic, and I longed to follow them.

Instead, I remained with Molijc, our silence as stifling as the air. Before, I had thought his talk of revelation, of being chosen by De Gofroy, was just that, talk. He had always been given to grandiose statements, never afraid of looking utterly ridiculous. But now I saw that I was wrong. He believed.

10

At my insistence, Molijc and Lasinha gave me access to all the Church records, financial and otherwise, so I could see for myself what the true state of affairs was. Not just the main accounts, which Frederik had largely emptied, but a list of all our assets, and a list of all the subaccounts that various fiefdoms like the Protectors and the Acolytes had control of, to say nothing of the various Protocol Centers and other official Church agencies.

I spent weeks combing through everything, trying to get a sense of it all. It was incredible and mind-numbing in equal measure. By the end, I felt I had a firm grasp on the true state of the Church, the number of faithful we could actually count upon, and the cost of maintaining the vast infrastructure that had been constructed over the years. Undoubtedly there were things that Molijc and Lasinha still hadn't shared with me, shadows of operations that I could only see hints of in the accounting, but I had no doubt that I would be able to discover everything given time.

It was clear to me that things needed to change if the Church was to survive this turmoil, and the storms to come, and hope to grow again. As a beginning, I centralized the organization of the various Protocol Centers and other official proselytization agencies, removing duplication in efforts wherever possible. The lands and buildings we owned that, in my judgment, were being underutilized were sold off to help pay our steadily mounting bills.

Dejian encouraged my efforts to reorganize the Church institutions. "It is good that you have taken an interest in the actual matters of the faith, instead of these esoteric matters that compelled you before," he told me one morning as we had breakfast.

We had taken to eating that meal together as often as his schedule allowed. Since his grand tour, he regularly left the campus to meet with the faithful, laying the ground for his succession and wanting to be seen by as many Regents as possible. He did not insist on my attending all these event with him, which was a relief, for I found them interminable. Dejian was in his element, though.

"I'm glad to be of service to the faith," I said, not rising to the bait. The "esoteric matters" he was referring to meant Meredith, I knew.

In spite of the evident trust he placed in me, he still had not forgiven me for my affair with her. Nor could I blame him. Though we shared the Grand Regent's quarters, we slept in separate rooms. He had shown no interest yet in resuming our relationship. For that I was alternately relieved and angry, but I tried not to interrogate my emotions on the matter too deeply.

For one thing, there was far too much to be done. My reorganization of the Church and its Hierarchy, which took the better part of six months, helped to stanch the bleeding, but it did not heal the wounds we had suffered as a result of De Gofroy's death and Frederik's betrayals. People continued to leave the Church in droves, and even those who remained did not visit the Protocol Centers as regularly or donate as much to the faith. It seemed obvious that, unless things drastically changed, the Church would die a slow death, strangled by lack of funds.

The faith would not die, of course. Those of us who believed would continue to do so regardless of the Church itself. But without the Church, how could we hope to achieve De Gofroy's vision? How could we cross over to the other worlds and search for the one true universe?

It was these questions that drove me. I had to make certain that the Church survived so that we had a chance to realize what De Gofroy, and so many others, had dedicated their lives toward. We owed it to them to see it done.

The other reason for my immersion in the minutiae of the Church's finances and infrastructure was that I knew Molijc and Lasinha were still hiding things from me. They were working with the Acolytes on something, which they said nothing about to me. As a Protector on the front lines of the battle to guard the faith, I had imagined that I knew all the Church's secrets, but now I knew that I did not.

The Acolytes were their own world within the Church, and Lasinha and Molijc seemed intent on creating another world apart as well. I could only hope I could convince them to allow me to enter it.

My suspicions only grew when I next saw Frederik. Lasinha had him brought from the Acolyte complex in Saskatchewan when we judged the timing right for Dejian to ascend to the Grand Regency. The plan was that he would meet with Molijc in an official and very public way, to dispel the rumors that still persisted. Following that, there would be a private meeting where Frederik would announce his intention to step aside.

It would be a tricky moment, or so I thought. Lasinha and Molijc were unworried. The stories about Frederik had dimmed somewhat in the months following his betrayal and initial disappearance, as his absence, and the absence of any further details, starved the fires. Lasinha and I had been carefully laying the groundwork, with our agents disseminating "rumors" to the effect that Frederik would be stepping aside in favor of Molijc, and these had gained some traction.

But it would all fall apart if Frederik was uncooperative. Or worse, if it seemed as though his resigning as head of the Church had been coerced in any way. Which it most certainly had.

"Don't worry," Lasinha told me, as we drove to the airport to meet the airship that was carrying Frederik. "Freddy will be a good boy."

"I trust the Acolytes know how to hide bruises," I said.

He laughed, which made me even more squeamish. "Have you ever known an Acolyte who seemed capable of resorting to violence? Frederik has not been ill-treated while he is there."

We came to the security gate by the airport's landing field and were waved through by the guard without a second glance. He was a Regent, as many of the airport staff were, something we had viewed as a necessity following the airship disaster.

"They've just been experimenting on him," I said, giving voice to my suspicions.

Lasinha clicked his tongue. "They're doing experiments with the Eye. I'm not sure what. You know how they are. But they wouldn't do anything to harm him. We still need him, after all."

Not after today, I thought. I did not believe him when he professed his innocence as to the Acolytes' intentions with Frederik. Despite his perpetual mask of casual indifference, Lasinha was, above all, careful and cautious. He would not allow a potential landmine that might disrupt Dejian's position, and our own, without knowing what the consequences would be.

That he wouldn't tell me what they were doing could mean several things. Perhaps he thought I would disapprove of the Acolytes' experiments, whatever they were. Even if that did not concern him, he might want to keep what they were doing a secret from me for any number of reasons. Did he still fear that I would return to Meredith and she would inform Osahi?

Never mind that she had done no such thing during our time together, at least not after the airship disaster. I trusted her more than either Molijc or Lasinha. At the end of the day, I knew what she was. With Dejian, I had believed I did as well, but now I was no longer certain. And Lasinha was too much like me, always slippery. Always just evading my grasp.

The airship was already docked when we arrived, the trolley stairs being put in place by the door into the main cabin. I pulled up near the stairs, and both Lasinha and I got out of the van, staring up at the door, waiting for someone to emerge. My palms were damp with sweat, though I couldn't have said why I was nervous. It wasn't as though Frederik was going to try to make a break for it on the tarmac. The real trouble, if it arrived, would come later.

A figure emerged at the door, stepping from the shadows of the cabin into the light. I was surprised to see it was Frederik. Even more disarmingly, he was wearing a suit, dark in color and conservative in cut, which was entirely unlike him. He descended alone and approached Lasinha, shaking his hand warmly, before coming to embrace me. I hesitated, glancing past him to the stairway, still expecting to see an Acolyte escort descending from the airship.

"Laila, you look beautiful as always," Frederik said, smiling and taking me into his arms.

His words left me cold. There was something in his face, his smile, his intonation that was wrong. When I looked into his eyes, they seemed vacant and unfocused somehow. Drugs, I assumed, though he did not move or react like someone who was under the influence. He seemed just this side of normal.

"Shall we go?" Lasinha said.

"Yes," Frederik said, climbing into the back of the van.

I glanced back again at the airship, but no one else emerged from its cabin. Lasinha smiled at me, one of his rare genuine smiles, like a cat that had caught a bird. We got into the van and drove back to the campus in silence.

Everything had been prepared by the time we arrived. A large crowd of Regents and Initiates was gathering on the lawn outside the Grand Regent's tower. A dais had been set up, draped with banners and symbols of the Church. There was an image of a Mayan calendar and, at the center of the stage, a massive illustration of the Hunab Ku, which De Gofroy had identified as the symbol indicating the many worlds and our collective consciousness.

We parked on the outskirts of campus and slipped Frederik through the tunnels that interconnected the buildings, emerging in the basement of the Grand Regent's tower, where Molijc was waiting for us. He was pacing and agitated, his face covered in a sheen of sweat, which surprised me. This was normally his element. It was as though he and Frederik had had their minds transposed in their bodies.

Frederik went to greet Dejian, just as he had Lasinha and I. Molijc ignored him, glaring at Lasinha. "Is he prepared?"

"They have assured me," Lasinha said quietly, glancing in my direction.

Dejian nodded. "Good," he said, ignoring Lasinha's signal to be quiet. "If he fucks this up, it will be on their heads."

A flash of displeasure crossed Lasinha's face, disappearing so quickly that I wondered if I had actually seen it. Frederik remained standing beside Molijc, waiting for him to shake his hand, apparently utterly oblivious to the conversation that had just transpired. It was a strange sort of obliviousness, I thought, but he did not seem unhappy. There was none of the despair that had overwhelmed him the last time I saw him, after he was abandoned by Arajuano.

"It will be fine," Lasinha said. "Let's get it done, and then we can move on with what is really important."

"The faith," Frederik said in a solemn voice.

"Yes," Lasinha said, favoring him with a condescending smile, which made Frederik practically glow.

I shuddered, despite my best efforts not to show my discomfort. Lasinha saw it, but I could not tell what he thought of my reaction; his expression was as unreadable as ever. If I had been forced to put a word to it, I would have said he was excited by my reaction, though I could not have said why.

I had no time to consider this, for Molijc announced himself ready and we went upstairs and out of the tower, mounting the stage, together, arm in arm. Frederik went ahead of us, waving and smiling as the crowd cheered. He went to the podium at the center of the dais, while Molijc and I stood behind him and to his left, doing our best to look reflective and impassive.

He pulled a sheet from inside the pocket of his suit jacket. I wondered briefly who had prepared it for him, though I knew it must have been Molijc or Lasinha. The question was definitely answered as Frederik began his speech. It began as we had more or less discussed, with Frederik telling the assembled that he had spent the last months in solitude contemplating the faith and trying to connect with the disparate parts of his father's souls across the veils of the universes.

"Though I have yet to find my father, neither his true self or any of his Regent beings, I have come to two realizations. One is that this is where my path lies now. I must see this journey to some kind of end, though I do not know what it will lead. But I realize that I cannot do this and see to you and to this Church. Someone else must guide us."

Frederik paused, looking down at the crowd to smile. "The second realization is that I know the man to do so. The man to guide and lead this faith. He has received a revelation from my father. A gift of the spirit denied to me. He has been chosen to lead this faith and to take us to the other universes. And I believe he will do so."

I did not hear the rest of Frederik's words, nor did I pay any attention to what Molijc said after in accepting his anointment as Grand Regent. The talk of revelation—Dejian's clear belief in it—shook me to the core. That we were standing here saying this to the faithful, when there was nothing in De Gofroy's writing to say that such a thing was at all possible, struck me as foolhardy in the extreme.

There were wild cheers from the crowd at both Frederik and Molijc's words, but from the stage I could see how false those were. Most were plants, Protectors sent out to make noise and hopefully bring the rest of audience along with them. The larger portion remained silent, or clapped tepidly. They appeared as unsure about what was being said as I was. I had no idea how this would all appear to those on remotes across the planet, but I could not imagine it would be any more inspiring than it was for those actually here.

After the speeches, we retreated to the Grand Regent's chambers, where we had a muted celebration with the High Regents and several other important figures in the Hierarchy. Everyone seemed awkward and guarded, hesitant to give voice to whatever their true thoughts were. Molijc moved through the room, talking with everyone and accepting their congratulations with a fierce energy, as though daring them to defy him.

Though I wanted to disappear and gather my thoughts on all that had just happened, I stayed at his side, accepting the blank-faced murmurs of delight that everyone gave. I could feel everyone's sidelong glances as we shifted on to the next group of Regents, could sense the whispered conversations. What would they be saying about us and all we had done to the faith?

Frederik was present for the first part of the evening, but Lasinha took him away as soon as politeness allowed. I saw him again much later as the party wound down when I stepped out to get away from the press of people and their endless, discreet stares. Massaging my temples in an effort to ward off the headache I felt approaching, I wandered from the main chambers, past the elevators, to the other side of the tower, toward a small alcove with a window that overlooked the whole campus.

Frederik was already there, staring out the window. He started at my approach, looking back at me with wild eyes. As I came closer, he backed into the alcove, as though he were trapped, with no idea of where to go. His expression was one of panic and fear, nothing like the person he had been only a few short hours ago.

"Frederik, what's wrong?" I said, reaching out to comfort him. He flinched at my movement, raising his hands to cover his face.

"Who are you?" he said.

"Frederik, it's Laila. What's the matter? You can tell me." I kept my voice calm and soothing, though the sight of him and his obviously confused state left me deeply concerned.

Frederik looked at me, as though trying to judge whether he could trust me enough to confide. It appeared he had made his decision, and was about to speak when an Acolyte materialized beside me. His sudden appearance was a shock to me, and it nearly undid poor Frederik, who cowered in the corner. It was the same Acolyte, I realized, who Lasinha and I had given Frederik to on the airship in Montreal. The same Acolyte who had cared for De Gofroy in those final terrible months when he was held in suspension.

The Acolyte twisted his ugly visage into smile. "Freddy, you shouldn't be out. Come with me back to your room."

It was as though he were addressing a child. Frederik looked at the Acolyte in terror before turning to me. "Please, don't make me."

"This is not your concern, Laila," the Acolyte whispered to me. He held out a hand to Frederik. "Come along, Freddy. It's time to go."

Weeping, Frederik went with the Acolyte and was led down the hallway into one of the rooms while I watched in horror, unable to summon any kind of reaction. I knew I should be stopping this madness, halting the Acolyte from whatever he was doing to Frederik. He was clearly in distress and unable to fend for himself. But I could only stand idly by.

The Acolyte emerged from the room where he had taken Frederik five minutes later. In all that time I had not moved, still processing what I had seen and what it meant. The Acolyte must have been on the airship and come to campus separately and in secret. Was it paranoia from Molijc and Lasinha, wanting to ensure that no link could be made between Frederik's fate and the Acolytes? But he could easily have joined us in the van, for no one had seen us entering the campus. The obvious conclusion was that they did not want me to know about his presence. But why?

These thoughts flickered through my mind as the Acolyte closed the door behind him and glanced in my direction. He grimaced a little seeing me standing there, and I thought he might come to speak to me. Perhaps he thought about it. Instead, he turned and went down the corridor toward the Grand Regent's chambers.

After a moment, I followed him, returning to the celebration. He was not there, I noticed, though I was not surprised. Neither was Molijc.

11

The ceremony anointing Molijc as the new Grand Regent took place a week later, without apparent controversy. Immediately following his ascension to the role, we set out upon another grand tour, visiting Protocol Centers and connecting Molijc with as many of the faithful as possible. It seemed to have its intended effect, for donations to the faith remained steady. There was a drop in the number of Initiates joining the faith, but that was to be expected with all the turmoil and rumor we had suffered through.

We could almost believe the worst had passed. For Dejian's part, he was certain the faith was now stronger. "Those who had doubts have been cast out, and those who remain have iron in their blood. They will be faithful vessels. We shall mold them for the battles to come with the Society."

"What battles are those?" I asked him.

"Our eternal struggle, of course. I have great hope that we shall find the means to cross over. If we do, the Society will menace us at every turn, even more than they do now. But people will flock to the faith."

I didn't know what gave him such hope. All our infiltration of the Society had managed to that point was to lose Ana so utterly that she might have been better to have suffered exile from the faith under Osahi. Of her fate, we knew nothing. I had long since abandoned hope of her returning. While Lasinha still professed confidence in her eventual return, his actions said otherwise. He no longer spoke of her, no longer asked his agents within the Society to send word. Nor did I, for I knew none would be forthcoming.

As we traveled, we worked hard to consolidate our hold upon the Hierarchy of the faith. Every Protocol Center and every church had at least one person who was loyal to us in a position of authority. There was no one to oppose us at the moment, with even Osahi nominally allied with us, but we all knew how quickly things could change. If we were seen to have failed the faith in some way, those remaining would turn against us.

When we finally returned to Calgary, I felt as settled and happy as I had in some time. I still dreamed of Meredith, but the agony of her absence had lessened to a bearable ache. Dejian, despite his grandiose statements about revelation, was a fine leader of the faith. He was as galvanizing a presence as De Gofroy had been, and he was as gifted at the Protocols as any of us. I still had my doubts about his alliance with the Acolytes, but for now I pushed those aside, as there could no doubt he was the best leader available for the faith.

He still had shown no inclination for us to resume our previous relationship, which left me conflicted. I was still unsure I felt anything like that for him anymore, and yet I longed for some physical contact, for something to replace what I had with Meredith. To help me forget her.

I was also left with some question of what to do with myself. Molijc expected me to be a prop that he could use to demonstrate his worthiness to lead the faith, my faithfulness to him evidence that others could put their trust in him. That held little interest to me, and I chafed under those strictures. I was not some symbol for others to use as they pleased.

I told him as much: "I've done this for now, because you asked me to, and I felt it was important to the faith and to your Grand Regency. And I will continue to do it. But I am going to return to the Protectors. That is where I can serve the faith best. Besides, someone needs to watch Osahi."

"Lasinha can do that," Dejian said, with a dismissive wave of his hand. "Osahi will play along because he can see which way the wind is blowing now."

I set down my fork, stopping myself from glaring at him. We were having breakfast in one of the Grand Regent's chambers. It was another thing that he still insisted upon, that we share breakfast after his prayers and meditation. Every day seemed to bring some new stricture that he demanded, from which I could not deviate. It was hard not to become infuriated and show my frustration.

I chose my words carefully, keeping my tone even. "De Gofroy chose all of us to protect the faith, not just you. I have my part to play too, and it is not just sitting here."

It was as though he hadn't heard me. "You have always been a faithful vessel, Laila. Of that there can be no doubt. But it is clear where your place in the faith is, where you can do the most for it. And that is beside me, helping me bring De Gofroy's revelation to the worlds."

It was his revelation, but I did not want to say that. Just as I didn't want to tell him that I didn't believe in his revelation, had no concept of what it even was. If I wanted to continue to influence the direction of the Church—and make sure that Molijc didn't go too far down the badger hole of his supposed revelation, as well as acting as a counter to the Acolytes and even Lasinha—I would have to keep silent on many things. But I could not entirely accede to his will, or he would simply ignore me.

"I will not do it," I said, my voice brittle. "There are things that need to be done. You can say that your revelation has told you that we shall overcome the Society and open the channels to the other universes. I have no doubt that it's true. But we both know doing so will take hard work, not miracles. And it will be Lasinha and I who will lead that, because there's no one else you can trust."

He glared, taken aback. Had he expected me to simply go along with everything he said? So it seemed. His obliviousness surprised me. It was as though he had forgotten everything he had known about me before.

"What do you have in mind?" he said, in a quiet voice. His eyes had changed, and I could see that his guard was down and that he was unsure of himself and the ground he stood on. Here was the real Dejian, one I had not seen in some time. Not since Meredith.

"I'm going to find Ana," I said, not even realizing that was what I had wanted to do all along. "I'm going to bring her back from the Society."

"And then what?" Dejian said, his voice bitter with recrimination. He, of all people, knew about the depth of my feeling for her.

I looked at him, a challenge in my eyes. "If she's done her work, we will cross over."

It was well on to morning, and I was in a deep sleep, consumed by a dream where I chased a hooded Traveler, who I knew to be Ana. Every time it appeared that I was near enough to touch her, my perspective would dissolve and I would see that I was, in fact, standing far from her. I climbed mountains, descended into valleys, and lost myself in a maze of streets that circled in on each other. She was always there, but never near.

More disturbing was the sense, growing throughout my dream, of someone watching me. It began as a niggling worry I dismissed as a distraction from my search from Ana. But it grew and grew as time went on, and thoughts of Ana became remoter and remoter. I never caught sight of the people pursuing, but I knew they were there. No matter what I did to lose them—run, circle back, or duck into alleys or stray doorways—they were there. Watching and waiting.

I was so possessed by this dream, by the sense of being hounded, that when my arms were pinned behind my back and a hood placed over my head, I thought it was somehow part of the nightmare. It was when I began to struggle and thrash, my elbow striking someone in a soft place in their body, and I heard someone mutter a curse, that I realized I was no longer dreaming. This was a nightmare come to life.

There were two of them, at least, and they led me from my quarters in the Grand Regent's tower, still in my underwear, to the stairwell opposite the elevators. Normally there would have been someone on watch there, which told me that whoever was on duty had been subdued or bought off. I made a note to remember to check the duty roster, for I was confident I would be able to escape this predicament and these bounds.

I was untouchable in the Church and its Hierarchy, except by Molijc or Lasinha, and this did not feel like it had their hands upon it. If they came for me, it would not be like this. They would do it in the light of day, in public, and in a way that would leave me with no way but to go along with them. No force would be necessary. They would sidle up and slip the knife in, all with a smile.

This, brutal and direct, with no subterfuge as to its intent, had Osahi's fingerprints on it. The only question was what he was after, and how far he was willing to go to get it.

As they led me down the stairs and then through various twists and turns through silent corridors, I made sure to pay attention so that I had a fairly good sense of where we were and where we were heading. It was to the basement of the Protector's House, further confirming my suspicions. I had been in those rooms before with Osahi, and I could not help recalling another night when I had been awoken without warning and brought to a basement interrogation room to witness Gabriel Arajuano's final hours in the Church.

A door was opened and I was taken into a room and deposited on a chair. My hands were still bound, the hood tight over my head. I was left alone—I could hear at least two pairs of feet leaving the room and the door closing—for what seemed like half an hour, though it was hard to judge how much time actually passed. There was nothing to distinguish one moment from the next beyond the growing ache in my wrists where the rope was cutting into them. At first, I fought against them, trying to see if I could work myself free, but all I managed was to have the rope dig in further.

Realizing there was no use to trying to escape, I surrendered, trying not to let despair enter my thoughts. I focused instead on why I had been brought here. What did Osahi want with me? It seemed unlikely he would dare to take Molijc, given he was now Grand Regent. And somehow I imagined that Lasinha was too slippery to let himself get taken as I had.

I could not see the end game here. Dejian would not accept my banishment from the Church—it would reflect too poorly on him, something he could not afford so early in his Grand Regency—and Osahi would know that. Molijc would never exile me, no matter what I did. He would want me kept close, so that he could punish me, as he was for my betrayal with Meredith.

Perhaps Osahi wanted to try to turn me against the others, though surely he knew this was the wrong way to go about it. This reeked of desperation and fear the more I thought about. What was Osahi so scared of?

"I know what you three are doing," Osahi said, his voice seeming to emerge from the darkness that enveloped me. Somehow, he had entered the room without my knowing. Or had he been here all along? Sweat formed on my face and neck, trickling down my back. I offered no reply.

"I know what you're doing," he said again, all insinuation. "And it ends tonight."

"I'm not answering your questions," I said, cursing my voice, which quavered with emotion. "You have no right to subject me to this."

"I haven't asked you any questions," Osahi said. "Nor do I intend to. Not of you, not of the snake Lasinha, and certainly not of that usurper Molijc. How you can sleep with him is beyond my understanding."

I almost laughed when he said that, but a quick bite of my lip stopped it. He was obviously not well informed as to the current nature of my relationship with the Grand Regent. Dejian would be happy to hear that Osahi believed us to be sleeping together, because if he did, then so did everyone else. That appearance was important to him, important to his conception of himself as Grand Regent, though I couldn't understand why.

It still did not explain what this was all about, why Osahi had risked so much to get me alone to interrogate. The answer to that came when he next spoke.

"I know what you have done. You've sacrificed the faith for your chance at power, all of you. I cannot believe it. If De Gofroy had only known—but Molijc saw to that, didn't he?"

I swallowed, trying to work some moisture into my mouth. This would be easier if he removed the hood and let me look him in the eye. "What have we done, Toma?" I said. "You insinuate, but you don't say. If you're going to accuse me of something, have the guts to do it properly."

"Don't pretend with me. Not now. I know now that you engineered Ana's exile to save her. She is with the Society as a *double agent* now. You're as blinded by your lust as Frederik was. You're her double agent. All of you."

"You've gone mad," I said. "Ana was always faithful, whatever her father did. And you know as much as I do about what's become of her. For all I know, the Travelers are doing to her what you're doing to me."

A chair scraped against the floor and I could sense Osahi sitting in it, looking me in the hood, so to speak. "I don't believe you," he said.

"You never will. That's why you wanted back in. That's why you wanted Frederik out. That's why, even though you have professed your loyalty to Dejian, you will never trust him. And you will do everything in your power to have him removed."

Osahi gave a bitter laugh. "You think me the power-mad provocateur, willing to destroy the faith if it means I can control the Church. But that is all projection. You three are the ones who see nothing but authority when you kneel for your prayers. I know I was too blunt an instrument for De Gofroy to ever let me into the light. And I knew too much for any of the High Regents to ever trust me. But I have always had what is best for the faith closest to my heart."

"We all have," I said, taken aback at the emotion in his voice. Was it at all real?

He seemed not to have heard me. Or, at least, he paid me no mind. "But you're not worried about any of that, are you? You'll take care of me and any others who defy you, just like you took care of De Gofroy. I can't believe I was so blind I did not see it."

His accusation was so breathtaking that it was some time before I could find it in me to respond. "What in De Gofroy's name are you talking about?"

Osahi leaned across from his chair, so that I could smell the perfume that he always wore and feel his breath upon the hood. "I know what Molijc did to De Gofroy. I know why his recovery was so, shall we say, protracted. Why he had to kept in stasis, and why he always had to be present when the Grand Regent spoke. And I know what the Acolytes have been up to when no one is looking."

My thoughts seemed paralyzed by Osahi's words. Was any of what he said true? The Acolytes were up to something, and Molijc had been at the center of it. But they were responsible for what had happened to Frederik. He was obviously their test case, but for what, I still wasn't sure. Molijc had been sick, suffered several strokes, and had died. I had watched my mother go through the same ordeal. It was no different.

I tried to speak, but only air escaped my lips.

"Don't pretend with me," Osahi said before I could try again. "Did you not see Frederik when he was here? He is not the same man."

"I know," I said. "I don't know what happened to him. I had nothing to do with that."

"Just like you had nothing to do with the airship."

I flinched at those words. "I would never harm a Regent," I said, fighting against the bonds that held me. "You know I wouldn't. And I wouldn't do anything to Frederik either, even though he betrayed the faith. Whatever else he is, he is a Regent. And De Gofroy's son."

Sweat poured down my face, running into my eyes, stinging them. If what Osahi said was true... But it couldn't be. It was impossible. He said nothing further, and I continued to fight against the ropes around my wrists, to no effect. His scent, I realized, was gone, and I could no longer sense his presence.

"Damn you, Osahi," I called out. "I don't know what you're talking about."

The dim hum of the lights in the room was the only response. I don't know how long I sat alone in the room, with only my thoughts to keep me company. They were no comfort.

At last someone entered and my wrists were untied. As I massaged the feeling back into them, the hood was pulled off me and Meredith looked down at me without expression. She gestured toward the door, and I stood and left the room.

12

The sun was still below the horizon, although it was near to cresting above, to judge by the odd feel of the darkness that I wandered through. The campus was empty at this hour, no one upon its pathways. Except me. I didn't have the strength, after my ordeal with Osahi, to return through the tunnels connecting all the buildings. Normally I would have done so without thought, and, at that moment, I probably should have. There were too many questions to be answered if the wrong person saw me.

But I could not face it, could not face anything. The universes seemed to have tilted on their axes, going askew, and pitching me toward an abyss which seemed to pull inexorably closer. I needed the crisp air of autumn in my lungs, the dampness of the grass on my shoes to remind myself that I was not living in some nightmare. That all this was real.

I returned before anyone in the Grand Regent's chambers had risen—even Molijc was not up for his prayers—and returned to my quarters with no one apparently the wiser as to what I had just undergone. Even I was not entirely sure.

Could I give any credence to what Osahi had said?

They were the ravings of an embittered, paranoid man. Nothing more. And yet...

The Acolytes had certainly done something to Frederik. I had assumed he was chosen as their test subject because it served both Molijc and their purposes to have Frederik out of sight and controlled. But had they begun their experiments even earlier? I could not believe it. Dejian, whatever he was, however power mad, would not have countenanced doing anything to De Gofroy. He was the founder of the faith, the Grand Regent. The reason for all of us belonging to the Church. Without him, we were lost. It still felt as though we were.

I paced about my room, unable to even think about sleep though I was exhausted. A nervous energy ran through me like a current, setting me vibrating at an intensity that frightened me. I was terrified of everything. Osahi and what he had done. The expression on Meredith's face when she motioned for me to go. And my own doubts about Molijc and the faith and the path we were on. Were we the Church's saviors or its doom?

One thing I was certain of was that we were not Society agents. Nor was Ana, though she might be now. She might have turned to them, just as her father had, when Osahi and De Gofroy pushed him to it. If she was, I blamed him for it. His paranoia and suspicion had driven her to it. The idea that we three—Lasinha, Molijc, and I—were now her pawns was beyond laughable. We had not heard from her in nearly four years.

Meredith had to have told him the truth behind her exile. I had trusted her entirely too much, given too much of myself to her. And then I had betrayed her.

I pushed thoughts of her from my mind, forcing myself to focus on the more immediate concern. Which was what the hell Osahi thought he was achieving by kidnapping me in the dead of night, to threaten me and insinuate that I had betrayed De Gofroy's faith and was a Society agent. It was laughable.

And yet I could not shake the seed of doubt he had put in my mind. The doubt that said something was very wrong with Frederik. That he was only the first, and there would be more like him to come. The Acolytes were up to something, but I had no idea what. And neither did Osahi.

He had gambled that perhaps I might. From what Meredith had told him, he would know I was the weak link among the three of us. In kidnapping me he hoped to find out something of what we were up to, or, failing that, to warn me of his suspicions.

I sat down to look at my hands, which I saw were trembling, whether from exhaustion or anxiety, I could not say. Osahi had given me his warning—that the Acolytes were up to something in concert with Molijc and perhaps Lasinha—and now he would wait to see what I would do. I stared across the room, wondering the same thing, feeling as though I were standing atop a precipice.

Unlike Osahi, I moved cautiously, not wanting to make a mistake and reveal my doubts and suspicions. I came at them sideways, as Lasinha and I always did. I could not confront Molijc, so I went fishing with Lasinha. He remained in his old office in the Protector's House, a place that was not at all indicative of the power he held there and within the Hierarchy.

After receiving me warmly, he offered me coffee, and we chatted of this and that. Agents that we had within the Society, problems of the faith that the Protectors were dealing with. I felt disengaged from it all, having spent so much of the last few months at Molijc's side. My agents were still active, people still reported to me, but they reported to others now too, and I felt less essential to the process.

Soon I would be irrelevant, if I wasn't careful, and I decided to sit down with Morris as soon as possible. If I was going to attempt any kind of investigation of Molijc and Lasinha's activities over the last few months, I would need people I could trust. And if I was to have any kind of influence upon the faith going forward, I would need Protectors and others who would answer my call.

When the pleasantries were finished, Lasinha smiled. "What can I do for you, Laila?"

It was no idle question. "Well, I'm sure Dejian has mentioned that I want to try to find Ana."

He raised an eyebrow slightly. "He hadn't, actually. I'm afraid I don't think we'll have much success there, given how little we've managed so far."

"All the same," I said, with an elaborate shrug, "I feel I have to try."

"And you want my help?"

"Not immediately," I said. "We don't have many resources. I don't want to tie them up in a wild goose chase. But I wanted to let you know what I was doing. Just so there are no questions later."

"Of course," he said, his face impassive.

I smiled my thanks. "That was all, really. I just wanted to keep you in the loop and get updated on things."

"Good," he said. He seemed surprised.

"One other thing," I said, feigning recalling something. "Have you been watching Osahi?"

It was his turn to shrug. "As much as anyone can watch him. You know what he's like. Why?"

I paused, choosing my words carefully. "It may be nothing. It may not be him at all. One of my people came to me with a rumor that she thought came from Osahi's camp."

Lasinha raised an eyebrow slightly, no doubt wondering if the agent I was referring to was Meredith. Good—let him wonder about that.

"Did Frederik seem odd to you when he was here?"

Lasinha gave me a slow nod. "Yes. He was not himself. I don't know what they've done to him. Perhaps Dejian does. He is the one the Acolytes deal with. They don't trust Protectors."

"With reason. We're always trying to get someone in their shop." I smiled. Lasinha did not return it, which was odd for him. "Anyway, I thought so too. And I wasn't the only one to notice. The story my source heard was that the Acolytes had operated on him, just like they operated on De Gofroy after his stroke."

I didn't elaborate, but I didn't have to. Lasinha stiffened visibly. "Osahi believes this, you think?"

"It doesn't matter," I said. "Just like it doesn't whether it's true. All that matters is whether people believe it."

Lasinha massaged his temple, as though warding off a headache. "I'll look into it."

I stood up to go. "You don't think there's any truth to it, do you?" An innocent, almost joking question.

"Absolutely not," he said, with a vehemence that surprised me. "You know Dejian would never do anything to harm De Gofroy or the faith."

"Of course not. None of us would."

Lasinha looked at me sharply, probably wondering if I was somehow commenting on his murder of the High Regents. I pretended not to see his concern, and neither of us said anything further. It took all my self-control to stop me from running from the building. When I stepped out into the sunlight, I gasped for air, as though I had been suffocating. Tears stung my eyes and I tried desperately to keep them at bay as people walked by.

The only time I didn't trust Lasinha was when I thought he wasn't trying to hide something. His answers at the end of our conversation, so insistent, told me there was some truth to what Osahi had claimed. Molijc and the Acolytes had done something to De Gofroy. I had to discover what.

I was careful in the weeks that followed my talk with Lasinha, reconnecting with my people among the Protectors and elsewhere and setting them the task of trying to find Ana. To anyone who looked closely, that was my main focus. And in truth, I did want to find her, if it was possible. But like Lasinha, I had my doubts.

These I expressed to Morris Loverne, along with our ulterior agenda, when I met with him in a Chinese restaurant called the Hong Kong Cafe in Vancouver, where he had been stationed to oversee the Protectors in the Protocol Center there. "We need to find out what Molijc and the Acolytes have been up to. Lasinha may or may not be involved. I don't know how much. But Dejian is the one in charge. He's the one with the answers."

If Morris was surprised, he did not show it. He sipped his tea and stirred the bowl, teeming with seafood, noodles, and broth, with his chopsticks.

"We should stay away from Lasinha regardless," he said. "He'll smell us coming a mile away."

"Agreed," I said, fighting to get my chopsticks and the noodles to cooperate.

"It's really not that difficult," Morris said, watching me.

I rolled my eyes. "You can't take the prairie out of the girl."

"You really can't."

I gave up on the food for the moment and pointed my chopsticks at Morris. "I want you to do some digging on the Acolytes. Whatever you can find. About what they were before the Church, why they broke with the Travelers. Whatever. I'm realizing we really don't know shit about them. Nothing that would attract any attention."

Morris nodded. "I'll pull together a dossier on everything known or suspected about them."

"Good. That's it. I'm going to look up Molijc and see what I can find about him. There must be some reason why the Acolytes made an alliance with him."

"You've still got access to De Gofroy's files?" he said.

"Maybe," I said, with a smile.

I did not get a chance to look at the files I had secreted away. When I returned to Calgary, Molijc and I were arrested by the Society of Travelers.

THREE

THE OTHER WOMAN

13

The remainder of the hiking trip passed in a blur. I remember little of it. I remember all of it. There are gaps when I was not myself, when Aeida was in command. He lusted for Suon, and so I did as well, and in the end, we spent three days engulfed in passion, even as I could not help but feel some revulsion for what was occurring.

She noticed that I was conflicted. But that was to be expected. We talked of nothing but how we were conflicted by what we did, and lying between us was the knowledge that, for whatever desire we might feel, we were still ultimately doing what we saw as necessary to achieve our goals. Hers were Osahi's. Mine, I do not know. Were they Aeida's or my own?

We talked of the strangeness of the universes we inhabited. The Society. The Acolytes. The Seekers. None of these entities existed in so many universes, where life went on in an explicable manner. One could look at events and trace their causes back through time. Not so with our worlds. The Society, with its opaqueness, touching everything but leaving no marks. It is impossible to trace what they have done. Just as it is impossible, even now, for me to say what the Acolytes have done to the Church.

Were we their faithful vessels? It often felt so.

And of the Seekers we know the least of all. Only that they posses abilities beyond those of any mortals, or so it seems. Who knows the truth of the matter. Does the Society do their bidding, or they it? In any ordinary universe there would be answers to these questions. There would be tangible facts one could point to that would explain the way things are. We are denied that and are left prisoners as a result. But of what?

Aeida's memories of his uncorrupted world, before Lasinha found him, make the strangeness of my life and my universe more apparent. Everyone accepts the logic of the Society without question. Even we, who oppose them and their ideas, do so on their terrain. Maybe it is just my involvement in the Church, which has utterly consumed me and left me isolated from the rest of the world, that has insulated me from reckoning with the bizarre shift our universe underwent before I was born. Maybe others are more aware of the seismic shifts that have spun the world, and whose reverberations we are still living through.

I do not know. It suddenly seems as though, with my belief in the universes as De Gofroy taught me broken, that I know nothing at all. Everything remains to be discovered.

These fears and doubts bonded Suon and I together, at least while we were alone on the hiking trail. Now that we have returned my own peculiar predicament is foremost of mind for me. I am afraid, deeply afraid, of what comes next. Aeida returned. He could not remain in command, not for long, and I believe I have banished him again. But he will return again, especially if I cross over to another universe, as I must if I am to retrieve my body. The next time he may be stronger; he may stay in control longer. I may be exiled to the void again, and this time I may not return.

The hike and the nights spent with Suon seem to have stilled the tremors in my hands, which is welcome. In spite of that, my control over my flesh seems more tenuous, even as the conflict is no longer rendered visible.

Everything about me seems tenuous, a product of happenstance. I am not in control. There is no control. Before, I worried about what would become of my body while I was exiled from it. What depredations would Molijc visit upon it? Now I fear that nothing of myself will remain by the time I find my way back to myself. Whatever shell of a person the Acolytes have crafted in there will be as much me as whatever creature inhabits Aeida's flesh.

Some of my dreams now are Aeida's. Even my idle thoughts. They drift in without my being aware, and I am back again on a Vancouver street following myself into a dive bar to meet Morris. Or stalking Ana at Lasinha's command, seething with jealousy as I watch her fuck Sebastien with the cameras I installed in his apartment. The release on her face, the peace that emerges, as she climaxes, inspires both despair and hate in me. Along with a need that can never be fulfilled.

I despise myself as Lasinha and I march up to confront her in the sushi restaurant. I do not understand the enormity of what I have done, but soon enough I will. Soon enough I will do far worse.

I want to cut these thoughts out from me. They are a cancer upon my being. Even Aeida wants to look away, to forget these sordid episodes. It is something he tells himself, that he would not do it again, knowing what he knows now. But I can see the truth lurking in the shadowed places he does not acknowledge. I should know—I have told myself the same lies.

There is something about that moment in the sushi shop that keeps pulling me back into the memory. His guilt makes him return there constantly, a sort of flagellation. All Aeida can see is the look on Ana's face as she realizes the totality of his betrayal. It is the moment he realizes, beyond any doubt, that she will never feel for him as he feels for her.

As the days go by and Aeida's presence in me recedes and I gain more of a semblance of control over my thoughts, I return to the moment to inspect it with my own eyes. It is only then that I realize what compels me to look. Not Ana, beautiful as always, righteous in her anger, and with no sense of what is to become of her. It is utterly heartbreaking, especially because I know I should have prevented it. I should have prevented all of this.

The woman with her. I do not recognize her, and Aeida does not know her. Lasinha does, though. I can see it in the way he looks at her during the conversation. Who is she? And why did Ana risk so much to smuggle her across to that world?

Suon remains near me whenever I venture out into Osahi's little village from my dormitory. She doesn't bother to disguise what she is doing, using it as an excuse to linger near me. We have an understanding, the two of us now. A secret that is no secret at all.

My true secrets I must guard against revealing—a dangerous prospect now that Aeida is a palpable force within me. Every time Suon is near, the conflict within me rises to the surface. Aeida lusts for her—perhaps I do too; I can no longer tell—and I fear what she will see within me. What she will report to Osahi.

She is different now. There is an ease about her when she is with me. There is truth in what she said about her conflicted feelings about her duties and the Church. By allowing a little infatuation into the mix of our staged romance, she feels she is defying Osahi, but in reality, she is only doing as he expected.

You can't help but fall a little in love with the person you are playing and who you know is playing you. Something has to ground you, and the mind creates it. That is what happened with Meredith and I. Or so I tell myself. The other thing the mind is adept at is lying to itself. No one can trust their own thoughts, least of all me.

It is a nearly week after my return from camping when Osahi calls me for another audience. Suon brings me to the building where he and De Vroes interrogated me, and we meet in the same room, all four of us standing awkwardly amongst the Acolyte's implements. He means to unsettle me by talking to me here, with De Vroes looming behind him, reminding me that it is within his power to return me to the state in which he found me.

He has been absent the last week—at least, I have no sign of him about the village. I wonder what he has been doing, how the revolt against Molijc progresses, and what of the Church remains. It was a dire situation when I was captured, and I can only imagine it has gotten worse. There may be no one left near Molijc who has not been sent to the Acolytes, except perhaps Lasinha. Even Meredith will no longer be safe now that I have escaped her clutches.

The whole situation is beyond belief, and I desperately want to find out what Osahi knows, but I have to restrain myself. I can only know what Aeida knows, on the off chance Osahi has discovered who he is within the Order.

"You're still enjoying your stay with us?" Toma says.

"I'm getting tired of doing nothing," I reply with a thin smile. "I didn't come here to go on camping trips. I came here to take down the Grand Regent."

A twitch of the eye is the only indication I get that Osahi is irritated with me. Good. I need him distracted somehow so that he doesn't notice how fragile I am. His absence has actually spared me from being discovered, in all likelihood, and now that he is back, I need to keep him off guard.

"I appreciate your impatience," he says. "But I'm not about to drop all my work just to help some random stranger who arrives at my doorstep because he kidnapped one of my agents."

"We saved Nicola," I say. "This place would be in the Order's hands right now, if not for me."

"She claims Morris led them to her."

"Then she's a fool," I say, though I know it may be true.

"Be that as it may," Osahi says, "you are here now and you potentially have some valuable information as a member of the Order. We should see what use we can make of you."

"There is something. It may be nothing, I don't know," I say. Osahi nods for me to continue, and I tell them about the woman who was with Ana when Lasinha had her arrested.

"I don't see why this is particularly important," Osahi says. "I think we should be focusing on who is in the Order. Who its agents are. So I can protect my people."

"I can give you all that," I say. "I can even tell you who Lasinha and Molijc suspected were your agents. I'll gladly do it."

I pause, and Osahi smiles. "But you want us to look into this woman for you."

"Yes."

"She was probably just one of Laila's people. She and Ana were close. Or a Traveler. I don't think she ever left the Society. Not really."

"I don't know anything about that. But I'm sure she wasn't a Regent. Lasinha told me all about Ana's associates in the Church when he had me start investigating her." A lie—Lasinha told Aeida little about any of the people he had him investigate—but Osahi will not know the truth. "She may be Society. I doubt it, though. Ana had to bring her across, and if she was a Traveler, she would have had her own means."

"Not necessarily," De Vroes says. Osahi glances at him, raising an eyebrow.

Interesting. An Acolyte who knows things about the

Society's inner workings. Also, it is clear from that raised eyebrow that Osahi doesn't trust me at all, and intends to share as little as possible with me.

I file those thoughts away for later and continue. "Whoever she is, she's important. Lasinha knew her. I'm sure of it. He definitely recognized her. And he didn't want Ana meeting with her. She knows something about Molijc."

Osahi is clearly not convinced. He crosses his arms and stares at me. "Okay. How do we locate this mysterious woman?"

"The Order will have her. She'll be one of the half-things now."

"So you want us to find this woman and restore her." Osahi shakes his head in disbelief.

"Don't act so surprised. I know you can do it." I look at De Vroes. "If you can't find the woman, you can find Ana. Restore her. She'll be able to tell you who the woman is and what she knows."

"And if I agree to do this, you'll give me the names of all the Order agents you know?"

"I'll give you everything," I say.

He smiles and holds out his hand. "Very well. We have a deal."

I take his hand in mine and we shake, staring into each other's eyes, wondering how the other is trying to betray us.

14

I am curious about the woman with Ana. No doubt she holds information that would be of use to me. But that is not why I have asked Osahi to look for her. I suspect she cannot be found. Lasinha is far too careful and covers his tracks too well. But Ana can be, and if I can have her restored, I will begin to right some of the wrong I have done.

My suspicion is that Osahi does not intend a serious search for this mystery woman, but he will have to at least give the appearance of doing so. It will keep me occupied while he tries to determine just how much he can trust me. For my part, I am hoping it will give me access to resources I can use for other purposes, though what those might be I am still unsure.

For the moment, nothing happens, and it happens slowly. I meet with Suon in my quarters and tell her all the agents I know of in the Watchers' Order. I give her all the universes I know the Order is active in and the code names Lasinha gave them. It is tedious work for both of us, and exhausting for me because Aeida is reluctant to part with much of the information and I have to hunt for it in the outer regions of his thoughts.

After spending the better part of the day wrestling with my own mind, Suon's hand upon my own is welcome. We move to the narrow bed with the thin mattress, and I surrender to the desire that consumes me, whoever's it is. I do not think about that—I do not think about anything except the light sparking in Suon's eyes as she sits astride me, moving her hips in abandonment.

After, as we both luxuriate in the aftermath of those sensations, I study her through narrowed eyes while she looks at the ceiling. There is an eagerness, a hunger for me, that is not fake. Or so I tell myself. It is dangerous to allow myself to believe that. This is her duty, and if she wants to extract a little pleasure to relieve the tedium of it, then I should not let that fool me into thinking she has any particular feeling for me. Above all else, I cannot allow any feeling for her to enter my calculations.

She feels me staring at her and looks over at me and smiles. A wounding, bruising smile, innocent and unadorned. Am I misreading her, misreading this whole situation?

"What are you thinking?" she says.

"Life is forever surprising me," I say. "The more I think I know, the less it seems I do."

She looks at me, unsure of my meaning. I lean across the pillow to kiss her, putting a hand on her hips. "Let's not worry about any of that right now," I say, as my hand begins to move of its own accord.

Suon returns to my quarters after dinner and we spend the night together, the first time she has done so here. She seems self-conscious in the cafeteria, although there is only a scattering of people there when we arrive, and they pay little attention to our coming and going. But she is unsure what they will think, unsure of what she wants them to think.

I wake up before dawn, darkness still shrouding the room, and watch Suon breathing for a time, telling myself not to feel what I am feeling. That it is a lie. A need born of loneliness. Which does not make it any less real.

When it is evident that I will not be able to return to sleep, I slip from bed, get dressed, and leave the dormitory. The air outside is crisp, with the feeling of autumn in the air, though none of the trees show any signs of it. The paths through the village are all empty, and quiet reigns. A bird takes flight from the trees just beyond my dormitory, the sound of the leaves rustling startling me. I look about sheepishly, worried someone has seen my reaction, but there is no one about.

I decide to wander, or at least give every appearance of doing so, and make my way toward the center of the village where the administration buildings are. The windows are dark within, as they are in every building. Only the watchtower at the village's far end has a glimmer of light escaping its windows, though on closer inspection, it may just be the reflection of the moon on the glass.

I take no chances, though, going nowhere near any of the buildings I know will raise suspicions from anyone who might be watching from above. When I get to the far end of the village and the other set of homes and dormitories, I loop back around, heading back to my bed. As I go, I try to think of what needs to be done, to get me closer to my body and my revenge.

The temptation is to simply find the transfer equipment in the village and send myself over to the campus to confront Molijc. That can only end in disaster, though. The return of the tamp and my endless, circular days under Meredith's watch. Even if I somehow manage to smuggle myself onto the campus and extricate my body, there will still be the matter of restoring myself to it. I will need an Acolyte.

As if summoned by my thoughts, I see De Vroes on the path ahead of me. He is walking toward the central buildings, presumably from his quarters. Evidently, he failed to notice me, or just assumed I am a Regent, unable to sleep, about for a walk. Which is true.

I follow behind him, careful to keep my distance and to make sure my steps are quiet. On the off chance there is someone in the tower watching me, I do not keep to the shadows, as is my instinct. Better to be visible if De Vroes should sense my presence. It will make for a much easier explanation than if he sees me skulking alongside some building.

He is clearly preoccupied, though, for he hurries on, head down, oblivious of the night and all around him. Fortunately for me, he heads along the path that leads to my dormitory, breaking off only as he comes to the strange suburban house, whose purpose is unclear. I pause to watch him and see that he goes to stand on the veranda, hesitating for a moment as if he is unsure.

I walk past the house, in case he chances to look in my direction, and head toward the nearest dormitory. Assuming that I am far enough away from the watchtower that they are unable to observe me, I double back to the rear of the house before I reach the dormitory entrance. I lean close, putting a hand on the siding for balance, and crouch to my knees, slowly making my way around on the far side of the house. Though the blinds all remain drawn, I make sure to keep my head low and away from the windows.

"What do you want?" De Vroes says in an angry voice.

I freeze, certain he has spotted me crouched alongside the house, frantically searching for a satisfactory explanation and coming up empty.

There is a response, a voice coming from within the house, but I cannot make out the words. I almost exhale in relief, but stop myself. The night is so hushed that any sound seems to carry. De Vroes' exclamation sounded like a thunderclap interrupting the silence.

After I regain my composure, I creep nearer to the front porch, slinking lower with each step, until I can hear the words of the man inside the house. He has just finished saying something about having a deal.

"We have a deal. We've been very clear on that," De Vroes says, in a tone that suggests this is not the first conversation they've had on the matter.

"And you've done nothing to live up to your end of it. I know what I was promised…and all I've gotten to this point is house arrest in the middle of goddamn nowhere."

The man's voice is muffled—he must be standing well back from the doorway—and his words are still difficult to make out. I dare not go any closer, though. His voice sounds vaguely familiar to me, though, I am certain. It is someone I know, and yet the intonation, the enunciation, are off somehow. Like another mind is speaking with that voice.

I know what that means: another Acolyte project. But De Vroes is not acting like he is speaking to some kind of kept thing.

"We will keep our end of the bargain and you will keep yours," De Vroes says. "In the meantime, you will remain here, quiet and out of sight. If you disturb me or Toma again, there will be hell to pay, I assure you."

"You need me—" the man starts.

"We do. Not as much as think, though. And you need us just as much. Or would you like us to return you to where we found you?"

There is no response, which tells me De Vroes has hit his mark. I hear the door shut and, a few seconds later, De Vroes' footsteps off the porch and down the path. I wait until I can't hear them anymore before I rise from the shadows beside the house and return to my quarters.

If Suon noticed my absence, she makes no comment of it the next morning. I am self-conscious about it, making stupid jokes about how deep a sleep I had that only invite further questions. When did I become so clumsy at this? I have always been certain of myself, careful and precise in my craft. Now it feels as though I am back with Ana in my first days as a Protector, where every conversation seems to lead me to brink of disaster.

Doubt consumes me. My questions about the faith and my place in it. Doubt about what there is for me beyond this world that has defined my adult life. What am I, if not a Regent? I even wonder about facing Molijc. Is it revenge I am truly seeking, or just some kind of closure? But what closure can I have without my body?

I tell myself that if he would promise to restore me, I would walk away from all this. But he will never let me do that. And I don't know if I could. Not yet. Perhaps someday.

Even Suon, whom I feel so certain about sometimes, leaves me wondering. In her unguarded moments—when she is looking at me and thinks I don't see her as we eat breakfast—there is a kind of happiness and desire in her expression that leads me to doubt what I know about her. She is Osahi's agent and she is with me because Osahi has told her to get close to me. But is there something more?

Once I would have been certain—even if I was utterly wrong—but now certainty has dissolved. I am left with only competing desires, confounding emotions, and the doubt that shadows everything I do. Meredith and Molijc conspired together to remove all my certainty, all that I am. Even now, I am unsure of what remains.

Adding to my general state of confusion is the question of who De Vroes was speaking to the night before. I cannot make sense of it. That voice—at once so familiar and so foreign—torments me. It feels as though I should know it intimately, and I wonder if my current state is having some effect on my other faculties. If I can figure out who they have hidden there, I may be able to discover what Osahi is doing. For he certainly has a plan to take back the Church from Molijc, and I have no doubt this man is part of it somehow, with all his talk of the deal they have in place.

I hoped that my arrival—Aeida's arrival—would serve

to make me the centerpiece of Osahi's plan to take back the Church. That is my best hope to be able to use his resources to my own ends, as I must if I am to restore myself. If I were to reveal who I truly am, he, undoubtedly, would make me integral to his plans. And he would use me as a bargaining chip with Molijc to buy himself more time, while I would be no nearer to my own goals.

After breakfast, I leave Suon to whatever work she has and go to the church for some peace so that I can think through what I must do next. Though it is tempting to return to the house tonight and find out who is there, I know that is likely to backfire. The man will see me as an interloper, not an ally, and I could rapidly find myself in trouble. The little trust I have built with Osahi and his people is the only currency I have now. I need to hoard it.

Ibrahem finds me as I am praying, or pretending to. He kneels beside me on the floor, where I sit cross-legged and with my eyes closed, near enough that I flick them open to see who it is. I resist a sigh. Evidently, I have not gained Osahi's trust yet if he is sending this fool back to try to draw me into some new scheme.

"You've been busy," he says with a hissing whisper.

I glare at him and look around the room. No one else is near us, and the few who are in church are lost to their own contemplation. Still, I do not want a confrontation here, so I decide to ignore him. He will not let me, though.

"Have you thought about what I said?" he says, as though he made some offer to me before. When I don't respond, he adds, "Osahi can't be trusted, you know. He's no different that Molijc and the Order. He wants the same thing. Everyone in line and in place."

That much, at least, is true. I keep my eyes closed, willing him to give up, but he is persistent, if nothing else.

"I know you've no reason to trust me. And I'm sure you've heard what's happened to Laila Johar."

This piques my curiosity, and I am unable to resist. "No," I say, glancing over at him.

He raises an eyebrow at me. "She's gone. Disappeared. No one sees her anymore. I've heard the Acolytes have her."

I am somehow disappointed that he has not thought up a more elaborate rumor for my fate. "So you want me to join a leaderless movement?"

"Not leaderless. There are those who remain in place. We are ready to strike when the moment is right. We can topple the whole thing, once we have Laila back."

Ridiculous. My people are scattered or in hiding. Morris' capture will have resulted in many more falling under the Acolytes' implements. There can only be a handful of us left. It makes me desperately sad to think about. I am alone and without allies. Except the Seeker, and I do not want his help. Not that he would give it, unless he saw some gain for himself and the Society.

"You'll forgive me if I am not filled with confidence," I say. My derision makes my voice louder than I intended, which draws a narrowed glance from a woman sitting toward the front of the church.

Ibrahem shakes his head and gestures for me to watch my voice. I am tempted to leave without another word, but something stays me.

"Look," he says, "maybe it doesn't seem like we're the horse to bet on. But we do still have people in key places. With Osahi's people. With Molijc. In the Order. And with what you know, well, we could do a lot. Maybe find what happened to Laila."

I choke down a shudder and get up to leave, my tolerance for Ibrahem's shenanigans at an end. Did Osahi think I was a fool? He has to know by now that I, or at least who he thinks I am, would not fall for so obvious a snare. I already rejected it once, so why try again?

There are tears in my eyes and my hands are shaking again. Without entirely realizing it, I have run from the church and am standing in the middle of the path, staring out into the wilderness beyond the village. In truth, I am staring at nothing, feeling utterly overwhelmed by my predicament. By how alone I am.

"What's the matter?" Ibrahem says, appearing at my side. He touches my shoulder, and I flinch. "Be careful. People are watching."

I bite off my retort and look at him. He appears concerned. I force the emotion from my thoughts and expression. "What if I told you I knew where Laila was?"

15

Clouds obscure the stars above, rendering the darkness near absolute as Ibrahem and I approach the citadel tower. The air is cool, as the nights here always seem to be, but my back and hands are damp with sweat. My nerves tighten my muscles and make it feel as though every step I take involves pushing against some invisible barrier.

Though I cannot see his face through the darkness, I can sense Ibrahem's anxiety as well. He was uncharacteristically subdued when we rendezvoused outside the church, the enormity of what we are doing settling upon him. It is one thing to talk of betraying Osahi, but another to actually do so, after so long staying hidden. There can be no going back, as he must surely realize. If we manage to do what we are setting out to, everyone will know we have betrayed them and Ibrahem will become the hunted.

It is a sensation I am intimately familiar with. That does not make this any easier. This is a dangerous game we are playing here, neither of us sure how truthful the other has been. And I know only too well the dangers of misplaced trust. But I cannot wait for Osahi; he is too willing to remain invisible and play the long game, knowing that he has the luxury of time. That is what I do not have. The longer I remain here, the more likely I will be exposed.

The door to the citadel is, unsurprisingly, locked, but Ibrahem claims he can open it. He also claims there is no one in the watchtower. It is only manned during the day, sometimes not even then. There are no inhabitants who live nearby in the area, no one who might stumble upon the village by chance, or so they have come to believe. The only threat is someone transferring themselves from another universe, as I did, and they have equipment to detect any channels opening.

The mechanism of the lock is simple and Ibrahem makes short work of it, leading me into the building. Once the door is closed behind us, we turn on the flashlights Ibrahem has procured. I do not ask how he has managed to do so, although flashlights in a place like this would be common enough that it would not be a strange request for those in the administration building. It is convenient all the same, as is his proficiency with the locks.

Ibrahem leads me upstairs to the watchtower, which is empty, as he promised. We keep the flashlights turned low and away from the windows, but some light will inevitably be visible to anyone who happens to look in this direction. It is three in the morning, though, and, as I know, no one is likely to be about.

"Here it is," Ibrahem says, hurrying across the room to a wall stacked with equipment.

As I cross over, I see that it is transfer equipment, some of the most advanced I have seen. Osahi has been busy, then, and he still has assets in the Society. I am not surprised.

"How do the alarms work?" I crouch beside Ibrahem, passing my flashlight across the equipment.

"Any channel that opens starts it. The alarm goes here and probably in Osahi's place." He means the building where Osahi and De Vroes interrogated me. "He and the Acolyte are always in there—one of them, anyway. So they can muster the troops."

"And it will sound no matter which way the channel goes?"

Ibrahem nods. "That's why we need to make it seem like someone is coming over. They'll think the Order has found them and they won't notice that we've gone across. At least not right away."

I think it unlikely that this ruse will fool Osahi for long. And unless we do something to obscure where we are going, he will be right behind us. I keep these doubts to myself. They are not relevant for the moment.

"You know how to use these things, right?"

I nod. "I did a lot of this for the Order."

"Do you think it will work?"

"Your plan?" I say. "Maybe. It will definitely get us out of here and where we need to go."

"Well, that's all we need." Ibrahem is brimming with excitement at the thought.

"Not quite," I say. "We can get there, but then what?"

He looks at me, not comprehending. "We get Laila."

"Sure," I say. "And then where do we go? Once we get her."

Ibrahem purses his lips. "Can't we hide out in the world for a bit? Wait until Laila can arrange for someone to extract us."

Can he be so great a fool? I have to choke down my rage. I keep my voice even, barely, as I speak. "We can try to hide, but people like Osahi and the Order know how to find people like us." To say nothing of the Society and the Seekers. "And Laila may have contacts, but she won't know where any of them are. Not if they're smart and want to stay out of the Order's hands. We need to organize an exit, too. No sense blundering in if you can't get out."

Ibrahem looks concerned. "Can we do that?"

I blink. "You're the one who's working with Laila. Don't you have contacts? People that can arrange this sort of thing?"

He blinks, his confusion apparent. "Laila has them. She'll know who to contact. We just have to get there. To her."

I stare at him, trying to determine whether he is the idiot he appears or something more sinister. There is something about his confusion, something about his constant invocation of Laila, that worries me.

"Have you ever met Laila?" I say.

"Of course not. I was recruited by someone else, someone who knew her. We didn't want Osahi to be able to trace me back to her."

"And how did you end up here with Osahi?"

"I worked for him in the Protectors. I always have. When the Order started, he began to move us out. The people he thought they might go after. He brought us here so that we could work on things."

Ibrahem shrugs, as if he can't explain what those things they are working on are. "Anyway. I came to realize that Osahi's no different than Molijc. No different at all."

There is a pit forming in my stomach, an awful sensation. "What makes Laila different?"

"Oh, she is," he says, nodding vigorously. "She is. She's not like them at all."

I stand up, unable to look at him any longer. "Come on," I say. "We're done here."

I walk out of the room and down the stairs at a quick pace, not bothering to glance back at him.

"Wait," he says. "We haven't finalized our plan. How are we going to get out once we get to Laila?"

"Leave that to me," I say over my shoulder. "Now come on. We've been here too long."

They are waiting for us at the bottom of the stairs. A dozen of them, all grim-faced. Several have weapons in their hands. I raise mine and am dragged outside by one of them. Behind me, I hear Ibrahem cry out.

"Don't tell them anything, Aeida."

Osahi and Suon are outside, hands in pockets against the cold of the night. He raises an eyebrow at me.

"He says he's working for Laila," I say. "But I don't think so. He's never met her. Doesn't seem to know anything about her operations."

"Who's he working for, then?"

"I don't know," I say with a shrug and a glance over my shoulder. "If you ask me, I think he's on his own."

"Don't be ridiculous, Aeida," Osahi says, staring hard at me. "A person doesn't just take it into his head to turn when he's been with me for over ten years. Something made him do it. And someone convinced him."

"I don't know," I say again. "I asked him about that. He just says you're the same as Molijc. Couldn't explain why. Couldn't even tell me who turned him."

"He's hiding it," Osahi says with authority.

I don't agree, but I decide not to argue and give a noncommittal shrug, looking past him into the darkness.

Suon looks at Osahi. "He hasn't been the same since the Order got their hands on him."

Osahi doesn't even glance at her, his eyes intent on the doorway. Ibrahem emerges with two people holding his arms to keep him from struggling. He looks around wildly, and sees me standing with Osahi and Suon.

"Don't tell them anything, Aeida. I beg of you."

I look away, unable to meet his gaze. He is dragged away, yelling and struggling to break free, to no avail.

"Someone turned him," Osahi says under his breath. He turns to stare at Suon. "De Vroes restored him."

Suon nods, but I can tell she does not agree with that assessment. I feel the same way. There was something off about all our interactions, but the extent to which they were not right was only made evident tonight.

"Someone turned him," Osahi says again, to himself this time. "He would not betray me."

He is looking into the darkness where Ibrahem and his minders have disappeared. It is as though Suon and I are not even there. She reaches out and takes my arm, leading me away, leaving Osahi alone.

16

Four days after that night, Osahi meets with me again. I do not ask about Ibrahem. He will tell me if he wishes, but most likely Ibrahem's fate will remain unspoken of, a threat and a promise lying between us. This is not the first time I have sat across from Osahi after sending someone to him to punish as he saw fit. In most cases I never found out what happened to them, though I knew enough to be able to surmise. Here I can guess too.

"Osahi's no different than Molijc," Ibrahem said. He is not wrong. For some reason he thought I was different, but there he is not correct. I am no better than any of them. I can only *be* better. But will I?

Osahi is pleased. "The names you've given me have all checked out. You've been very useful. Probably set the Order back months, if not longer. You've given us a chance. Maybe more."

I smile. "More, I hope." I don't ask what he has done with these people. Some he will keep in place to feed false information to Lasinha and the Order. Others he will remove to extract information from. "If there's anything else I can help with, just let me know."

"I have something in mind," he says, looking

thoughtful.

"I'm up for anything," I say with false bravado. "Any news on my mystery woman? Or Ana?"

"No sign of the woman. I expect she's gone. Lasinha will have hidden her well away. Ana seems to be moved from one Order site to another. Difficult to get to her, even if we could manage to pin down her location. I won't risk my people on that, not unless you can prove that what this woman knows is important."

"It's obviously important," I say, unable to hide my need for him to allow this. "She knows something about Lasinha he doesn't want known. It could be about Molijc, it could be about him."

"It could be about Laila. Or Ana herself," Osahi says. "We don't know. I'm not risking my people for maybes and hopes. I've seen what the Order does to those it captures. If I'm going to ask people to chance that, I want to be sure."

I'm disappointed, but I cannot blame him. This was always the most likely outcome of my coming here. Osahi using me for what I know and stringing me along until he thinks he has all he needs. And then, like Ibrahem, I am gone.

"What do you have in mind, then?" I say, trying again, unsuccessfully, to hide my emotions.

"Don't be so disappointed. This may help your cause." He smiles, and I shiver. "We're going to take one of your Order people. And we're going to be careful about it. You're going to help us. I want to make sure he thinks it's an Order extraction."

"All right," I say. "And what do we do once we've got him?"

Osahi's smile broadens. "You're going to ask him some questions."

The windows to the citadel tower have been blacked out for the transfer, on the off chance that the man who is about to arrive sees something that will allow him to identify where he has been brought. It is unlikely, but Osahi does not want to lose this hideaway. He is taking an incredible risk just by transferring someone here, but he must be sufficiently confident he can obscure that trail. Perhaps Nicola, whom I have not seen since my arrival here, can help in that regard.

I am alone in the room, though Suon and a few others are behind the nearest door, ready to act if necessary. It will not be, I am sure. The man who is coming across will be disoriented and exhausted. He will be assuming the worst and afraid for his life. He is right to be, and I do not intend to let him forget it.

His name is Menardo Ocampos, an Order member from one of Lasinha's worlds. He is not important, at least not that I can recall, but we have met on several occasions. That is why Osahi has chosen him. It is a test, of sorts, for my usefulness. For Osahi has discovered that most members of the Order, or at least those who have some knowledge of me, still believe I am at Lasinha's side.

That is not surprising. Lasinha and Molijc would not want to broadcast that one of their selected has betrayed them, so they will keep Aeida's disappearance a carefully guarded secret. There will be suspicion and rumors, just like my own absence from myself is a subject for much discussion, but nothing concrete. Always deniable, if necessary. Molijc cannot stand the thought of anyone seeing the Grand Regent as fallible.

I can feel the channel beginning to form before I see it, a vibration that seems to travel deep into my being. A song played at pitch just beyond my hearing. I feel ill, as though my whole body might come undone. Aeida surfaces within me, but I force him down. My hands start to tremble, and I clench them tight at my side.

If just being near a channel causes this kind of reaction, then I will be hopeless if I cross again. I will not stay together. The thought makes the shaking in my hands worse, and I push it away, hoping that those watching from the other room do not see the distress on my face.

Three figures materialize on the other side of the channel. They are standing in a room not unlike this one, anonymous and filled with transfer equipment. Two of them hold the man in the center firmly by the arms. His face is covered by a hood and his hands are shackled in front of him. As the channel solidifies, they lead him across to our universe. He seems to shrink as he gets closer, cowering at what he believes awaits him.

After they are across, we wait a moment for the channel to close. I gesture to the guards to set Menardo down on the chair we prepared for him. He sits uneasily, his hands shaking. The two guards move to stand behind him, ready to act if necessary and near enough that he will sense their presence.

A red light flashes behind them on the wall with the shelves of transfer equipment, indicating that the channel has been severed. Beside that light there is another, and I wait for it to signal. It is a warning system that will tell me whether our transfer was tracked by someone. I glance between it and Menardo as I wait, can feel the tension and fear emanating from him. The light flashes green—all clear—and I am ready to begin.

First, though, I pause, studying the man's body language some more. He is short and diminutive, a slightness that is exaggerated by his cowering. Aeida's body will appear to dwarf his own, especially if he remains in his chair. I can imagine his thoughts, the doubts and questions that will be haunting him. His imagination will be torturing him, telling him that he is doomed, soon to be an Acolyte plaything. He works for the Order; he will know what results from interrogations like these.

I take a steadying breath, hoping that the effects of the transfer have passed, and step forward, making sure that Menardo can hear me. He starts at the sound. I gesture to the guards, and one them steps forward and removes the hood. Menardo blinks, looking around wildly. The guard has returned to her position behind him in the shadows. There is a circle of light in the room around me and Menardo, focused upon his eyes.

"Do you know who I am?" I say, taking another step closer to the chair so that he can make me out.

He blinks furiously, his mouth opening and closing. He nods.

"Good," I say. My voice is calm, welcoming. "Do you know why you're here, Menardo?"

"I've done nothing wrong," he says, frantic.

"Do you know why you're here?"

I wait as he looks at me with pleading eyes. He knows he has done nothing to betray the Order, but doubt is beginning to assert itself. He believes they do not make mistakes, that what they are doing is essential for the faith. That what he is doing is essential to the faith. But if that is true, he must be here for a reason. How did he fail?

"Please," he says. "I beg of you. I've done nothing wrong. I swear it. I've done all that was asked of me. Nothing more."

"You are here," I say, as if he has not spoken, "because you have betrayed the faith and the Order."

"I haven't," Menardo says, leaping from the chair to face me. One of the guards steps forward and forces him roughly into his seat. He winces in pain. "I haven't. I swear upon De Gofroy."

"Do not use his name in my presence. If the Grand Regent were to hear that you had done so, it would be unpleasant for you."

"I swear to you, I don't know what I've done." He is weeping now. "There's been some kind of mistake."

"There has not," I say. "The Order doesn't make mistakes."

He has no reply for that. I look him over with a studied indifference. He does not meet my eyes, looking miserably down at the floor. I should not be taking pleasure in this, but I feel a surge of glee at that expression and the knowledge that I have total power over him in this moment. It is terrible, irresistible thing.

"What did Lasinha tell you to do?" My tone suggests that he has not done what was asked of him.

"I did exactly what he said. To the letter," Menardo says, looking at me as though I might give him some clue of what I expect him to say. I give him a little scowl, as though to say that I want to help him, but this is not the answer I am looking for. That is all it takes for the dam to burst.

"Is this about the woman?" he says. That surprises me, and it takes a great deal of effort to not betray my interest.

He doesn't appear to notice. "I did exactly what Lasinha asked me. When the Acolytes were done with her, I hid her in my world. I put her where no one could find her. Not even Lasinha." He sounds oddly proud of this, before remembering himself. "And I haven't told a soul. Just like he said."

"Is that so?" I say, making it clear I don't believe him.

"It's true. I swear it upon—" He catches himself from saying "De Gofroy" again just in time. "Anyway, I don't know who she was."

"And that is all?"

Menardo lifts his bound hands in anguish. "My god, yes. I mean, I haven't even done anything else that would even matter. I'm nobody in the Order. I'm not trusted me with anything important."

Except that. What, I wonder, are the odds that this lowly functionary, arranged as a test by Osahi to see if I still have any currency in the Order, would know about the woman I want him to find? It cannot just be a coincidence, I tell myself.

"You have betrayed the faith, Menardo Ocampos," I say, as though pronouncing a sentence.

"Please. I have only done what was asked of me."

"Indeed," I say. "If you wish to continue in the Order

and prove your faith and obedience to the Grand Regent, then you will continue to do so."

"Yes," he says, nodding and gulping for air. "Of course."

"Good. Tell me where the woman is and how we can find her."

Menardo is aghast. "I can't," he says, his voice barely audible. "Lasinha specifically told me to tell no one. Not even himself."

"He also told you not to tell anyone about her. And you've told me. What do you think will happen if he finds out you've broken your word?"

Menardo's eyes widen slightly, as he realizes this is not quite the predicament he thinks he is in. It is something far worse.

"But he told me."

"Do you think Lasinha is the only authority in the Church or the Watchers? There is a higher one, in case you have forgotten. You can assume that he is asking the question."

Menardo looks at me, suspecting a trap of some sort. He is wondering if this a test Lasinha has set before him, or if this is a real demand from the Grand Regent. A demand like this can mean only one thing. Lasinha has betrayed the faith and all his followers are now in doubt. Menardo takes a shaky breath, contemplating a universe where the ground beneath his feet is no longer as solid as he believed.

"And if I refuse?"

"Menardo, you know you can't. One way or another, you will tell us what we want to know and you will be returned to the faith. How that happens is up to you. Are you a faithful vessel?"

He doesn't answer, staring at the floor, the enormity of the choice before him draining the blood from his face. When he looks up, I can see the decision on his face before he speaks.

"You can find her in Arequipa." He stops, choking back a sob. "The Casa de Manila."

17

The Casa de Manila proves to be a restaurant, two blocks north of the Plaza de Armas in the center of Arequipa. It is in one of the many colonial buildings that are scattered throughout the heart of the city, most converted into banks, hotels, restaurants, and shops. Tourists wander about the streets, most heading for the Convento de Santa Catalina, which is just down the street.

Suon and I will go there later, to keep up appearances, but first we settle down for lunch in the restaurant. In spite of its name, it offers standard Peruvian dishes, potatoes, rice, and meat. The staff appears to be Filipino, and I catch one of them speaking in a language other than Spanish. The accent is similar to Menardo's, so I trust that we are in the right place.

It took some convincing to get Osahi to agree to let me come here. At first, he refused to allow that the woman Menardo spoke of was the same one Lasinha arrested with Ana.

"It could be any woman," he said. "There's no reason to think it was that woman. I can't afford to send people off around the world on wild goose chases."

But I would not be denied. The woman's description,

which I extracted from Menardo, was close enough a match that I thought there was little chance this was some other body Lasinha had buried. And there was the fact that he had made her disappear, rather than subjecting her to the Acolyte's procedures.

"Why would he do that?" Answering my own question, I said, "Because he doesn't want the Acolytes to find out what this woman knows. Or anyone else, for that matter. He wants her out of reach of anyone in the Church. Doesn't that tell you something?"

"Yes," Osahi said. "But I suspect it tells you something different."

"It tells me that whatever she knows is dangerous to him."

I am not sure I entirely believe that. Lasinha is not above killing someone, and if she is truly a threat, that is the cleaner method to deal with it. The fact that Menardo is stationed in this universe, as I discover when Osahi finally relents and allows me to proceed, also gives me pause. It is very convenient that we are able to conduct this investigation without transferring to another universe and potentially alerting the Watchers to Osahi's location. Just as convenient as the fact that Ocampos appears to be a low-level functionary in the Order, while the Church has little presence in this world.

That it even has any is shocking to me. I had assumed Osahi would place his hideaway in a pristine universe to ensure that no Watchers stumbled across his people. Though no one is just stumbling across this place. And the Watchers would make the assumption I did and never think to look for him in a universe where they had people.

Still, it's all a little too neat, as though Osahi is trying again to keep me busy and distracted and, most importantly, away from the village. I cannot help but wonder if this is related to the stranger in the house in some way.

At the same time, I can't deny that it is a huge relief

that I do not have to cross over the channels in search of this woman. Such an attempt would leave me utterly unraveled. I felt the aftereffects of being in the vicinity of a transfer for two days following my interrogation of Menardo. And that was not even a true opening of the channels across the universe.

I ponder the Casa de Manila's menu, trying not to think about the fact that I may be, for all intents and purposes, imprisoned in this universe, unable to risk crossing over. Suon catches my eye and smiles at me. Since coming to Arequipa the day before, she's appeared more at ease, more herself, as if some burden has been lifted from her shoulders. I cannot stop myself from wondering if this is some act she is putting on for me, if this whole thing is an elaborate charade. All I have is doubt now, about everything.

"What are you thinking?" Suon says.

She is talking about the menu, and perhaps about the Casa de Manila and our work here, but her question paralyzes me momentarily. Is my disquiet visible upon my face?

"Definitely not the guinea pig," I say, trying to keep my tone light.

"Why not? They say it tastes like chicken," she says with a teasing laugh.

"I always think people who say that must never have had a chicken in their life. Anyway, I think I will stick with the menu of the day. Always a safe choice."

The waiter comes by to take our orders. There are two other waiters, all wearing slightly formal vests over pressed white shirts. Which seems odd for a place like this, at least to me. At the far end of the long room that the restaurant occupies there is a bar, behind which a woman prepares coca tea and other drinks. Unlike the men, she is wearing sunglasses, ripped jeans, and a tight t-shirt of a band I do not recognize. Her face is as lovely as her expression is inscrutable.

Suon notices me staring at the bartender and raises an eyebrow. I shake my head. "Not her. They wouldn't have her this visible anyway."

From the outside, the building we are in appears to be two stories. It is unclear what lies above the restaurant, though there are no signs for any other businesses, and no obvious way to get upstairs. There are windows on the upper floors, but it is impossible to see anything from the street. It does suggest that there are apartments there. Or perhaps something else.

Menardo did not say much beyond the fact that the woman was in this building. "I left her keeping to them," he said to me, with a broken shrug. It is clear that he wanted to know as little as possible about the woman, who she was, her connection to Lasinha, and what became of her. He knew such knowledge was dangerous, and he discovered just how dangerous it was.

The woman notices my attention and returns my stare. I can sense her gaze behind the sunglasses, the questions she is asking herself. She brings our tea and water over, nodding at me as she does.

Suon looks at me. "Interesting," she says. There is a hint of jealousy in her voice.

"That's not good," I say. "She may remember us now."

"Does that matter?"

I shrug. "It may. It may not."

"Does it change anything?"

"No," I say. "We go ahead as planned. First, though, we need lunch, and then the convent."

That evening, after a day of being tourists and wandering about the lovely streets of Arequipa, we return to the Casa de Manila. The restaurant is shuttered and the surrounding streets are empty. The windows on the floor above the restaurant are dark as well. A quick search of the perimeter reveals no other entrance on the main floor, but there is an old-fashioned fire escape down the back of the building, leading up to the roof and past a window on the second floor.

It looks old and rusty, liable to groan under someone's weight, so we do not attempt to climb it. The streets around us are far too quiet now to risk it. We will need to find another alternative, and, as we scout the surrounding area, we do. There is another building with a fire escape that looks far newer at the far end of the block. We use it to climb atop and begin to make our way across the rooftops to the Casa.

As we come to the roof of the building beside the Casa, Suon goes still in front of me. I do as well, frantically casting about for what is causing her to stop. I do not see it immediately through the darkness, only a portion of the illumination from the streetlights below reaching us. When I do, I drop to my knees, pulling Suon down with me, so that we are obscured by the small lip on the edge of the building.

The light makes it difficult to say for certain, but it looks like the bartender from the restaurant who stands staring off into the darkness, smoking a cigarette. Her profile is to us and she is lost in thought; otherwise, she would surely have noticed our approach. She finishes her cigarette, grinding what remains beneath her heel, and returns through the door that is open behind her, pulling away the cinder block she used to prop it open so that it closes as she disappears below.

Suon looks at me and shakes her head with relief. I can only nod. She opens her mouth to speak, but I shake my head and gesture below. There may be a window open through which the woman can hear us. We wait five minutes to see if she will return, and when she does not, we scamper across the roof. Suon investigates the door, while I prowl around the roof, looking to see what, if anything, might be revealed there.

We are both careful to keep the tread of our feet light and try not to make a sound. I return to Suon by the door, and she gestures to indicate she can manage the lock. I shake my head. Now is not the moment for that. We need to find out more about what lies behind it before we risk anything. And we need to be certain the woman is asleep.

After a final lingering glance around at the rooftop, as if the Casa de Manila might reveal its secrets, I follow Suon across the rooftops and we descend back to the street.

I return to the restaurant the next morning alone, taking a seat at the back near the bar. A waiter comes by, and I wave away a menu and ask for a coffee in my meager Spanish. The bartender isn't behind the counter, but she emerges a moment later when the waiter disappears into the back. She is wearing the same uniform as yesterday, dark, tight pants and another music t-shirt, and the same sunglasses.

I notice they are shaped somewhat like an insect's eyes, a distant echo of the Seeker's appendages. It provokes some momentary discomfort, making me question again whether it was a good idea to come here. Suon suggested it after we returned to our hotel the night before.

When I asked her why, she said, "Did you see the way she looked at you?"

"She caught me staring at her," I said. "She was wondering why. Who we were. She's on guard against strangers."

"No," Suon said. "We don't know that she's involved. And she has no reason to suspect we are. I know what that look was."

I was not sure, but I relented, unable to think of a better approach. We need a way into the upper floor of the building, and the bartender can provide it.

She brings me a cup of coffee, along with a saucer of milk and a bowl of sugar, setting it down wordlessly. I smile and thank her, but she is already walking away without a glance in my direction. She disappears into the back, and I am left alone with a solitary waiter who is busy setting cutlery on the tables at the front of the restaurant. I watch him and wait, lingering over my coffee.

When the waiter is done with the tables, he goes to stand outside the door, chatting with those passing by, trying to entice them into the restaurant. As soon as he is gone, the bartender materializes from the back. She busies herself behind the bar, looking, but not looking at me. I make a show of studying the ceiling and walls, which are painted with frescos that look as though they are original to the building. There are saints and Virgin Marys, the usual colonial artwork.

"Would you like some more coffee?" the woman says, in faintly accented English. Perhaps Filipino, perhaps Peruvian, I cannot quite place it.

"Please," I say.

She retrieves the pot and pours me another cup. Retreating behind the bar, she pours another for herself and looks down at me. "Where's your wife?"

"She's not my wife. We're just traveling together," I say. I hold up my left hand and wiggle my ringless fingers as evidence.

"You didn't answer my question."

I grin. "She's off to look at the condors. I didn't feel like hiking for a few days. I prefer the city life."

She nods, as though that is an acceptable answer, and heads into the back. I return to my study of the walls, pondering the life of saints and the faithful.

I am almost certain that Suon was wrong, that our conversation to this point is not a prelude, but an end, when the bartender returns to stand over me. She stands in that way that some women do, one foot to the side, hip jutting out just so.

"What are your plans for the next two days while your friend is gone?" she says.

I am careful not to smile. "Just hanging around, seeing what there is to see. Do you have any suggestions?"

"Maybe," she says. "Why don't you come by around

nine tonight? I can see what I can think of."

"I'll do that."

She nods and returns behind the bar. I finish my coffee and pay. She barely acknowledges my presence, but as I leave, I can feel her gaze upon me.

Her name, she tells me, is Martina. I give mine as Joseph, resisting a shudder as I do. The restaurant is quiet, with only one waiter on duty, and he is cleaning up. From the kitchen I can hear laughter. She is still wearing her sunglasses, though the sun set long ago.

"What would you like to do?" she says, stepping around from the bar.

"I'm open to suggestion," I say.

"Ah," she says. "I was supposed to think of something, wasn't I?"

She smiles, and I smile in turn. The waiter is watching us, while applying himself to the task of not appearing as though he is.

"Would you mind coming upstairs for a minute?" She gestures above. "I'll just get myself ready."

I nod and follow her upstairs. There is small landing on the second floor with doors to the building's apartments, of which there are four. A fifth door nearest the stairway presumably leads to the staircase to the roof. Martina takes me in through the second door from the stairway into a long, narrow apartment.

It consists of one large room, including both the kitchen and living spaces, with a single door leading off to one side, presumably to the bedroom and bathroom. Martina takes me by the hand and leads me toward the couch under the windows at the room's far end. As she does, she takes off her sunglasses, setting them on one of the end tables we pass.

When we are at the center of the room, she turns and looks up into my eyes, her hands upon my arms. I hear an excited intake of breath and realize it is my own.

Something about her eyes and her still-inscrutable expression is intoxicating. I feel giddy and want to laugh in delight.

She kisses me, and I taste something bright and alluring on her lips. I pull her into my arms hungrily, my tongue seeking hers, ignoring the sudden intrusion of Suon—her anger and her certainty as she tells me what Martina is about—into my thoughts. She remains there as Martina extracts herself smoothly from my arms, a small, knowing smile on her face.

I want her, in a way I have not wanted anyone in this flesh. Except Meredith. Always Meredith.

I do not notice the numbness spreading through my lips until it is too late. "What?" I say, but I cannot finish the thought. My voice sounds odd and muffled. I look at Martina and she returns my gaze without emotion, watching as I collapse to the floor. My last coherent thought is that Suon was wrong, and I feel a desperate urge to laugh.

18

There is darkness and then light. I gasp in shock and pain, struggling to turn away from it, but the light is everywhere. It intrudes even my thoughts when I close my eyes. A memory follows. Blue and green lights and the void, exploding outward. The endless universes extending on in all their glory and my endless selves crying out in agony.

A voice from somewhere. Husky and sensuous. "I don't know. He's not from this universe. I would put money on that."

A pause. Quiet, from which I soon distinguish sounds. The hum of electricity; the hiss of air through a fan. Traffic and laughter from an open window.

"Can't you get hold of Menardo? I need to know how to proceed."

I react groggily to the mention of that familiar name, which draws an interested grunt from Martina. *Wonderful.*

"He's secure. Don't worry about that. Worry about finding Menardo. That's your concern. If something's happened to him, we'll need to go higher to get answers."

Even in my disoriented state, I know that will mean disaster. Higher up in the Order will take them to Lasinha eventually. And he will know who I am. I fight against my grogginess and try to open my eyes so that I can see where I am, but they will not cooperate.

"Good. I'm going to see if I can get some answers from him. Hurry. I don't want him here much longer."

I must still be in the apartment upstairs, I decide. That is good, because it means two things. This is not a large operation with a lot manpower and infrastructure at their beck and call. And Suon will know where to find me. Can she extract me on her own, or will she need to get help from Osahi?

Martina says a curt goodbye. I can hear her set down the phone and walk over to me, and then feel the slight whoosh of air as she kneels at my side. A hand grasps my shoulder and gives me a rough shake, scattering the light and dark in my head into a jumble. I moan.

"Who are you, Joseph? And what are you doing here?"

"You invited me," I manage to say, though it emerges as more of a mumble.

"No," Martina says. "That's not why you're here. You would have fucked me, but that wasn't why you came here."

She is musing to herself, and while she does so, I try to get to my feet but fail even to raise myself off the floor. What the hell has she given me? I am awake and more or less aware, but unable to see or move. Even speaking is difficult, requiring thought. That is also sluggish, though not so slow that I miss the fact that I am not bound in any way.

"So who are you, Joseph? You might as well tell me. I'll get the answers one way or another."

I don't reply, trying to focus my awareness to determine where exactly I am. Definitely the apartment, near an open window, so toward the back of the room. Martina had to walk quite a distance to reach me, so I must still be in the main room of her apartment. Which suggests she is not worried about any visitors or strangers stumbling upon me. If I can get myself to the window somehow, perhaps I can yell for help.

"Fine," she says when I don't reply. "We'll do it the hard way."

She gets up and walks away, her footsteps soft on the hardwood floor. She is gone so long that I worry for a moment that I somehow missed her leaving the apartment. Eventually she returns, hoisting me up so that my head is cradled against her breasts.

The cold glass of a cup against my lips informs me that she is trying to get me to drink something. I try to fight, to seal my lips and to spit out the liquid that she pours in there. My mouth will not cooperate, though, and she is able to tip my head back and force the liquid down my throat. She sets me down on the floor and I do not hear her go.

"Aeida. Wake up."

Darkness. A breeze stirs across my legs, cool and light. There is a warm breath upon my cheek.

"Damn it, Aeida. We have to go."

The whisper floats around my head, as if separated from its body. If it possesses one. It may be in my head. Aeida. Who is that? Me, or one of me?

I blink, trying to peer through the shadows, unsure if they are in my mind or outside of it. The universes have collapsed in on themselves, and there is no distinction between the worlds out there and the ones within me. They are many. They are infinite.

Warms lips upon my own. "David. Please."

"Suon." There are so many memories. So many eyes looking upon the same memories. Which ones are mine? All of them.

"Yes," she says. "Come on. We have to go."

I reach out with a hand, or at least I think I do. Nothing is functioning. I can't move.

"Quiet," she says. "Let me help you."

I am afloat, upside down, or right side up—I don't

know. The world has spun from its axis. I try to work with Suon as she drags me to my feet, but we seem at cross-purposes. Finally, I cease any movement and let her carry me along.

My sight returns gradually. I can see outlines of shapes in the darkness. There is the couch and the end tables. The dining table and chairs. We are moving toward the door. I am able to put weight upon my feet, though not enough to walk on my own.

"Almost there," Suon says, more to reassure herself than me, I think.

We come to what I believe is the door. Suon fumbles with it, trying to swing it open while keeping me upright.

How are we going to get out of here? I say or think, I am still not sure. Nothing seems solid. Part of me wants to sound the alarm. Part of me wants to slip silently away into the night. A strangled gasp escapes my throat.

"Quiet," she whispers.

It doesn't matter. The door swings open to reveal Martina and one of the waiters from the restaurant below.

"David Aeida. Suon," she says, nodding at each of us in turn. My vision of her blurs. I am weeping, I realize. "I wonder what the Watchers' Order will have to say about the two of you."

FOUR:

THE FIRST CROSSING

19

The room was familiar, as all such rooms are. Small and square, with a table at its center and chairs on either side. I was made to sit on the side facing the observation glass. Different Travelers sat opposite me, depending on the day. Their uniforms made their faces seem all the same. And their questions were unchanging and unceasing.

"Are you the High Regent from the Church of the Regents known as Laila Johar?"

"Have you or any of your known associates participated in attempts to cross over to other universes?"

"Have you in any way attempted to subvert the Protocols of the Society?"

"Who are your agents within our ranks? It is an offense against the laws of all nations for someone to subvert the Society of Travelers."

There were more. They continued on and on, hours at a time, the questions wrapping around on themselves until we were back at the beginning and the same queries were being launched at me like blows to my temple. My responses were irrelevant. I knew that, and so did they. Yet I was expected to say something. So I denied; I obfuscated; I told them to go fuck themselves.

When I grew tired of that, I asked them why they had arrested me. By what right, by what law, was I imprisoned here. We both knew the Society could act beyond the law if it felt its own interests were at risk. But that was hardly the case here. Though we had tried endlessly to infiltrate the Travelers' ranks, and had succeeded to a degree, we had never gotten close to gaining the technology required to cross over. Subverting the Protocols of the Society, to use their parlance.

They knew that as well as I. If we had managed to insert a few agents they didn't know about—and that was always the debate Lasinha and I had: did the Society know about all our agents within their ranks?—they had surely managed to infiltrate the Church to a far greater extent. We were still crippled by what Gabriel Arajuano had done, though we had managed to stanch the flow of Regents abandoning the faith.

So the question was, what did the Travelers think they had to gain by arresting Molijc and I? I could not fathom it. If they were hoping to crush the faith once and for all, this was a poor way of doing it. Even now, Lasinha, Osahi, and the other High Regents—assuming they had not been taken as well—would be using our arrest to rail against the Society. This act confirmed everything we claimed about the Travelers. It gave us power, where simply ignoring us would slowly starve us of credibility.

It did not surprise me, though. This was what the Society was. They wanted to be absolute in all the universes they had infiltrated, so of course they would not be able to resist arresting us when they saw the opportunity. It still left the question of why they were doing so now. That, I assumed, would be revealed soon enough.

Hours passed in the interrogation room. Time seemed to slow down and stretch out. At some point the questions stopped, though they continued to echo in my head long after. I was taken back to my cell and left alone, only to be returned to the interrogation room for a further session. This was done again and again until I had no sense of how long I had been there.

Or how long I would remain. I tried to avoid thinking of that. It was best not to. The Society could take people without consequence, and they could remain lost in their various black sites for years. Or so it was said. No one knew for certain what happened to them. This was the potential fate that awaited me, endless days like this, an infinite number of pointless questions.

But I couldn't worry about that. The Church could rouse outrage against the Society, was doing so now. People distrusted the Travelers, even those who thought us members of a cult, and it would be easy to curry sympathy and to have governments put pressure on the guild to release us. Dejian and I were not nobodies who could be disappeared without consequence. Or so I fervently hoped. The truth was the Society could do as it pleased, likely without consequence, no matter what the Church did.

People came and left. Even when I was alone, I could sense people observing me through the mirror. In my cell, it was the same. There were people watching always. The room was dark, absolutely without light, and then so bright I had to close my eyes against the glare. Sleep was impossible, and so was staying awake and aware. I was disoriented and confused, unsure of my own thoughts, my own being.

Yet I still felt no fear. This was all as expected. Both of us had played our parts without variation. Now what mattered was what came next.

I dozed intermittently, starting awake when I imagined a presence nearby. Always I was alone in the darkness. I could not recall the last time the Travelers had come to drag me to the interrogation room to question me. It felt like days, but I knew not to trust my impressions. They had brought food only twice since my last questioning, and they had been feeding me regularly before that, so it seemed only the better part of a day had gone by.

I felt feverish, my cheeks hot and my mouth dry. I kept dreaming, strange and vivid visions that seemed as though they must be real, even as I knew they weren't. Asleep or awake, I dreamed them.

Travelers would arrive at the door to take me out, and I would slip free of their grasp, only to find myself lost in a maze of corridors in the midst of the vast facility from which I could not escape. There I remained, waiting for the Travelers to find me and return me to my cell. I would fall to the floor weeping gratefully and tell them all I knew of the Church, the Protectors, and the Acolytes.

There was a presence that came and went as I lay in this trance, half awake, half asleep. At first, I thought it part of my hallucinations, but as the feeling grew more persistent, I began to pay more attention to it. There was someone there, on the other side of the wall, I felt certain. The feeling was palpable.

Without even realizing it, I found myself backing away from that presence, moving into the far corner of the cell, as if I felt something reaching out for me. A cold and distant manifestation, looking down upon me as though I was an object to be dissected and studied. I had never felt so exposed.

The realization of what this meant brought me to my feet. It was a Seeker. The Travelers had brought a Seeker to interrogate me. They would find out everything. Most important of all, they would find out about Ana. If she wasn't lost already, she would be now.

The Seeker remained observing me for several hours, by my best estimate. Time had flattened out and I existed in that moment, terrified of what was to come. I tried not to think of Ana, fearful that I might somehow reveal my thoughts. A ridiculous idea, for they weren't mind readers.

Though no one was actually sure what they were capable of exactly.

Nor could I remove Ana from them. I was weeping without realizing it at the thought that, in the end, despite all I had done, I would destroy her. It was awful to contemplate. I was also reminded of how much I had missed her these last years, how much of an anchor she had been for me. With Dejian and Lasinha hiding things from me, and Meredith gone, I had no one I could trust.

Ana had been that. She had borne my youthful desires with patience, and remained a friend through it all. And I had failed her.

The presence of the Seeker vanished as suddenly as it had appeared. I trembled at its absence, wondering what it signified. The answer came soon enough. The cell door flung open and two Travelers entered, ordering me to my knees. One handcuffed me and the other placed a hood over my head. They lead me out down the corridor to the left, the opposite direction from my normal interrogations.

This was all so different from the norm that had been established that I panicked. The Seeker, I was certain, had to be behind this new procedure. That was who awaited me at the end of this journey. I began to fight against my guards, trying to throw them off and break free, though I knew there was no hope of escaping. Even if I did, I would only succeed in losing myself in the complex, just as in my dreams, and bring further punishment down upon myself.

The guards seemed to pay no mind to my struggles, tightening their grip a little upon my arms, but otherwise not even breaking stride. I lost count of the turns we took along the corridors and the doorways through which we passed. There was a trip on an elevator, though I could not tell whether we went up or down, and an ascent up a short set of stairs. At the end of it all, I was dizzy and shaking with fear.

The guards came to a halt and one them knocked on a

door. A voice, muffled and indistinct, told them to enter. They brought me within and set me upon a chair that felt the same as the one I sat upon in the other interrogation room. I was filled with a sudden certainty that this was the same room, that the hood would be removed and I would find myself facing the same interrogators. They would ask me the same questions, I would give the same answers, and I would be returned to my cell to begin this whole game anew.

Footsteps told me that my guards were exiting the room. They had not removed my handcuffs or the hood. The door closed, the lock clicking into place. I waited.

Someone approached and the hood was pulled off my head. "Hello, Laila," Ana said.

20

"What are you doing here?" I said, unable to stop myself.

The sight of Ana left me reeling, the dizziness I was already suffering from redoubling, nearly sending me tumbling from the chair in a faint. I bit the side of my mouth to ensure I was awake, that this was not some cruel vision brought on by the Travelers.

It was not. Ana was there before me, wearing the black uniform and red insignia of the Society. She was breathtaking, even with the attire and the severe expression that she held as she stared at me. It was like she was looking at a stranger, and in a way, she was.

Four years. That was how long it had been since I sent her away to save her from Osahi. Lifetimes had passed for both of us. Lives had been lost. And so much more.

I began to weep despite myself. Ana did not appear to notice.

"I have some questions for you." It was impossible to tell from her voice what she was thinking. "Tell me what happened to my father."

My eyes narrowed. What was she playing at? To other Travelers, I had obfuscated and denied when questions of Gabriel Arajuano and Frederik came up. But I couldn't do

141

that to Ana. He was her father.

I took a deep, unsteady breath, gathering myself. "You would know better than I. The last time I saw him, he was getting on a Society airship." I did not mention the Seeker, hoping that if I avoided mentioning them, one would not appear.

"So you're saying he was a Society agent?"

"I don't know, Ana. Osahi always claimed he was. De Gofroy obviously believed it. I've seen nothing that would say one way or the other."

"But you saw him getting on a Society airship?"

She doesn't know, I realized. *They haven't told her.*

"I did. He was definitely working with the Travelers then. But I don't know. Exiling him out may have pushed him toward the Society. Maybe he wanted revenge. Only he knows."

A wave of emotion passed over Ana's face, but she quickly forced it aside. She stared at me with level eyes. "How many people were forced out from the Church for being apostates? How many were banned for being Society agents?"

I couldn't look at her. "I don't know."

"You've never counted, have you? I have. Two thousand, one hundred and five. That's how many there were last I looked. Do you know how many agents the Society has sent to the Church?"

I met her gaze, but didn't answer.

"No more than ten in the time you were in the Church. They gave me access to their records."

"And you believe them?" I said.

"More than you."

Ana stared at me, a challenge in her eyes. My temptation was to argue, to say that I'd saved her from banishment from the faith. At what cost, her expression seemed to say.

Without another word, she turned and strode from the room, the door slamming shut behind her. I opened my mouth and closed it, wanting to find the words to call her back and apologize for all that had happened. None came, and I remained where I was on the chair, my wrists handcuffed. The lights flicked off a moment later, and I was left alone in the darkness.

The moments stretched on, each more excruciating than the last, as I was left with only my thoughts to haunt me. I recalled the day I sent Ana away, how I had justified it to myself. Now I saw that it had all gone wrong.

I should not have been surprised. Most of the agents Lasinha and I had in the Society were disaffected members of the guild. Ana was not that. She had left the Church, no doubt disillusioned by what had befallen her and her father. The Society would have preyed on that. They would have cultivated her sympathies, just as we cultivated their disaffected.

In the end, she would have known, as I had never admitted to myself, that she could never return. Not with Osahi in the Protectors. Not with all that had happened with her father and with her own disappearance. Everything she did as a Traveler only further cemented her place among them and made extraction from it impossible. They would hunt her for the rest of her days if she left them.

This was inevitable. I saw it now. How had I not before?

When Ana returned, she brought food with her, the lights coming up as she entered. She set the plate of chicken and rice on the table in front of me and loosened the cuffs from my wrists. I ate in a frenzy while she stood over me, watching, a closed expression on her face. When I was finished and sipping at the small glass of water, she sat across from me and spoke in a low, flat voice, looking at the corner of the cell.

"You're going to tell me everything I want to know. That's your only hope of getting out of here. Do you understand? They don't give a damn. They'll keep you here forever, no matter how much the Church screams about it. I want to know everything. About Molijc. About Lasinha. And Osahi."

I laughed, a bitter, corrosive laugh. "You're my biggest secret. What more is there to tell? You know, better than I, that the Society has agents with us. You probably have a better idea of what Dejian is up to than I do."

Ana got up and paced around the room. "I don't have patience for any more lies, Laila. I want the truth. And I want it all."

She had to be bluffing, saying that I would remain here forever if I didn't cooperate. The others had said that too. But with Ana, I could almost believe it. I had seen her lie before, and I knew when she was telling the truth. But now I was not sure.

"Everything I've said has been true. You know I would never lie to you, Ana. You're my friend. I believe in you."

She stopped her pacing and glanced at me, raising an eyebrow, as though she were surprised to hear I considered her a friend. "I want to know about Molijc. How did he really get to be Grand Regent?"

I shrugged. "You know him. It's always been his burning ambition. Even when De Gofroy chose Frederik as his successor, Dejian was setting things up so he could succeed when the time came."

"And you supported him?"

"Of course. We couldn't very well keep Frederik in charge, could we? He was a disaster for the faith."

"But the Grand Regent chose him. Just like he chose you to protect the faith," Ana said in a mocking tone.

"I know."

Ana returned to her seat, leaning across the table. "I want to know about Molijc and the Acolytes. What are they doing? What did they do to De Gofroy?"

I blinked, recalling Osahi's accusations. I knew Osahi would never ally himself with the Travelers—whatever else he was, he was a loyal Regent. What did it mean then when both were peddling the same strange story? Was this a rumor that she had grasped hold of, spread by Osahi, or was there something they could see that I was blind to?

"Dejian is the only one who knows what the Acolytes are up to. You'll have to ask him yourself."

"Perhaps I will," Ana said. "But you've seen their handiwork yourself. Haven't you?"

"I don't know," I said, though I did.

"Frederik."

"I don't know," I said. "He's not the same, but that could be anything. Maybe they've kept him in a place like this for too long."

Ana smiled faintly. "You know that's not true."

"I'm telling you what I saw. That's all. I don't know anything else."

"You can't hide forever, Laila," Ana said, crossing her arms and leaning back in her chair. "You'll have to deal with this sometime."

"So will you," I said. "You can't hide what you are. You're a Regent. You sat at De Gofroy's feet with me. I know you believe in the Protocols. Let them guide you."

"That time is over," Ana said bluntly.

"They are the truth and you know it," I said. "You've been too long in these shadows, living this pale life. Come back to us."

Ana glanced over her shoulder, emotion plain upon her face for the first time. "We'll talk again," she said, abruptly standing. She turned and left, and the darkness fell around me again.

When it became clear that Ana was not going to return for some time, I lay on the floor and tried to sleep. The room was growing colder, and the laminate of the floor seemed to exude a chill that entered my bones and would not leave. I could almost see my breath forming clouds as I exhaled, though I knew that was impossible. Though I had no idea where the Travelers had brought Molijc and I, it was not so far that we had traversed seasons.

I was aching and felt ragged by the time Ana returned, the lights flashing awake as she strode into the room. She stared down at me wordlessly as I struggled to my feet. I had managed a little sleep during her absence, but my mind felt sluggish and my body drained. As I looked at Ana, I felt emotion well up within me and tears sting my eyes. I forced my gaze to the table and tried to gather myself.

"Are you ready to tell me the truth?" Ana said, her words clipped. She sat down across from me.

"I've only told you the truth," I said, looking at her as steadily as I could manage. "I'd like some water. And I need to use the bathroom."

Ana ignored my request. "I want to know everything you know about the Acolytes."

"If I tell you, do I get to use the bathroom and get a drink of water?"

Ana would not answer.

"Fine," I said with a shrug, standing up. "I'll just go right here."

I pulled down my pants and started to squat. For a moment it appeared as though Ana was going to call my bluff, but she relented. "Fine. Fine. I'll arrange for a bathroom and some food and water. Once you've answered my questions."

"Okay," I said. "All I know about the Acolytes is what De Gofroy told us, nothing more. When I was more active in the Protectors, I tried to get some people inserted there, but they're impenetrable. De Gofroy was the only one they would deal with directly. And now it's Dejian. If you want to know why he's Grand Regent, that's as good a reason as any."

"What about Frederik?"

I sighed in irritation. "It's like I told you. The Acolytes took him after… He came back after, to step down and to anoint Dejian. He was different. I thought he was drugged at first. But I saw him after, later, and he wasn't himself at all."

"What do you mean?"

I could sense Ana's anticipation of my answer. This was the crux of why she was talking to me. "I'm not sure. It could have been drugs of some sort. Side effects. But I don't think so. It was more like he wasn't there. Like there was no one there."

Ana nodded as though I had confirmed her own impression of the situation. She was lost in thought, and I said, hoping to catch her off guard, "I've missed you."

A flicker of emotion danced across her face before she regained control. "You sent me here."

"We had to. But it wasn't supposed to be forever."

"How, Laila?" Ana said, her anguish apparent. "You join the Society for life. You don't leave. There's no going back from this."

"We can protect you," I said, ignoring the absurdity of what I was saying.

"You can't even protect yourselves. You'll be lucky if they ever let you out."

I fell silent. There was nothing to say to counter that cold reality. The Society had taken Dejian and I without our even realizing they were moving against us. For all I knew, they had taken everyone in the upper Hierarchy. All the High Regents might be here in this complex, might be cutting deals for their lives, just as I was trying to. For it now seemed to me that I was parlaying with Ana for my life, or at least my freedom.

"What do you want from me?" I said, putting my hands on the table as though in surrender.

"You'll get no favors from me," Ana said, as if she understood my train of thought.

"Fine," I said, in a quiet voice. "Don't forgive me; don't forgive any of us our trespasses. We deserve whatever revenge you want. But remember the faith.

147

Remember the Protocols. You know the truth of the universes. You know that these people are telling are lies. We are multiples, longing to be singular. You have seen your other lives. De Gofroy helped you to achieve that. Don't forget it. Help your faith. Be faithful to the truth, if nothing else."

"It is not that easy," Ana began, but I interrupted her.

"Nothing is. Nothing can be. All I ask is that you remember the Protocols. Let them guide you."

Ana turned and left without uttering another word, but I had seen the expression on her face, and I allowed myself to hope.

As I awaited Ana's return, I tried to calm myself by performing the Protocols, silently mouthing them to myself. As always, I felt the universes open up within me, their fabric going from opaque to transparent, and I could see all the unending shadow Lailas in the other universes going about their lives. Some shared my predicament; others lived very different lives. There were multitudes upon multitudes, and in some universes an absence. But all of us were shadows, half-things, and we all felt it keenly, for the true Laila was beyond us. We were her vessels, seeded throughout the universes, and she awaited our return.

I had nearly reached my desired equilibrium when I felt the Seeker's presence again. It was there for a moment and then gone, but my spine was tingling and my whole body went rigid with fear. Had I misread Ana? Had she decided that she could not get what the Travelers wanted out of me and turned me over to the Seeker's implacable gaze?

The idea was terrifying beyond measure. The Society was fearsome enough, intimidating in the way that any institution was. Justice, or what they saw as justice, was their end, and they did not care about the means it took to reach it. But the logic of the Travelers was understandable. It was the logic of governments, of authorities, across worlds and time.

The Seekers were something else entirely. They had come after the Society had, though it was unclear when. There were rumors the Society had discovered them in one of their crossings, or that the Seekers had discovered the Travelers. It was often said they controlled the Society, but I didn't believe so. They worked with the Travelers when their interests aligned, but they did not see themselves as the universes' policemen in the same sense. What they sought, no one seemed to know. They knew what you wanted, not the other way.

The Acolytes, of course, were nearly as secretive as the Seekers, though they had arrived in our universe with the Society and as their allies. But they were more explicable, at least for someone who belonged to the Church of the Regents and had some inkling of their works. They were engineers, repurposing Society technology—whether developed by the Travelers or imported from some other universe—as they had done with the Eye. As they were doing with whatever they had done to Frederik.

The Eye was obviously connected in some way to the Seeker's implanted eyes. The source of the technology had to be the same. And there were those who said that they had once been allies, even part of the same larger guild in some other universe. There was no way to tell whether any of these stories had any truth to them, or if it was all just supposition and innuendo.

As soon as the Seeker's presence vanished, Ana returned to my cell. Something had changed, I could see immediately, by the expression on her face. There was a new resolve. Had the Seeker been to see her and, if so, what had been said?

She walked behind me and pulled down a small camera perched in the top corner of the cell, which I hadn't noticed, but which I had always assumed was there. After placing it at the center of the table, so that I could see it was off, she sat across from me. To be certain, and to see what her reaction would be, I picked the camera up, smashed it against the table, put it on the floor, and crushed it under the heel of my shoe until it was in a dozen pieces.

Ana watched me, not even blinking. When I was done, she said, "I cannot just set you free. They want to know everything. They want it all."

"What about the Seeker?" I said.

She was taken aback by my question. "What Seeker?"

"Don't play games with me," I said. "I felt one just now. And I felt one just before your men came to bring me here. There was one on the Society airship when your father was with Frederik in Montreal."

"I don't know anything about that," she said. "They may have called in a Seeker when Frederik and Gabriel went to ground. And they may have someone in here for you guys, or for something else. I don't know. I don't have anything to do with them, believe me."

I hesitated. She was earnest. I could almost allow myself to believe. It was not as though I had any other choice. I noted her reference to her father by his first name. That too was interesting.

"If there's a Seeker involved in this, we're both lost," she said. "They made me sit with one when I first came in. There's no hiding anything."

"True enough," I said. There was every possibility she was lying to me. It was the simplest explanation. Far more likely than my presence stirring the remnants of the faith in her heart. But the Regent in me wanted to believe she could be brought back.

"What do you need from me?" I said. "I've told you everything. I haven't lied."

"We need to give them something," she said.

I made a helpless gesture, telling her that there was nothing more to give. It was not entirely true. There were De Gofroy's files, in particular those I had removed and secreted away. There might be things in them that would provide the answers they were looking for.

Ana thought for a moment. "Then we have to tell them what they expect to hear."

"What will they expect to hear?"

"We can tell them you suspect Molijc, and the Acolytes too, of doing something to Frederik. And that you're willing to work with us to find out what it is. But the only way to do it is to let you go. Let Molijc and Lasinha go too. You'll have to agree to inform on them."

I shook my head. "I'm giving you everything in this deal. They get an agent at the top of the Church who is beholden to you for releasing us. What do I get?"

"That's the best I can do," Ana said. "They don't want to let any of you go. They want the Acolytes stopped."

"If they want to stop the Acolytes, then why extract us? Go after the Acolytes."

Ana didn't answer. Was her silence a sign that some Acolytes had been arrested, or did she just not want to tell me the reason why the Society would not confront the Acolytes directly? Perhaps she didn't know.

"You have to give me something," I said. "Dejian and Lasinha are going to want an explanation for why we've been released. You're my explanation. I'll tell them you arranged to get us released in exchange for my agreeing to work for you."

"You can't tell them that," Ana said. "What good would that do?"

"That's exactly what I'll tell them. Because it's what they want to hear. You released us because you're still a Regent and we're letting the Society believe I'm working for them. And to prove it, you're going to give us the equipment to let us cross over."

"I can't do that. They'll never let me do that."

"If they want a useful mole, that's the price they'll have to pay," I said, sitting back and crossing my arms, as though I was prepared to remain in this cell indefinitely. They knew they could break me, but so did the Protectors, and the longer I remained here, the more certain Osahi and others would be that I had turned and the less useful I would be to the Society.

"They won't agree to it," Ana said, emotion creeping into her voice. "It goes against everything they believe. It's their fundamental purpose for being."

I shrugged. That was of no consequence to me. "I'm betraying the faith by agreeing to do this. Putting myself in danger as well. You know what Lasinha is capable of. I need the transfer equipment or you're sending me back to my death. Or worse."

Ana shook her head. "They won't," she said.

"You can convince them this is worth it," I said. "This is what you came here for. This will make all of this bullshit worth it. Don't you see? All of this can be made right. And if we do this, maybe we can bring you back then. Maybe we can hide you in some universe the Society won't find."

Ana did not answer. She would not look at me, biting at her lip as emotions warred across her face.

"I know you want to come back. You can't hide that from me. You were born a Regent. You're more of a Regent than I can ever hope to be. Your faith needs you. We need you."

Ana swallowed and met my eyes. Hers were red with tears. "And what about when I need you? Will you be there?"

"I will," I said. "I swear it upon De Gofroy."

21

"You're certain the lights are supposed to do that?" Molijc said, with an eyebrow arched theatrically.

I did not bother to answer, intent on the transfer device and the other output readings. Ana had told me precision was essential—seconds mattered if we were to hide our crossing in the signal of others. Dejian sighed, making his displeasure known. He would be sharing a knowing glance with Lasinha as well, I knew, but I did not pay either of them any mind.

We were in a basement suite of a house in the midst of a vast swath of suburbia. Hundreds upon hundreds of nearly identical houses, lining crosshatched streets that were all named variants of whatever community we happened to be in. Community, a ludicrous name to call these places, though no more ludicrous than the street we were on: Crosshaven Manor. A third, or maybe more, of these places were empty, a consequence of the vicissitudes that had befallen Calgary in the years since the Society's arrival, the ensuing wars and the collapse of the oil industry. This one, the Church had taken over surreptitiously several months before in preparation for this day.

One of the outputs spiked and my heart leapt in my throat. I adjusted one of the knobs experimentally and felt relief flood my veins as the signals returned to their previous levels. Ana had been very clear on that matter: our signal had to fall within range or the Travelers would notice us piggybacking on their transfer channel. Agents would be dispatched in both universes to track down the stray signal. A Seeker might even be contracted from the guild to pursue those who dared to subvert the universes.

We would disappear back into the Society's network of holding sites, this time never to emerge. And I would have failed Ana again.

The first transfers would be the most difficult, because we had nothing to send back to balance them, which, Ana said, helped disguise a crossing. Ana had chosen one of the universes frequently trafficked by the Society for a maiden transfer, where an odd, lopsided signal would hopefully be lost amidst everything else that was going on. Once we had established transfer points in other universes, we could set up exchanges, provided we knew the Society schedules. Ana had promised me those would be coming. From there, the universes would be ours to explore.

"Is everything all right?" Lasinha said in a conciliatory tone that only infuriated me further. He was the one whispering in Dejian's ear, telling him that he should be watching me, and yet when we were all together, he acted the peacemaker.

"Just have the transfer box ready to go," I said without raising my head.

Our current location, and the place we were transferring ourselves to, had been chosen by Ana. The four-bedroom split-level here had an abandoned factory on the other side, the sort of place where an unskilled hand could easily create a channel without dropping someone in midair, or worse. The factory could be used to establish a transfer point, a junction in a universe separate from the Church, where we could begin our search of the universes. That was the theory, at any rate.

It was impossible not to wonder, as we all watched the lights move toward synchronicity, whether Ana had betrayed me. This was a moment from which there was no turning back—not that there was any question of our not seeing it through—but we were undeniably subverting the Protocols of the Society. In my nightmares, we walked through to the warehouse and were greeted by a dozen Black Robes, Ana looking on without expression.

"Something is happening," Lasinha said. "You can feel the air changing." There was excitement in his voice that he couldn't hide.

"How can we be certain we won't be walking across to the inside of a mountain?" Molijc said.

"Because Ana arranged it," I said, not taking my eyes from the outputs. There could no mistakes today.

There were still sudden fluctuations in the readings, where our outputs went outside the range of the Society transfer channel currently being opened, theoretically rendering our activity visible to the Travelers. As I adjusted our signal, I realized I had no way of knowing if those fluctuations were significant enough to attract the notice of the Society agents. I could only hope that they were not and that there was enough traffic that they would not be paying this discrepancy any mind.

"She is a Society agent," Molijc said.

The questions following our release lingered. Molijc, Lasinha, and I had been the only ones taken by the Travelers. Lasinha and Osahi both said that their agents within the Society had no explanation for why we had been taken. That, in itself, was not surprising. None of them were deep enough within the Society's inner sanctum for them to be trusted with such sensitive information. Our release, after two weeks' imprisonment and questioning, had been just as sudden and inexplicable.

I knew the reason for both, of course. If Ana was telling me the truth. That was the question everyone had now. Osahi, predictably, had no doubt she was a Black Robe. That was what he had always suspected. Dejian, to my surprise, seemed to agree with him. Her long, unexplained absence and the nature of our arrest and release convinced him that she had abandoned the faith.

Lasinha I could not get a read on. In my presence he was supportive of Ana, or at least of the opportunity I had worked to arrange. What he said to Molijc when I wasn't present, I didn't know. I had begun to suspect it was something else entirely.

"She's a Society agent because we asked her to be." This had become my standard response.

"They turned her," Molijc said flatly. "You cannot tell me otherwise. It's the only explanation for her silence all these years."

"If you can't trust her, you can certainly trust me," I said, returning my attention to the transfer unit. "I haven't been turned." An awkward silence followed, and I could feel both Lasinha and Molijc staring at me.

Part of their mistrust stemmed from the fact that I had not told them everything. I had given them a semblance of the truth. Ana had been chosen to interrogate me because the Travelers felt she might be able to get more out of me than the other Black Robes had. Instead of questioning me, though, she had offered a way out. I would act as a double agent, which would give me an excuse to meet regularly with her, where she could pass me the secrets of crossing over.

Best of all, in my role as double agent, I would supply the Society with information on our activities. False information, with enough truth thrown in to keep them on the hook for years.

"We have a conduit to Ana now," I said, "and the means to cover our tracks."

It made sense, but they were still suspicious, and rightfully so. For though I professed my faith in Ana, I wasn't certain I could trust her. She was torn in her loyalties, and she, and her minders, would not accept the misinformation campaign I'd proposed to Lasinha and Dejian. I would have to provide them with real information about the Acolytes and Molijc. It was a fine line I needed to walk, and I was not at all certain I could manage it.

For all I knew, they had made similar deals with their interrogators, although both claimed that they had said nothing to the Travelers. "We've done nothing wrong," Molijc had said after our release. "Granted, not for lack of trying, but we haven't subverted the universes. Yet. They'd no right to arrest or to keep us, and they knew it."

Part of Dejian's reluctance to place his trust in Ana stemmed from his fear at what we were doing. Until now all of this had been talk; there had been no real possibility of us crossing to other worlds in search of our true selves. It had been fantasy. Now that it was becoming reality, he was feeling doubt—about himself, about the faith, and about his claims of being De Gofroy's chosen.

But Dejian could not stay away from this, no matter the risk. I had offered to conduct the test without him present so that the danger would be mine alone, but both he and Lasinha had refused. Neither of them wanted to be absent from this momentous occasion should it prove a success, leaving all the glory to me. Our names would be spoken with awe throughout all the universes if we could manage this feat.

First, I had to open the channel.

The lights—blue and green and yellow—began to pulse rapidly and approach synchronicity. My breath caught in my throat as I watched, and I could feel the others go still behind me, sensing the moment was at hand. I checked the outputs one last time and saw they were still within range. I looked from Lasinha to Molijc.

"Are we ready?"

They both nodded, faces taut with anticipation. The lights went synchronous and we all looked, unsure what we should be seeing or what was going to happen. I was about to check the lights again, certain that something had gone wrong, when I felt the air begin to shift. As I blinked, a new universe was unveiled before us.

It was difficult at first to comprehend, my mind refusing, almost, to believe what was there before it. One instant all I could see was the empty living room, and the next it opened up and there was the warehouse floor, with its cavernous ceilings and dim lighting. All of us stood dumbfounded, unable to reconcile these two simultaneous existences and unwilling to do anything that might interrupt them.

Finally, I regained my senses and looked down at the channels. They still held within normal parameters, but that would not last. Ana had said we had less than thirty seconds once the channel was opened for the universes to pull apart and the channel to dissolve.

I took a deep breath and stepped forward. There was no obvious threshold from one place to the next, but I could feel very clearly when I had left one universe and entered another. The air felt different. I felt different. There was a gravitational pull I had to fight, something clinging to me from one place and then pulling me into the other as I went further.

Molijc and Lasinha followed behind me, and we turned in unison to watch as the channel dissipated, the living room vanishing, leaving only the factory floor visible, the sun glinting in through some faraway windows. It was some time before anyone moved or spoke, the enormity of what had just occurred settling upon us.

"We should check the perimeter first," I said, my voice sounding very loud in that vast space.

Lasinha nodded, and we both began a thorough search of the premises. The main floor, where we had crossed over, was empty, as were the surrounding offices. I went to the back of the warehouse, following a long corridor from the offices to what at one time must have been the shipping and receiving area. Everything was empty, with the dust-filled scent of encroaching decrepitude.

I slipped out one of the back doors and made a circuit around the building. It was surrounded by a moat of cracked and broken pavement from what once had been the employee parking lots. The back and sides were fenced, while the front had an embankment leading up to the street. It was covered by grass and weeds, recently trimmed, their pungent aroma filling the air.

I walked up it to the street, where I had a better view of our surroundings. To my left I saw a set of traffic lights changing from green to red in one direction. There was a strip mall there, and behind it loomed a voluminous store, with an ominous neon sign perched atop it. I did not recognize the name. To the right were more buildings like the one I had just come from with empty parking lots. Were they all abandoned, I wondered?

The sound of a car approaching caused me to flinch, and I ducked back down the embankment, heading for the entrance to the building, certain that the Society had arrived. The car went past without stopping, and I resisted a laugh of glee. Lasinha stuck his head out the door as I approached.

"What's so funny?"

"Nothing," I said. "All clear."

He nodded. "What's out there?"

"More of this," I said, gesturing at the building. "It should work."

Lasinha nodded again, and we returned to the main room, where Dejian remained. He was looking around the room, whispering to himself, a mixture of wonder and elation on his face.

"This is why I have been chosen," he whispered. He was speaking to himself, not even acknowledging our presence. "This is why De Gofroy granted me his revelation. He has chosen me as his vessel to take the Regents to our true selves. And we shall do it."

The fierceness with which he spoke took me aback. I glanced at Lasinha and saw that he was smiling in approval. He caught me staring at him, and that smile quickly vanished, replaced by his usual blank look. A chill came over me, and I had to resist an urge to shudder. In that moment, I could see how Dejian, with Lasinha's help, would use this to solidify his hold on the Church. The story of the revelation would be tied to our first crossing, and people would believe it was destiny.

It was not. So many had suffered so much to arrive at this moment. It was not something that Dejian had conjured from De Gofroy's true self.

But even my disquiet could not quell the glow I felt. We had crossed over. We had done what De Gofroy had left for us to finish. And this was just the beginning. From here, we could go anywhere.

22

The central library in Vancouver had ornate red-stone colonnades snaking out from its entrance like arms beckoning people within. I entered and took the elevator to the fourth floor, where the history section was. I wandered through rows of shelves aimlessly until I arrived at the Mayan history section. As I lingered there, someone passed by, a woman wearing stylish boots I recognized. I stayed where I was, pulling a book out at random and placing it on another shelf, before wandering away.

I made my way back to the elevator, my head down, my eyes ostensibly focused on the floor. As I stepped back into the elevator, I saw my shadow from the corner of my eyes frozen by the row I had just left, wondering whether she should investigate the shelf to see if I had left some sort of message for a contact—or if she should follow me.

To the annoyance of the ESL students in the elevator, I pressed the button for each floor below. They glared at me as the elevator stopped at each floor in succession and I did not exit. I paid them no mind and left, passing out the main exit through the sensors in the flow of a crowd of students, teenagers, and retirees. Staying with them, I went back out the main entrance and made a sharp turn left into the sushi place set in one of the colonnades. I sat in a booth facing the door, perusing a menu held so that I could look over and see as my shadow walked frantically past, looking left and right.

When she was gone, I got up and left the restaurant, looking toward the street corner where the woman was hurrying, hoping to catch sight of me. I ducked back into the library and walked across to the exit on West Georgia, where Morris was waiting for me in a dark sedan. I stepped into the car and he pulled out into traffic.

"Head back around the library," I said, and he nodded, navigating the traffic.

We ended up on Robson, heading west, and I saw my shadow, still on the corner, looking around, hoping to spot some sign of me. I stared straight ahead as we drove past her.

"Did she spot us?"

"Definitely," Morris said.

"Good," I said. "Make sure we don't have a tail and drop me off near Waterfront."

He nodded and said nothing, his eyes flashing between the road ahead and the rearview mirror. I looked in the side mirror, trying to ascertain if anyone was following us. There was no one that I could see, but Morris took a circuitous route anyway.

As we drove, we talked quickly about his investigation into the Acolytes. "I can't get anyone close to them to talk, but I think I've managed to locate all their sites. I can send them to you."

"Good," I said. "The usual secure channels. What about their activities? Anything?"

"No. They were doing a lot of stuff for a while. A lot of activity. Purchases, expenses—you can find it all if you know where to look. The accountings been disguised, though, so no way to really tell what they've been spending on. I'm trying to trace some of the purchases now. Whatever they were doing, though, they seem to have more or less stopped."

"When?" I said, though I suspected I knew the answer.

"Not long after you were arrested, actually."

"Curious timing," I said.

He nodded and pulled up into a hotel drop-off lane about two blocks from the train station. "Good luck," he said.

I shrugged and didn't say anything, ducking out of the car and setting out on my way.

I kept a tight clamp on my anger as I walked toward the train station. That I had to take such elaborate precautions to thwart people within the Church—and not just people, my ostensible allies—should not have been surprising by now. I could not help it, though; it still stirred me to anger, for the danger they were putting both Ana and I in.

The year that followed our first crossing had passed with dizzying speed. We journeyed to a dozen different universes, establishing way stations in each from which we could explore others. After the initial giddiness of crossing had worn off, we set to work at building the infrastructure we would need to explore the universes. The task was utterly daunting. There were untold numbers of universes. How were we to find any trace or clue of the one universe amidst all the others? We could search for lifetimes and be no further ahead than we were now.

Molijc and some of the other scholars of the Church studied De Gofroy's words, seeking any clues the Grand Regent might have left. As always, it was in the Mayan calendar that we found the information we needed. It existed in each universe, following the same cycles and counts, ending with the same cataclysmic rebirth. The creation of the many universes from the one. This was the trail the true beings had left for their vessels, scattering clues throughout the universes, for those who understood and could follow them. They would lead us to them.

I sat at the front of the first car, the farthest down the platform, where I could easily see anyone who entered. There were no familiar faces, no familiar clothes, no one who had happened past me earlier in the day. Both Osahi and Lasinha—Molijc, really—had taken to having people follow me. They did not trust Ana or me, refusing to believe in the bounty I had brought them, always suspecting a noose closing in.

I felt it myself, every day, especially on days such as these, when I had to meet with Ana. I wasn't sure of anything with her. Our meetings, infrequent by necessity, were fraught with tension and things unspoken. Ana was careful not to reveal any of her thoughts to me, while I was constantly worried we were being observed.

There had been precautions in everything related to the crossings from the beginning. We had to take care about who knew about them within the Church, for fear that the Society would be alerted to our activities. The way stations we chose were in universes the Society did not have a presence in, and where there was no knowledge of the truth of the many universes or our ability to traverse them. It was safer that way, we reasoned, keeping our operations as much out of sight of the Society as possible.

Lasinha chose a few trusted agents from among the Protectors to manage the way stations, seeing to some himself as well. The rest were locals who were brought to the faith. sub-Regents, we called them, as they could not officially be a part of the Church. They formed a shadow Church known only to the High Regents and a few others we trusted with that knowledge.

Osahi was one of them, of course. We had to involve him in everything, for it would have been foolish to attempt to hide a project like this from him. Lasinha argued against it, still not trusting the High Regent and wanting to keep the Protectors separate from this new organization we were forming.

I overruled him, something I regretted occasionally.

Today especially, for I was fairly certain the woman stalking me earlier had been one of his. Likely trained by Meredith. That thought only added to my anger and despair, which was not a good state of mind to be in before meeting with Ana. She would only unsettle me further, and I needed to be calm and focused. I could not afford mistakes.

I was risking my life and my freedom to acquire the knowledge we needed to cross over. I had to provide Ana with lies that would satisfy her and her masters in return. They were never satisfied, and nor would they ever be, I suspected. That was not the nature of our arrangement.

At what point would they decide I was delaying, providing them with a trickle of truths and half-truths, all to get more tech and information from Ana? Would it be today? That assumed that Ana had her masters' agreement to provide me with what she had, which I was not certain of. She might be doing this on her own. She might be doing this all for the faith, risking as much as me. I did not know.

That was why none of them trusted me. They all suspected I was withholding something. And I was, from each of them.

The train reached Burnaby, Joyce Station, and I exited, following the crowd down the stairs from the platform to the busy street below. I headed to my left, crossing over to a quieter stretch of road, lined with Filipino markets and restaurants. There was a hardware store, and I ducked within, standing in one of the aisles, watching to see who might be following me.

When I was satisfied that there was nothing amiss, I left the store and took a long, rambling walk before arriving at the condo building where Ana had secured an apartment for our meeting that day. It was one of those vast, bland monstrosities, with glistening glass and edges, covering an entire block. I entered the main lobby and retrieved the key from the lockbox, which Ana had supplied me with the code for. Recalling her instructions, I went to the third floor and the farthest unit on the one side, facing the back alley.

I didn't bother with knocking, just unlocked the door and entered, then locked the door behind me. Ana wasn't there yet, though she would have observed my entrance, and would now be waiting to see if anyone had followed me. No one had, I felt quite certain, though I could never quite dismiss the nagging sense, always present, that someone was watching me. It was so ever-present that I felt worried when it wasn't there, as if something truly calamitous might now befall me.

While I waited, I looked around the condo for clues as to what kind of place I was in. There was little to identify anyone who lived here, which made it a safe house, or the home of a certain kind of single man in his twenties. I found myself smiling and wondering if Ana had a lover. What did she do with him? What was her passion? Surely her life wasn't all this, as mine was slowly becoming, now that Meredith was gone.

I heard the door open behind me and turned to watch Ana enter. "I don't have much time, so let's make this quick," she said, pushing a hand through her dark hair. "What are you smiling at?"

"It's good to see you."

"I'm not your friend, Laila," she said. "Not anymore. Now, what do you have for me?"

"I'm still your friend," I said. "Whether you want me to be or not. I said I would be there for you, and I will."

One of the reasons why meeting Ana always left me off balance was how apparent it was that she did not need me, while I needed her. The closest thing to a friend I had in the Church now was Morris, and ours was strictly a working relationship. Agent and minder. That was what Ana was trying to create with me as well, and I knew why. It would make things simpler for her if this all went sideways, as it inevitably would. We both knew that, but I was so lonely, so isolated now that I had cast Meredith off that I wanted Ana to be a friend, even if it made things more difficult for her.

Ana scowled, choosing to ignore what I said. "What do you have for me?"

I stifled a sigh. If I truly wanted to be her friend, then I had to do this. This was what she needed from me.

"Not much. It's like I've been saying—they've gone quiet. I was with Morris before I was with you, and he said the same thing. Lots of activity until you arrested us. Not much since. You scared them. They know someone is watching."

Ana frowned. "That's not good enough, Laila. I can't go back and tell my bosses that."

She paced back and forth in the area between the living room and the dining area, being careful not to go near any windows, though all the blinds were closed. I had made sure of that in my first sweep, knowing how she liked our meetings to go.

"Look," I said, in a pleading tone. "I know it's not good enough, but we have to go carefully here. We can't let them know we're looking at them. We can't let Molijc know either. If they get wind of it, I'm done, and where will your bosses be then?"

"We've given you the keys to kingdom, Laila," Ana said with a tired sigh. She reached into the bag she carried over her shoulder and pulled out a thumb drive. "This is the schedule for the next month. I need more from you, though. People are starting to ask questions about me."

"Morris has found a bunch of accounts and purchases. We don't know what they are yet, but we will soon. Once we have that, I'll give it to you, I promise. That will at least give you an idea of what they were working on."

"I need to know what they're doing now." Her voice, which had been pitched low so that only I could hear it, rose sharply and her face flushed.

"I'll talk to Molijc," I said, though I had no intention of

doing so. There was no point in that. All he could talk about now was his revelation, how it had become a reality. He had been chosen to transform the faith and to achieve all that De Gofroy had envisaged. We were on the cusp of something transformative, he was certain, and he was directly responsible for it. I couldn't stomach hearing it anymore.

"See that you do," she said, and handed me the thumb drive before turning to go.

I waited five minutes before I followed her out the door, locking it behind me. As I started down the stairs to the lobby, I began to weep, taking care that I didn't make any sound. I couldn't afford to attract any attention here. By the time I reached the front door of the building, I was composed and went on my way.

23

Though it seemed impossible that day, two months later, Ana returned to the faith. Everything changed following that, the reverberations echoing outward across all the universes.

It began one day when Lasinha came to see Molijc and I as we ate breakfast. He still insisted that we do so every day I spent upon the campus. We did little else together anymore, as I refused to attend all but the most important official functions of the Church with him. My work in establishing the crossings was too important for him to demand that I remain by his side, the dutiful companion.

"Ah, good," Dejian said as Lasinha sat at the table with us. "Join us. Lasinha has momentous news concerning the multiverse project."

I blinked, my heart lurching. Lasinha smiled at me, his eyes impassive, while Dejian had a vicious grin. Since my last meeting with Ana, he had become increasingly suspicious of me. No doubt because the agents Lasinha had following me were unable to find anything out.

I often contemplated telling him that it was because Lasinha was either an inattentive or poor trainer of his agents. Osahi and Meredith were masters by comparison, able to insinuate people near me without my being aware until it was almost too late.

"One of my agents has been brought into the inner sanctum of the Society," Lasinha said.

I raised an eyebrow, my mouth going dry.

"He has access to everything. Cloaking devices, signal scramblers. The full Society crossing schedules. All of it."

"That *is* momentous news," I said, barely managing a smile.

How had he done it? I almost didn't believe it, wanted to dispute what he said. It was impossible. We had never come close to infiltrating the Society, except in the case of Ana, and she had been turned. But I couldn't very well say that. It would reveal that I too was a Society agent of a sort, and that the price for all I had gained for the Church was still to be paid.

"Even better," Dejian said. "We can bring Ana home."

Now I understood. Whether or not they had an agent in the Society, they didn't want Ana, and by extension me, to be in command of the crossings. They did not trust either of us.

"How can we do that, exactly? The Travelers won't just let her leave." To say nothing of the fact that I doubted very much she would be willing to do so.

Lasinha looked at me. "We can make her disappear. Send her to another universe. I have one where I've been acting as the Adjudicator. She can stay there, and we can bring her back when the trail goes cold."

"They won't stop looking," I said, despair overwhelming me. I worked hard to hide it. Once Ana was no longer a Society agent, I would no longer be needed to act as go between. Molijc would expect me to return to his side and they would be free to do as they wished in the other universes. "I don't know if she will come back. I don't know if she trusts us to keep her safe."

Dejian reached out, squeezing my hand. I had to resist a shudder. "Talk to her about it the next time you see her.

See if she wishes to rejoin us."

I promised I would, though I was certain I knew what the answer would be. No matter what, it felt as though I was assuring my own doom.

To my shock and consternation, Ana agreed to return. It seemed she had been expecting me to ask. There was no trace of surprise on her face as I outlined Molijc and Lasinha's plan.

"Of course I will come back," she said. "Why do you think I gave you the transfer equipment and all that information? This is my only hope. My only way out."

"They'll come after you," I said quietly, looking over her shoulder at the other customers in a Vancouver coffee shop.

I felt exposed, but Ana seemed unconcerned. She had chosen the place, the first time she had selected a public venue for our meeting. That had set me on guard, and her ready agreement with my offer of escape and asylum in another universe only increased my wariness. I hadn't told her why Molijc and Lasinha wanted her out of the Society, and she had not asked, had just accepted, without question.

"They will," she said, with a sharp nod. "They won't stop."

"And if they send a Seeker?"

A shrug. "They will. But they need to know what world. You and Lasinha are good at what you do. You've proven that. I've been watching the last year. At first, they could track where you went, but not anymore. I know which universes they know about, and which they don't."

I digested what she said, still unsure. Had this all been an elaborate ruse to see if we were capable? I doubted it. The Society had turned her. She had said so herself.

"You told me we weren't friends. You made it clear you were an apostate." I tried to keep my voice even.

"I had to. They were listening. They heard everything

we said. They still don't trust me. Even after all this time. Even after letting the Seeker interrogate me. They don't trust anybody, not even themselves. You don't understand what it's like there."

"Are they listening now?" I sat back and crossed my arms.

Ana stiffened, her eyes flashing with anger. "You sent me to them. You asked me to trust you. I did all that you asked. I gave you the path to other universes. I convinced them to give this all to you, and now that you have it, you can't be stopped. They can't control it anymore. And now I've done all I can for you and I want out of this. I'm tired of always looking over my shoulder. Get me out. Trust me like I trusted you."

I swallowed. It was hard to control my emotions. "I don't know if I can protect you." Or myself, but that I did not say.

"You can try. That's all I ask," Ana said. She put her hand over mine. "Remember what you promised me. Be there for me when I need you."

"I will," I said, hoping that would be true.

Ana returned and disappeared again into another universe. I did not see her, dared not, for fear the Society would follow me to her. Lasinha was the only one who knew where she was. No one entered the universe she was in, though he told me there were still some transfers carried out from it.

"Normal traffic," he said. "In case they were watching it before. We don't want to raise any suspicions."

That set my mind at ease somewhat. If the Society took me, I would not be a danger to her. That was my greatest fear, that they would seize me again and I would somehow inadvertently reveal where she was. Why they didn't was a source of mystery to me. They had to suspect I was involved in her disappearance, that she had returned to the Church. Yet they did not. Nor did they reach out to me, or try to put another handler in place to see if I would continue to provide them with information.

The worry ate at me. I could not sleep and I became indifferent to everything, even submitting to Dejian's demands that I remain at his side for official Church functions, leaving my work on the multiverse project to Lasinha.

"It's a precaution," he said. "A matter of safety for Lasinha and the others." It was not, but I did not have the strength anymore to deny him.

Every day I expected to be dragged from my bed in the dead of night or to see a van pull up alongside as I walked around the campus or the city. I almost looked forward to that moment. It would have been a relief had it happened, but it never did.

Finally, after six months or more of unrelenting darkness, I could take my despair no more, and I left Calgary. I did so without consulting Dejian, though I knew he would be furious and suspect me of betraying him. Let him believe what he would, I determined. I was the one who was living under the sword of the Society, after all, my future foreclosed.

I had to talk to someone about what I was going through, I knew instinctively, but I had no one to turn to. Ana, who knew of the peril of my existence, was gone and unreachable. Meredith, who would have understood and comforted me, I had turned away for the faith. Now that act seemed pointless. What good was the faith and life itself without her words or touch?

I turned to the only person I knew who I could trust, Morris. We were not close friends, ours was not that sort of relationship, but I knew beyond doubt that I could rely upon him. He had been with me almost from the beginning, a constant and stable presence. I told him almost everything about the double life I had been leading with Ana as a Society agent, and how I still wondered if she had truly rejoined the Society or was acting at the behest of her superiors.

I told him how my days and nights were haunted by the ghosts of the Travelers in my peripheral vision. Why had they not taken me, if Ana and I had so completely betrayed them?

"They probably haven't sent anyone because they know Ana was their only currency with you," he said, calm and sensible as always. "I agree it's a very real danger that they might disappear you again. But they haven't so far, so they must see some value in keeping you where you are. Time is on their side. They can always come to you whenever they want. But if you don't, maybe you learn more. Maybe you get more value to them."

"I have the ear of the Grand Regent and his closest ally. How much more valuable can I get?"

"We still haven't figured out what the Acolytes are doing. And you said that's what they were interested in?"

"Yes," I said. "That's all they cared about."

"If they take you out now, they might not learn anything. But if they keep you in place..." He let the thought linger.

I could immediately sense how right he was and felt a wave of relief come over me. For the moment, I was safe. So long as the Acolytes and their project remained a mystery, I would be potentially more valuable to them free. I intended to keep it that way.

"You haven't found anything about what they're up to?" I said.

Morris looked at me sharply and shook his head. "No. They're as quiet as always. They've gone dark. And I can't seem to untangle all the information we talked about before."

"The expense trail," I said.

"Yeah," he said, biting his lip. "It's damn annoying. I'll keep at it, of course."

"Of course," I said, not wanting to say that I hoped his difficulties continued.

"In the meantime, I've heard of something else that's very concerning. Molijc is forming a new group within the Church. The Watchers' Order."

"What is it?"

He shrugged. What in De Gofroy's name was Dejian up to, I wondered? And did I want to find out?

After my talk with Morris, I felt more myself again. I could see the path out of the forest I had gotten myself trapped in. Rather than returning immediately to Calgary and my duties at the Church, I took a ferry out from the Vancouver to one of the islands north of the city, found a bed and breakfast in one of the villages there, and spent the better part of two weeks forgetting who I was and what lay before me.

When I returned to the airport in Calgary, Dejian had someone there to meet me, and I was ushered immediately into his presence atop De Gofroy's tower. I felt as though I was entering a new room in a different building as I was brought into the Grand Regent's audience chambers. The floor had been replaced with what looked like marble, and the furniture was all ostentatious and new. There were stands and shelves filled with Mayan artifacts—steles and ceramic vases, gold and clay figurines, and fantastically painted vessels.

Where had all this come from? I had not been gone long enough for all these renovations and additions to have taken place, which meant they must have occurred while I was still there. As I had descended into the abyss of blackness that was my despair, I had spent most of my time in my quarters, but I still must have passed through this room at least once a week. Yet I had somehow failed to notice the renovations taking place.

What else had I missed during those lost months? It was a terrifying thought, but I had to force that aside and try to calm my mind for what I knew would be a confrontation.

Dejian received me sitting upon a high-back chair that was throne-like. He looked down upon stiff-backed and imperious, as if he expected me to kneel before him.

"Where have you been, Laila?"

"I needed some time on my own," I said. "I had to get away from the Church and all this. I've been having difficulty sleeping. The Society has—"

"You were meeting with the Travelers," Dejian said.

"I wasn't. I can give you the name of bed and breakfast I was at. They'll confirm I was there."

"I'm sure they will." Dejian sneered. "I'm growing tired of your constant betrayals, Laila. I once trusted you absolutely, and now I wonder what it was I saw in you."

"Who was it that put you in that chair?" I said, unable to contain my anger. "Who secured our release from the Society? Who gave us the universes? I did. And who now stands under suspicion of the Society for doing so, and bringing Ana back to the faith? Me. You dare to question my faith, given all that I've done for the Church. For all Regents."

Molijc stood from his chair and walked over to me, small, taut smile stretching his lips. I could feel the anger, barely contained, pulsating from him with each breath he took. "And yet. And yet."

"And yet what?" I said, unable to control my emotions. "If you have something to say, say it. If this is still about Meredith, you should know as well as I do that I haven't seen her since you told me to stop. I haven't seen anyone else since, if you must know. If it's about something else, I deserve to know what I'm being accused of."

"What were you doing meeting Morris in Vancouver?"

"My duties as a Protector," I said. "We meet regularly. I'm sure you know that as well, since Lasinha has someone following every time I go out there."

Molijc seemed about to shout, but managed to stop himself. When he spoke it was in a calm voice, dripping with hate. "Until you are willing to tell me what you are doing, you are not to go anywhere without my permission as your Grand Regent. You will see to your duties beside me, but you will do nothing else with the Protectors or with the other worlds. If you earn my trust again, I will reconsider."

I laughed, which shocked him. "I'll do nothing of the sort. My duty is to the faith, not to you. De Gofroy didn't just ask you to see to it, in case you have forgotten. You don't command me, Dejian. Without me, we wouldn't have the universes."

Without waiting for a reply or a dismissal, I turned on my heels and left the chambers, heading for the elevators. I could feel his fury about to explode behind me, and I wondered how many of his precious artifacts would be missing when I returned.

I went to find Lasinha. He was in his office in the Protectors' Hall. Seemingly nothing about it had changed in all these years. As Dejian sought out accouterments of splendor and power, Lasinha seemed to yearn to disappear in plain sight. He did not appear surprised to see me, but then, he never did.

As I sat across from him, I had cause to wonder about him and his relationship with Dejian. Was it this invisibility that caused him to escape Molijc's rage and suspicion, or was I simply not aware of similar episodes where Lasinha was on the receiving end? It was certainly true that Lasinha had done nothing to betray Dejian like I had with Meredith, putting everything we had worked for at risk over an affair with a woman I had never been certain I could trust.

Lasinha seemed to be considering me as I was him, a finger to his lips, before he spoke, smiling. "Did you enjoy your time off?"

"It was restorative," I said, nodding. I left aside whatever grievances I felt at his constant surveillance of me. That came from Molijc. Lasinha, at least, had clear enough eyes to see what was going on.

"And now you've returned," he said. It was a question of sorts.

"We need to talk about Dejian," I said. "He's just finished telling me I'm not to leave his sight, nor am I to continue my work for the Protectors. What the hell is going on with him?"

Lasinha frowned, his smile fading slightly. "Our arrest by the Society changed him, I think. And now, with our work in the other universes, he's more aware than ever that of how precarious our position is. If they find out..." He let the thought linger. "I think you know a little of that agony."

"More than him," I said. "I'm the one they'll come for first."

"Strange, in a way, that they haven't," he said. Seeing my expression, he held up a hand. "Oh, I've no doubt of your loyalty, Laila. It was merely a comment. As much as I hate to say it, because we could use your help with the multiverse project, it's best if you stay away from it. Until we can sort out what the Society is thinking."

"What about your agent?" I watched his expression closely.

Lasinha nodded. "He is looking into this as best he can, without raising suspicions. In one sense, Ana's return has bought us time. They think they've sealed their ship of leaks and they aren't paying close attention, so we've been able to get some good things out of there. I'll tell you about them when we have the chance."

"That would be good," I said. "I'm not willing to step aside entirely. More importantly, we need to talk about Dejian. I don't like how he's changing. First this nonsense about a revelation—I still don't know what the hell that was about. And now he's seeing enemies around every corner. At the moment of our greatest triumph."

"It's been a difficult transition for him," Lasinha said. "I think it would be best if you don't do anything to attract to much notice in the next little while. Do what he expects and he'll come around. I'll talk to him too."

"I'm not going to be his pet."

"No one's asking you to," Lasinha said. "Just be predictable. Let him know what you're doing. When he asks you to be with him for events, do it. This too shall pass."

I felt none of Lasinha's confidence. Molijc would not be so easily mollified. And if I did this now, he would expect it to continue. Still, it was not as though I had any better choices at the moment.

"I'll try," I said. "I'm not going to stop my work for the Protectors, though. That's important to me. It's important to the faith."

Lasinha inclined his head in agreement and smiled. I left feeling no better about anything, and more certain that things would continue as they were. Nothing would change. Molijc would continue to mistrust me and Lasinha would be whispering whatever

I returned to my quarters. Molijc was absent from the Grand Regent's chambers, and no one else intercepted me. I was left alone and spent the rest of the afternoon carefully going over my rooms to see what observation equipment concealed within. There were two cameras and several listening devices. I removed all but one microphone, letting them think I had missed it somehow.

When I was certain I was unobserved, I pulled out what looked like a small router and set it up in the corner of my sitting room, tucked in beside the real router. I even connected a cable between them to make it appear as though it was there to boost my router signal. As with all routers, it had a bank of green lights in front, blinking intermittently. The one on top was the only one interested me.

I could see it whenever I entered the room, and if I passed a hand near it, I could feel a slight pull, the gravity of another universe drawing me near. It was Ana's protection against Molijc, Lasinha and the Society—a dead man's switch. So long as she remained in the universe, she would keep the device that sent this signal working. If something happened to her, I would know within a day.

For the first months of her return, I had been so convinced I was going to be taken by the Society at any moment that I had been unwilling to have the device away from my person, though it was large enough to make it difficult to conceal. Now I felt confident they would not take me, at least not while questions remained about the Acolytes and Molijc. If I had my way, those questions would not be answered anytime soon, and I would remain in these quarters for a long while.

24

For most of the next year, I followed Lasinha's advice, or at least gave the impression of doing so. I appeared with Molijc when he wanted me to, and left most of my duties as Protector to various agents I trusted. This included Morris, of course, and I visited Vancouver to see him as often as I could. If Dejian suspected something of me, he offered no comment. He was in good humor most of the time, excited about the progress Lasinha was making in the other universes.

Morris had little to report about the Acolytes when I saw him. Part of this was my doing. I had him attend to various other matters that I told him I could only entrust to him, which was not entirely true. They were important, but mostly I wanted to keep him busy and unable to dedicate his full attention to the Acolyte question. If he suspected me of delaying him, he did not say anything.

The other constant in my life was the light upon the false router. So long as it continued to blink, I told myself that all the rest of this was worth it. I was doing what I needed to.

The routines that I fell into almost made it possible for me to forget about the threat of the Society seizing me.

That changed one afternoon after I met with Morris in our usual place near the central library. I wandered northeast toward the old Chinatown, my mind on where I would stop to eat. As I was looking at the storefronts near Pender and Carrall, a Black Robe appeared on the street before me.

Instinctively, I turned to flee, but as I did so, a large SUV pulled out of traffic and came to halt beside me. Doors flew open and hands seized me, pulling me into the vehicle while I struggled to break free. Frantically, I cast my eyes at the passersby on the street, but everyone was careful not to watch what was happening. They recognized the black robes and the unmarked vehicle with blackened windows, and wanted no part of what was taking place.

The woman who had confronted me on the street got in on the passenger side, and the driver maneuvered us back into traffic amidst squealing tires and my stream of endless curses. I felt equal parts terror and rage. Fear at what was going to happen to me and anger that I had been so clumsy as to let it happen. My terror dissolved as I saw the man sitting on the bench opposite me in the back of the vehicle, leaving only a teeth-grinding fury.

Toma Osahi. He wore a disdainful expression and one of his ridiculously extravagant suits.

"Damn you." I slammed my fist against the door. "Do you know what Molijc and Lasinha are going to think when they hear about this? Unless that was your man following me earlier."

Osahi shook his head and waved a dismissive hand. "I'm sure you can think of something to explain it to them. You're very skilled at that, I understand."

"Fuck you," I said, rubbing my sore knuckles. "You know, if you want to talk, all you have to do is ask. We're on the same goddamn campus."

Having the woman dressed in Society robes was especially infuriating. Lasinha's agent would report it, and all the work I had done to allay Dejian's suspicions would be lost in one moment. All these months of patiently waiting, lost for nothing. It would almost have been better if it had been the Black Robes seizing me, though I knew that wasn't true.

"As you note, you're being observed by the Grand Regent. I can't risk him knowing about this encounter."

I snorted. "You don't want him to know about the all the wild accusations you've been throwing around?"

Osahi frowned, as though my display of emotion was uncalled for. "He's getting rather paranoid, in case you hadn't noticed. But then, you haven't noticed much of anything lately, have you?"

I glared at him. "What are you talking about?"

"The Watchers' Order."

I looked past Osahi out the vehicle, trying to gather my thoughts and see where we were going. The driver turned onto Granville, heading across the bridge and out of downtown.

"I don't know anything about that," I said, thinking about all he had said. It was startling to realize that my lost months and the aimless ones that followed had been obvious to everyone else. What else had Molijc been up to aside from redecorating? The Watchers' Order, apparently. Morris had talked a little about it, but he was still unsure what exactly it was. A group to handle the crossings was his guess, separate from the Hierarchy, specifically my people and Osahi's.

"I don't believe that," Osahi said. "At any rate, you're about to find out."

"Where are you taking me?" I said, tired of the games he was playing.

Osahi stared at me, and I began to feel the depths of his anger. "To see the consequences of the Grand Regent's new order."

"Tell her your name," Osahi said to the young woman. I recognized her. She had followed me several times when I had been in Vancouver to see Morris and Ana. The last time had been right before Ana had come over, when I had shaken her off in the central library.

She gave a blank smile to Osahi and turned to me. Her eyes seemed to dart around, never quite meeting mine. "Jennifer Rostencraft," she said. "Regent and Protector of the True Faith."

"A pleasure to meet you, Jennifer," I said, offering a smile and hiding my annoyance at Osahi and this entire situation.

We were on the second floor of a subdivided house in the Kitsilano neighborhood. There was a child crying below us, distant and furious. The apartment we were in was sparsely decorated with cheap furnishings and bland prints on the walls, all anonymous. A safe house, then, one that Osahi would get rid of as soon as he was finished with me here.

Jennifer was sitting in a squat chair whose upholstery clashed with that of the couch. Osahi and I stood before her. The black-robed woman stood behind Jennifer, watching me, while the two others who had accompanied us on the journey were by the door, presumably ready to stop me from fleeing. Only the driver remained in the vehicle.

I could not fathom why Osahi thought he needed such a guard to keep watch over me, but I ignored that question to focus on the woman. She was why Osahi had brought me here. There was something off-putting about her, something not quite there, though I couldn't have said why I thought so. She nodded as I stared at her, still refusing to meet my eyes. I could feel her discomfort rising, and I glanced at Osahi.

He nodded at her. "Tell the High Regent what you do for the Church."

"I am faithful vessel," Jennifer said. "I am a Protector of the Faith."

"When did you join the Church?" Osahi said.

Jennifer blinked, momentarily confused. "Four years ago," she said.

"When did you join the Watchers' Order?"

A cloud passed across her face as she struggled with some hidden pull of emotions I could not identify. "Six months ago," she said, and her blank expression was restored.

"What do you recall of the last six months?"

"I have been a faithful servant," she said, looking pleased with herself.

Osahi grimaced. "And your last four years in the Church?"

She considered his question, frowning in concentration. It was difficult to watch. At last, she said, "I don't remember."

"What about Laila?" Osahi said. "Do you remember her?"

Jennifer looked at me, still careful not to meet my eyes. She shook her head.

"What about your childhood? Your mother and father?"

"They were…" the woman began, before seeming to lose her train of thought. "I don't… I know them, but they aren't there."

At a gesture from Osahi, one of the women dressed as a Society agent led Jennifer away. I heard the door to the apartment open and close and footsteps sounding down the stairs that led to house's front entrance. Osahi watched me, expressionless, though I could still feel his simmering anger.

"This is what they have done. This is the Watchers' Order. It's what they did to Frederik. And De Gofroy himself."

"You're saying the Acolytes are behind this?" I said, pretending disbelief. I knew he was right. This was the Acolytes' work. Jennifer had the same affect I had noticed in Frederik when he appeared for his abdication. There, but not there.

"Who else could do that?" Osahi said, waving a hand. "This is the Church Molijc and they want. Are you and Lasinha going to continue to support him?"

"What proof do you have of what happened to her?" I said, hoping that he would reveal that he had none, that this was all supposition. I thought of the small router secreted in the inner pocket of my jacket. If the Society found out about this, they would take me, and Ana would be lost.

"Jennifer was one of my agents here, as I'm sure you recognize. She did a lot of surveillance for me here. When Lasinha came, she followed him. Same with Molijc. The last time she followed Dejian out east, toward Abbotsford, or Chilliwack, I don't know. At least, that was her last report, that she was heading that way.

"She was gone two days with no word. We worried, but hoped that her communications were compromised and she would turn up. Eventually she did. But she was like that. She doesn't remember anything. And she's... Well, you saw for yourself."

I had. It was impossible to deny, and yet I sought to. All the misgivings I had about Dejian, and the Acolytes, seemed to be blossoming into nightmares before me. How much did Lasinha know, I wondered? He had to know everything; he must be a part of this new Order. And I knew that he would not blanch at killing Regents, so doing whatever had been done to Jennifer and Frederik would give him no qualms. Osahi was right: this was what they wanted.

"I suppose you want something from me," I said, putting a hand to my head. It was difficult to concentrate on anything.

"I don't know what our Grand Regent intends with this procedure and his new Order. By the time we find out, it may be too late. Regardless, we are coming to another time where everyone will need to decide on which side of things they stand. I know where I will be. I don't know about you, Laila. I'll be waiting for your answer."

He spoke quietly, his voice pitched so that only he and I could hear his words. When he was done, he turned and left, and I heard the two men follow with him. They closed the door and left me alone. I sat in the chair Jennifer had occupied, staring at the same empty wall she had, trying to organize my thoughts and decide what needed to be done.

I did nothing, returning to Calgary and acting as if nothing had changed. But everything had, and I just did not know it. I stayed in my quarters, avoiding Osahi and what I imagined were hordes of Black Robes scouring the city for me. Neither Molijc or Lasinha mentioned my trip to Vancouver or my kidnapping by Osahi. Perhaps Lasinha's agent hadn't seen what happened, though I found that difficult to credit. I was not sure whether this was a reprieve or if the noose was tightening around my throat without my realizing it.

My paranoia spiraled and I became certain that the only thing I could do to save myself was to do nothing. If I didn't act on what I knew, the Society would never know and they would never seize me and Ana would be safe. If I did nothing, Molijc and Lasinha would be satisfied I was not a threat to all they were planning.

In the midst of this rationalization of my terrified stasis, Morris messaged me. I ignored him. I knew, or thought I did, what he wanted to talk about. Nothing good could come from it.

This lasted a week or more, during which I spiraled into despair once again. In the midst of that darkness, I told myself I was playing into Dejian's hands. That I should be working to stop him. I imagined myself going to confront Lasinha, to demand to know why he was going along with this madness. In my fevered visions, Lasinha would just smile in that way he had, as if it made all the sense in the world. Perhaps it did to them. After all, I did not know what they were doing.

One afternoon I sat in my living room, contemplating the wall and working myself into a paralysis of thought about what I should be doing. It was easy to continue to do nothing, to let things drift along as they were. I knew it was wrong, and, more importantly, I knew wrongs were being committed against the faith in its name. Yet I remained where I was.

At some point, as the shadows lengthened across the room, I noticed the false router, tucked in beside the true one. The light atop it had stopped blinking. I stared at it for what felt like a minute, unable to comprehend what I was looking at. My mouth went dry, sweat beading on my forehead, as I stared at the router, willing the light to return. It did not.

I frantically tried to recall the last time I had looked at it and seen it blinking. Even through my depression of these last days, I had made certain to look at the router several times a day. It was the beacon that guided me out of the darkness always. Ana needed me, so I would do what I could to keep this despair at bay.

I told myself it was impossible, that the false router was just broken or defective. The mechanism that connected it to its mate in the other universe was presumably a delicate one. Surely it could falter. Reluctantly, I went across the room to inspect it. When I put my hand near the false route, the pull was gone. And so, I realized, was Ana.

I went to see Dejian, to confront him. To find out what had been happening while I was lost to myself.

He was in his personal chambers, a room where he went for prayer and reflection. There were paintings of De Gofroy on the walls, along with images of the Mayan calendar. The center of the room was empty of furniture and had a symbol of the Hunab Ku graven into it. Dejian was sitting upon it in meditation when I entered. He smiled upon looking up and seeing me, and gestured that we sit at the back of the room, where there was a small table, cups, and a pot of tea.

It had been a long time since I had seen him so at ease in my presence. It frightened me more than the outbursts of anger, which I had come to expect and mostly ignored these last years.

"Tell me about the Watchers' Order," I said.

He looked at me serenely. "It is the bulwark against all those who would seek to ruin the faith. It is the instrument through which we will achieve all we promised De Gofroy."

I swallowed. "I've seen the Order's handiwork. It looks to me like a betrayal of all that De Gofroy believed."

Dejian's poise vanished and his face flushed. He brought his fist down upon the table, rattling cups and spilling tea. "Of all people, for you to speak to me of betrayal. Don't you dare, Laila. Don't you dare."

I did not reply, waiting for him to compose himself. When he did, he continued. "This is necessary for what we are trying to do here. The crossings must be protected from the Society at all costs. The faith is nothing unless we find our true selves. You know that as well as I. And you know that the Travelers have agents among us. You worked with the Protectors; you know they were constantly trying to infiltrate us."

It was true, or at least I believed it so. Ana had said otherwise, though, that there had only been a handful active during our time in the Church. But perhaps things had changed now that they were desperate to unearth what the Acolytes were doing.

"What have you done to these people? What did you do to Frederik?"

Dejian smiled. He was proud of himself, clearly, and excited to finally be revealing his secret. "They call it a tamp. You put a wall in the mind where a person's memories are. They still remain much the same in terms of their personality. They are who they are, after all. But they are more compliant."

I looked at him in horror. "You are robbing these people of who they are."

"No," he said. "We don't scrape their minds. Well…not in most cases. Only when it is absolutely necessary. And even then, not entirely. We simply repress their deviant thoughts. They are no longer apostates. They are faithful vessels."

"There is no justification for this," I said, but Molijc held up a hand.

"We are all vessels. We know this. Our true selves are elsewhere. And the selves we have in this universe are but a part of their shadows. If we put a tamp in someone's mind, it is not their true self we are harming. And if doing so ensures their loyalty, ensures that the faith is protected from Society incursions and we can continue our work finding our true selves unmolested, then it is worth it."

I felt ill. He looked at me triumphantly and my hands began to tremble. I wanted to ask about Ana, about where she was, what had befallen her, but I dared not. I didn't want to make him aware that I knew she had been taken. The only hope I had in finding her now was if he and Lasinha remained unaware of how much I knew.

Lasinha was another matter. I could hardly believe he had gone along with this, and yet, at the same time, I absolutely could. He was a cipher, his loyalty to Dejian the only thing about him that was readily apparent. The rest, his endless smiles, who was to say what was real?

"Lasinha agrees with this," I said as Dejian watched me carefully.

"He is a faithful vessel," Molijc said. It was both approval and a threat. His unspoken question: *Are you?*

No, I wanted to say. *Not anymore. Not like this.*

"He leads the Order?" I said, and Dejian nodded. "What about the multiverse project?"

"They are entwined together," Dejian said. "The multiverse project can be handled only by those whose faith is unquestioned. Those who we know are uncorrupted by the Society. The Order is that vessel."

"I thought the Protectors guarded the faith," I said. It was hard to keep how appalled I was out of my voice, to keep my expression neutral. He believed it all, without any doubt. It was no different than his talk of revelation, of De Gofroy speaking to him directly.

"Osahi cannot be trusted," Dejian said, with a sad shake of his head. "I am not sure of the other High Regents." *And you*, his expression seemed to say.

"So he will go under the Acolytes' knife?"

Dejian gave me a cold smile. "As you know, our friend Toma is far too wily to allow himself to be taken by the Order. Or anyone, for that matter. I must say, I have had cause to regret agreeing with you on allowing him to return to the Church. It has led to problems and will only lead to more. Lasinha was right about that. And a great many other things."

Such as? I did not say the words, though I dearly wanted to. Most of all, I wanted to flee this room and announce to anyone who would listen that we were being led by a madman. A madman whom I had made possible.

"What would De Gofroy say about this?" I said, still hoping somehow to make him realize the horror of what he was doing.

He was unconcerned by my question. "He speaks through me. Since my revelation, my voice is his. His essence is powerful, and his selves can reach across the universes to guide me."

I could think of nothing to say, and sat there dumbfounded, fighting to stop myself from crying. The despair, which had vanished when I first realized Ana was gone, returned now with full force. Everything was lost, and I was one of the authors of this doom.

"What are you thinking about?" Dejian said, his tone gentle, conciliatory.

I had to resist a shudder. "It's what I am trying not to

think about."

"You're still worried about what we are doing?" he said. "I understand. It left me uncomfortable at first as well, when the Acolytes came to me with their ideas. But it must be done. There are enemies in our midst. You know that better than I. Evil must be met with force; we cannot quiver and hide from it. The future of the Church, of all its work, is at stake. The Travelers will see us ruined."

I didn't reply. His answers felt rote, a speech he had practiced many times before, and which he was now unveiling to me. I was left lost, filled with questions, the answers to which were almost too disturbing to contemplate. What were the Acolytes playing at here? It couldn't just be about protecting the faith, could it? They must have been working on this for long before they made their alliance with Dejian. Which meant they must have conceived it for some other purpose and saw in Molijc someone whose goals aligned with their own.

Couldn't Lasinha see how dangerous this was? We were giving the Church over to the Acolytes. Already they were their own entity within it. Now, with the Watchers' Order, they would control it.

"I can see you're troubled by this," Dejian said, interrupting the torrent of my thoughts. He took my hands in his. "But you know that I need you, now more than ever. Your faith has always been a light to me. You have been a fine vessel. A true vessel in these faulty times. My secrets are yours."

His words surprised me. He needed me, and others, but especially me, to understand why he was doing this. The necessity of it. Why did it matter what I thought, after so much had passed between us, after he had shut me out for so long, trusting me with nothing? It did, though. Still.

He was staring at me, with a warm smile, and I met his gaze. *My secrets are yours.* Not anymore.

Dejian got to his feet, staring across the room, his mind casting forward to the next thing. I was forgotten. "I must speak with Lasinha today." As he spoke, there was a knock at the door.

"You trust him?"

"He's been with us from the beginning," Dejian said.

So have I. Another thing best left unsaid. Instead, I said, "We've always served the faith in our ways."

"Yes," he said, giving me a distracted smile.

He did not hear what I said, or did not understand its true meaning. I had always served the faith, and would continue to do so. Now I saw the only way to do that, and to save Ana, was to stand against Dejian, Lasinha, and the Acolytes. I had few allies left within the Church whom Lasinha and Molijc had not managed to take away from me. Morris was one. Osahi could be one, if we could find a way to trust each other.

I knew the path to that was through the person I should never have sent away. Her absence these last years was the reason I had become inattentive, lost to darkness, and unable to truly understand the abomination Molijc was creating. If I was to stand against him and all the power of the Church he could now marshal, I would need her.

Dejian was at the door, opening it, sharing a glance with who entered. "You know Meredith, course."

I did.

FIVE:

RETURNING

25

The world is fractured. There are many parts, many pieces. Somewhere there is a whole, but not here. Here there are multitudes. And beyond are the endless universes. The thought of them, of what they represent, makes me want to weep with joy. My other selves are there. I can feel their vibrations reaching me through the places between. The places where no one can go.

My head aches. Darkness and light. How long have I been here? It feels like weeks or months must have passed, but I know it cannot have been that long. Lasinha would be here if that was the case.

I am near a wall, and I use it to lever myself up in fits and starts so that I am sitting, propped up against it. The apartment, or the room I am in, is empty. Martina is gone, but that is not surprising. She will be downstairs standing watch, secure in the knowledge that I am going nowhere. Suon is not here, and that is surprising.

I try to call out her name, but the words are faint and indistinct. It sounds like someone else is speaking them. There are a thousand voices in my head and none of them agree on anything. Or so it seems.

My mouth is so dry that it is difficult to swallow. I look

in the direction of the kitchen and think of water. It is beyond my capability now to get there, to even stand up. I might be able to crawl along the floor, reach the bathroom, and drink from the toilet bowl. A thought unpleasant and alluring in equal measure.

I close my eyes and listen to the pulse sounding in my temple, its steady rhythm a comfort. A relief from cacophony within me. My multitude of selves. They will not be silent, though I try to quiet them. I can wait, though. This is my place. And, as always, time is on my side.

Lasinha is sitting across from me, smiling. He is always smiling. And never smiling. It is a strange thing, but many things about him are strange. Or so it seems to me. I should be worried to see him here with me now, but I am not. This is a memory. Of course.

"The faith is in our hands now," he says. "De Gofroy wanted it this way."

I nod, momentarily confused. Whose memory is this? It is so difficult to keep things separated now. I am many and I am one, but that one is not the many. The one is dangerous, that is the real threat, not the many.

Lasinha stands and dissolves, and reappears on the other side of me. Still smiling. "Molijc trusts you. I trust you. You would not still be a part of this if he did not. I hope we can prove to you that your doubts are misplaced. This is necessary. The Society has infiltrated us so deeply that this is the only hope we have."

I nod, though I do not agree. Yet I do. This is essential. The faith demands it. The faith demands sacrifices of us all. We are only vessels, and what happens to us in service of our greater work is of little consequence in the vast war we are involved in. No matter how monstrous it might be.

Lasinha is not smiling. His face is shadowed. "Everyone has their secrets. Everyone. Don't forget that. Even the Grand Regent."

"Even you," I say.

He laughs. "Even me."

For some reason, I am thinking of Ana. Though thinking of her always leaves me confused.

"The important thing is that our secrets not be made to harm the faith. Especially his. You understand, right?"

I do. There are files somewhere. Laila has them.

My hands are shaking. They are vibrating at the incorrect frequency for this universe. There are harmonics. I must try to match them to it.

Suon appears. Where has she come from?

"Aeida. We have to go."

I nod. "Yes. Lasinha."

She looks at me. "What about him?"

I stare at her, trying to find the words to explain what I mean, but they do not come. The meaning of what I was trying to say drifts away, and I look past her to the doorway. How long until Martina returns?

"Can you walk?"

I shake my head. It feels as though I am drooling. "Something is wrong."

Suon peers at my eyes with concern. "Whatever she's giving us is affecting you much more than me."

"Where were you?" I say.

She stares at me before sighing. "Don't worry about that now. Rest. I'll figure something out. We haven't checked in with the citadel in at least two days. They'll be looking for us."

I don't want them looking for us. I don't want to escape. Is that right?

No. The Order has me. Martina will get in contact with Lasinha eventually, and he will realize whom she has captured. I exult at the thought.

"You are certainly chatty this evening," Martina says, as she cradles me in arms, forcing me to drink her foul concoction.

I cannot remember what I was saying. Have I revealed anything I shouldn't have? It seems likely. I am not even sure who I am. Anything I say will expose that.

The liquid begins to take hold within me, and my vision begins to swirl. Martina lets me slump to the floor and goes over to where Suon lies, mumbling incoherently. As I lie on the floor, I see two of them, then one, then three, bathed in shadow and light.

Martina sets the cup on the floor and crouches, lifting Suon's limp body up. She looks away, reaching to find the cup. I blink and everything changes. A blur of movement and a collision of shapes and forms. Nothing coheres; nothing takes hold. Someone gasps, the air going from their lungs.

Someone is talking and saying something about Lasinha and how he cannot find out, how he must find out. A man's voice. My own. Not mine.

The world goes solid and the light begins to go from it. I fight to keep my eyes open, but it is no use. The last thing I see is Suon crouched over Martina, forcing her to drink from the cup.

"Come on." A whisper and a caress brings me back to the world.

Nothing is straight. I am out of alignment with this universe, my vibrations setting it off. I try to say that, but it is no use. All that emerges is one word that is no word at all. A cup appears at my lips and I shrink back, but the hand at my neck will not let me. Crooning words and the clear smell tell me that it is water. I drink greedily.

After that, I am left alone. Gradually, sense and feeling return. I can see the world as it is. I am myself, or as much of myself as I can be. My memories of the last days are unclear, not quite there. Not quite my own. That frightens me.

Suon returns. "Can you walk?"

"I can try," I say. The words come out more or less as I intended.

"Let's go, then. I don't know how much time we have before someone gets suspicious."

With her help, I get to my feet and we lurch toward the doorway. The hallway is empty, no sounds emerging behind any of the other doors. Suon pauses to listen. When she is satisfied, we attempt the stairs. It is a painstaking, exhausting process for both of us. She offers no complaint, and I try to stay silent, though my mouth seems to have a different master, constantly wanting to chatter and announce our presence.

There is a short corridor at the bottom of the stairs that lead to the restaurant. Before it there is another door, and Suon takes me there. It opens out into a small courtyard, enclosed by a stern-looking gate, on the other side of which is the street and freedom. I breathe deeply of the air, my whole body trembling.

Suon is careful to let the door close silently behind us. It is late in the night, the moon visible above us to the west. The air is cool and exhilarating. My head feels clear for the first time in days. Suon takes my hand.

"Wait," I say. "We need to look for the woman."

"There was nothing in any of the apartments. They were all empty. Martina was the only one there."

"We have to question her," I say, wondering how Suon could have managed to escape the room and look at the other apartments.

"It'll be a few hours until she wakes up. By then it'll be morning and the other people from the restaurant will be back. They'll look for her. I don't know if they're in the Order, but we can't take that chance. I'm sorry."

I glance back at the building, still reluctant to leave without finding out more about what happened to the woman with Ana on that last day. It is futile, I realize, especially in my current state. I cannot be taken by the Order, despite what other thoughts in my head might say.

I nod to Suon, and a sad smile forms on her lips.

No one is visible on the street, and the only sound is our footsteps as Suon guides me to the gate. Outside we pause, to ensure there are not cries or alarms. Silence reigns and we start forward again, making our slow way down the street and away.

26

Our return to Osahi's outpost is as painstaking as our escape from Martina's clutches. We do not return to our hotel room, on the off chance that Martina and her compatriots in the Order traced us to there. Instead we take a room on the outskirts of Arequipa, near the bus station, largely frequented by couples looking for a night alone together, and wait for me to recover.

It is several days before I become myself again and we can make our back across the continent. During that time, I live in constant fear that I will say something to Suon that will reveal my true nature. Or that Aeida will seize control again, however briefly, and try to return to Martina. He wanted to be captured by the Order, though I cannot fathom why. They will just tamp us both again, leaving only the simulacrum of a person, Joseph Aurellano, on the surface.

Something else about him worries me, though I cannot quite say why. While we were drugged and he was in nominal control of this body, he kept thinking about the multitudes within, as if there were dozens of people within this mind fighting for control. There are only two of us. Aurellano can only exist when we are banished to the void.

That banishment, and this whole creation—for that is what it is—is inherently unstable. Aeida and I will forever be fighting, forever be overwhelming whatever walls the Acolytes build within here. We cannot be stopped; the mind cannot be contained.

The thought that there could be others of some form or another within this already toxic stew frightens me. I try to dismiss it, but I can't. There is always the possibility that I have missed something. Aeida is very perceptive in his way.

Suon is unfailingly solicitous as she cares for me, working tirelessly to ensure that we are safe from the Order and that I am able to travel. She cares for me deeply, I think, though which of me she cares for, I do not know. That is a thought best not dwelled upon. I possess many of those now.

We take a bus to La Paz when I am well enough. It travels through the depths of the night, and we lie on uncomfortable sleeping berths. Sleep eludes me, and I am left alone with my thoughts and the hum of the bus as it ascends and descends through the Andes. Sometime in the night, Suon awakes and sees that I am also up. She leans across from her berth to kiss me.

"Why are you up?" she whispers, sitting up to look around. We are the only two awake on the upper level of the bus.

I shrug. "Never could sleep on a bus."

She nods, settling back down into her berth, looking as though she is going to go back to sleep. "How did you get caught by her?"

I glance over and see her eyes are closed. "She invited me upstairs. I thought you were right about her. She caught me off guard."

Suon does not reply, and I wonder if she is asleep. Finally, she says, "I was right about her. I saw the way she looked at you. And the way you looked at her. If the circumstances had been different…"

Her eyes are open now, glistening, as she stares at me.

"But they weren't," I say. I hesitate, not sure what else to say.

Suon reaches out and takes my hand. "I love you," she says. "I would leave the faith for you."

I squeeze her hand. There are many things I could say, but I do not trust myself to say them.

Osahi is gone when we return to the village. I find De Vroes in the building where they interrogated me. He eyes me warily.

"Toma is away for a few days. He'll speak to you when you're back."

It is a dismissal, but I ignore it. "I'm sure he will. Did he know he was sending me on a wild goose chase?"

"He didn't know what you'd find."

"I still don't know what is to be found there."

De Vroes shakes his head. "We're not sending people back there. Bad enough to find out the Order has been in this universe all along. We can't risk exposure."

"Will you leave?"

"I think so," De Vroes says. "We can't chance staying here. That's what Toma is doing now. Securing us a new site."

He looks past me, toward the door. He is lying or wants me to leave. Probably both. I cross my arms and lean against the nearest wall, making it clear I have no intention of going anywhere.

"So tell me," I say. "What kind of Acolyte are you? I've never heard of one leaving the guild. Certainly not to work with the enemy."

"We are all Regents. No one is the enemy here."

I snort and roll my eyes. "Please. You've seen what the Acolytes have done. To me and to others. You've probably done it yourself. Why leave? Or does Osahi intend to install his own loyalty program with the Acolytes?"

De Vroes looks uncomfortable and, for the first time

since I met him, unsure of himself. "I've left the guild," he says. "I agree with their aims, but not their means. Just like you and Toma believe in the faith but not the Grand Regent."

I study him for a moment, thinking of the multitudes within me trapped in this false flesh. "Can they reverse what they've done? Can you?"

There is too much need in what I've said. I think of Ibrahem, his desperate need to fix what he knew was wrong, yet could not understand.

De Vroes looks at me curiously, as though I have confirmed something for him. That vanishes and his expression turns neutral. "I managed to reverse what they did with you, didn't I?"

I shrug noncommittally, my lips pursed.

"It's difficult. And the results are not always assured. Especially for some of the more difficult procedures they've done. Some of them may be irreversible, or not entirely reversible. They're still trying to perfect the application of it. Everything else for them is secondary."

I smile distantly, an inexpressible ache forming inside me. "So there is no plan to return everyone to normal when we've triumphed over the Society."

De Vroes' faint smile reflects my own. "No. There isn't. We're not going to triumph over the Society."

I have more questions I want to ask, but I am suddenly exhausted by his answer. There is no winning here, only survival. I will not be restored to my own body, not entirely and not in the way I expect. The hope that I have clung to these last weeks seems foolish. Entropy does its work in all the universes and is not entirely reversible.

Osahi finds me the next day in my quarters with Suon. She has not spoken of her declaration of love since she made it somewhere past Cuzco, and she has chosen to ignore my failure to reciprocate. It would have been a simple thing for me to answer, to give her the words she wanted, and yet I was unable. Am unable to still.

If she is lying, as I suspect, and simply trying to leverage what she hopes are my affections, all the better to reply in kind. If she is being truly honest, then it is cruel to withhold those words. Even if I am unsure whether I mean them. That does not seem to be something that I can know about myself at this moment. Should I say that—she deserves some explanation surely—or will it reveal too much about my tortured state of being?

I am exhausted by my thoughts on the matter, as exhausted as Osahi appears, his eyes red from lack of sleep. He looks from Suon to me with a jaundiced eye and dismisses her with a curt nod. When she leaves, he turns to me.

"You've been talking to De Vroes, I hear?" It is an accusation.

"I wasn't aware that was forbidden."

Osahi grimaces. "Don't play the fool, Aeida. I have neither the time nor the patience. Why are you asking questions about the Acolytes and their methods? You were in the Order. Surely you know them better than anyone."

I am sitting on my bed, and I get up to face Osahi, so I do not feel so much like a child quailing before an adult. "Less than you'd think, really. In case you haven't noticed, the Acolytes don't talk much about what they do. Or why. I was just curious why your man had left the guild. I don't know anyone else who has."

"Who's to say he has?" Osahi says with a sneer.

"Him being here tells me," I say. "Besides, as someone who's been their plaything, I have a vested interest in what they do. And what happens when you try to turn someone back into what they were. You know as well as I do that it doesn't always work like you would hope."

"No," Osahi says, his expression grave. "No, it does not." He is thinking of Ibrahem, no doubt, and others as well. How many has De Vroes tried and failed to return entirely?

I decide to press my luck while I have him somewhat off guard. "We need to return to Arequipa. That woman who captured us has answers. She knows where Menardo put the woman with Ana. If we can find her—"

"Out of the question," Osahi says with a wave of his hand. "Absolutely not. We don't know how much help this Martina has on the ground there. If she has any sense—and she clearly does; she managed to capture both you and Suon—she's already sent word to the Order, and they'll have more people in this universe soon enough."

"It may take time, though," I say, even as I know he is correct. "She can't reach Lasinha directly, or both of us would be in the Order's hands already. There's a window now where we can get in before Order brings their forces to bear."

"There is indeed a window," Osahi says grimly. "And I intend to use it to get my people out of this universe before the Order floods it and starts watching the channels too closely. We're not going to waste our time chasing ghosts."

"We don't know that she's dead."

"Come, Aeida, don't play the fool. You worked beside Lasinha for how many years? The man will kill if he thinks it's necessary. Make no mistake."

I have too, of course, but he does not know that. What if he knew, what would he do to me then? A question I hope not to find the answer to. There are many things he must not find out.

"We have to try," I say, though I know the cause is lost.

Osahi shakes his head. "We do not. I owe it my people to do whatever I have to keep them out of the Order's hands. That is my only responsibility here. Everything else is secondary."

He seems to lose himself in thought for a moment. Perhaps it is that he is waiting for me to argue further. I don't have the strength to do so. I tried and failed so utterly that I nearly lost myself to Aeida. If I am to try again, I might only succeed in ensuring his victory.

"Besides," Osahi says, a small grin forming on his lips, "I've found Ana."

I stare at him, unsure what to say. "Where is she?"

"On campus, with the Grand Regent and the rest of the Order."

My heart sinks. He was unwilling to risk an assault on the campus before, and he will certainly not be willing to do so now that his base of operations is potentially exposed and the threat of the Order is imminent.

"And we are going to get her," he says. "I have a plan that will allow us to get her and secure my people from the Order. You can be a part of it, if you wish."

"Of course," I say without hesitation.

Osahi clasps my hand. "Good. We'll talk more in the next day or so about our next steps."

I smile and watch as he goes. Part of me is exultant that I may manage to free Ana, and, more importantly, restore myself, while the rest wonders what sort of trap I am walking into. It does not matter, I realize. I will go regardless.

27

The problem, as Osahi describes it, is that they can no longer trust the channels leaving this universe.

"They're almost certainly being monitored. Everything will be traced back to its source. Here. Unless we can suitably disguise it. Which, as you know, is difficult. Fortunately, we have someone who is something of an expert on hand."

Here he gestures to Nicola, who is part of our little coterie, along with Suon, De Vroes, myself, and a few other of Osahi's chosen lieutenants. They are all careful not to look at me and whisper to themselves so that I cannot here. They don't trust me, with good reason. Not only am I a newcomer, I am the reason they have to abandon all they have built.

We are atop the citadel overlooking the whole village. It is being manned continuously now, regardless of whether there are alerts for transfers. There is now the possibility, however slim, that someone could approach without transferring from another universe, and it must be guarded against.

Nicola appears to be much better than when I last saw her. There is color to her face, but she still has a sour expression, especially when she looks at me. *I saved you from the Order*, I want to say to her, but I keep my own counsel. I have put her and all these people in danger from the Watchers by what I did.

"If it were just a few people we're moving, it would be one thing," Osahi continues. "But we need to move everyone as quickly as possible. I don't want to risk staying here any longer than I have to. In talking about this with Nicola, we've come across a solution."

He turns to Nicola and nods for her to continue.

"Okay. So, the problem is the Order is here in this universe. We have to assume they have a transfer point established here and can respond rapidly if someone there traces the signal to here. Which means we need to hide our signal. They'll be expecting that. They know all our tricks. They use them too. It's one thing to hide your signal when no one knows what universe to look in. It's another when they're looking."

She looks around from face to face. "But they won't look that closely at a signal going directly to an Order way station. Why would they? It has to be one of their own. So we send someone there, with the channel disguised as they would. That's our cover. It will have to be a scheduled transfer, otherwise it might attract attention."

"Will one transfer be enough?" Suon says, looking doubtful.

"No," Osahi says. "We send as many people as we can under cover of that first signal. The rest will follow once we have control of the way station. We can send transfers of whatever to this universe and use it to cover the rest that we need."

"The Order will know that one of their way stations has been taken," I say.

"They will," Osahi says. "We won't have much time."

"Or any," I say.

"Perhaps," Osahi says, allowing himself a small grin. He turns to Nicola.

"When the Order realizes the way station has been taken, they'll look at the signal for the origin and for any markers, right? To figure what they're dealing with exactly. I can't disguise the origin of the signal, but I can make it look like it's the Travelers."

"They'll think it's a raid," De Vroes says with an approving nod.

"Exactly," Osahi says, his grin broadening. "They'll be in a panic, more worried about getting out of there and figuring out how compromised they are than anything else."

"I don't know," I say. Everyone looks at me, and I flush under their scrutiny. "They'll also pay more attention to what we're doing. They'll be wondering why all these transfers are going on immediately after. Somebody will look, and they may figure out what's really going on."

"I agree," Nicola says, ice in her voice. I wonder why she has such a strong dislike for me. "That's why it would be better to have more than one transfer of Society origin, to make them think it's a wide-scale raid."

"And that," Osahi says, gesturing to me, "is where you come in. We send you and a few others directly from the way station to the Church. They'll assume it's another raid for the Grand Regent, and they'll do whatever they can to get him out of there. In the meantime, you can get Ana."

"They might want to get Ana out of there too if they think the Travelers are coming," I say, frowning, trying to think the plan through. "They may think she's the target."

Osahi shrugs. "That's a possibility. We get her if we can. If not, you get out of there. Your main goal is to create enough of a diversion for us to get everyone out of here. That is our priority."

"And how are we supposed to get out of the Church once we're there?" I say. "They don't have any transfer equipment there that we can use. At least, not so far as I know."

"You'll carry the equipment with you," Osahi says.

"It'll have the coordinates of the transfer set in, so you can get out as soon as possible. It'll take you to a rendezvous point in another universe. We can move you again from there. We'll have equipment there we can use to hide your trail from the Society and the Order."

He provides some more detail on the specifics of the way station raid for the others there, but I only half listen to what he says. It is clear that I, and whoever comes with me, is to be sacrificed so that Osahi can get his people out. Even if we manage to find Ana and get off the campus and into another universe, we will be marked by our transit. The Travelers, and perhaps even the Order, will be able to follow us to the rendezvous. Maybe Osahi has equipment that can scrub the signal from us so that only a Seeker might be able to track us. Unfortunately, I happen to have a Seeker on my trail.

But I am not important to Osahi. Neither is Ana. He still believes, no doubt, that she is a Traveler. And he may be right. Regardless, he will sacrifice us both without a second thought if it means he can secure his people and keep his rebellion alive. I don't blame him. I would do the same.

As for me, I have no choice. I must go to the campus, no matter how foolhardy it may be, no matter how impossible the odds. This may be my only chance I have to get my body. I don't know how I will get myself back into it, once I do have it, but that is a problem for later. The more pressing question is whether I can remain in command of this body after I cross over. If the past is any guide, the side effects will be fierce, and eventually I will succumb to Aeida.

So I will be racing against two clocks once I am there, both of them quickly running out. The first is how long it will take the Order to determine our ruse and realize the Travelers are not descending upon them. The second is the one inside me that will determine when I weaken enough to allow Aeida to escape his bonds.

If I am lucky, I will have a few hours. If not, there will be a few desperate minutes followed by agony.

"Questions?" Osahi says, looking at me. It is as if he is daring me to point out what his intentions are.

But this is what I wanted. This is why I came here. Even if it all ends in disaster, I will go.

Osahi asks me to stay after he adjourns the meeting and everyone else leaves the citadel. He sits across from me with a solemn expression. Exhaustion lines his face, which I did not notice earlier.

"I'm putting all my trust in you," he says. "There are people who were in this room who think I am a fool. Especially after what you managed to do in Arequipa."

"I know," I say. "I can feel it."

"This plan doesn't work without you raiding the campus. It's risky. I won't lie. There's a very good chance you will be captured by the Order."

"I know," I say. "The same goes for your team at the way station. But if we don't go—if we don't try—then everyone is captured by the Watchers."

Osahi nods. "Good. I'm going to send Suon with you. She's an excellent agent, as I'm sure you realize. She can recommend some people to work with."

I nod my agreement, though I am surprised he is willing to sacrifice Suon in this mission. Has her proximity to me tainted her in some way in his mind? Or was her talk of dissatisfaction and doubt not simply words Osahi primed her with?

"She is in charge, Aeida. Let's be clear on that. You won't be chasing after Ana at all costs just to get the answers you want. When she says it's time to go, it's time to go."

"That's fine," I say. "I understand completely."

"Good. Go get ready. The next few days will be long ones, I fear," he says, with a wave of his hand. He turns to look out the window down at the vast surrounding wilderness, as though trying to take in the image of it one last time.

Suon lingers at the bottom of the tower, waiting for me. We walk back to my quarters, neither of us speaking, both absorbed in our thoughts.

"Did he tell you I'm coming?" she says as we pass by the house with its mysterious guest. Another mystery, among many, the answers to which consistently elude me.

"He did. What do you think about it?"

"It's a suicide mission," she says. "Even if they think it's a Society raid, there will be too many Order people willing to try to stop us, just to make sure we don't get to the Grand Regent."

"The odds are not in our favor," I say. "But still."

"But what?" Suon says. There are tears in her eyes.

"We have to go," I say, putting a hand around her. I lead her to my quarters and sit beside her on the bed. "We owe it to everyone here to help them get out. And who knows? We may get lucky."

We won't, I think. But I may be able to craft some of my own luck. The problem will be my state after the transfers. I need Suon there, I realize. Whoever else is with us may just abandon me to my fate. Even if they don't, they won't be willing to help me in what I need to do.

"We should talk to Osahi," I say. "There's no reason you have to lead this. He can get volunteers, I'm sure."

"He won't," she says. "He's sacrificing both of us. He doesn't trust us."

"Don't be ridiculous. He trusts you," I say. *He sent you to watch me*, I resist the urge to add.

"Not anymore," she says. "Not now."

I look at her, wondering if this is the final layer of the deception Osahi sent her upon. The weight of the moment to come seems to sit upon her. She looks as exhausted as Osahi, as worn to the core of her being. I wonder if I look the same to them. It is hard to know what I look like, what my expressions are from second to second. For all I know,

I have revealed myself to them a dozen times or more.

"We should leave," she says, looking at me, her eyes insistent. "Tonight. Now."

"What do you mean?"

"Why are we sacrificing ourselves for these people? For this faith?" Suon says with a fierceness that takes me aback. "I don't believe anymore. I don't. You're the only one I care about here. Let's just go and disappear. Leave this fight to them. Let them destroy themselves."

Is this another trap that Osahi has set for me? It seems late in the game for that, but he is unceasing in his efforts, willing to force anyone to service his plots. Even if they are unaware.

I shake my head. "We can't. I can't. I have to see this through to the end."

I want to believe Suon. I want to tell her I do. And her vision is enticing. But it is also impossible. My body lies in another universe. And no matter what universe this body finds itself in, I am certain the Seekers will be able to find me.

Suon begins to cry again, and I put my arm around her in a feeble attempt to comfort her.

"But you can go. You should go. There's no need to sacrifice yourself for this, if you don't believe in it anymore. I have no choice." I hesitate, wanting to explain why, but unable to. I tell myself it is because it would be dangerous for her to know, which is true in a way. "Don't ask why. I can't explain. But understand, I'm here to the end, whatever that may be. You don't have to be."

Suon looks at me. "I know why, Aeida. I know."

I feel my hands start to shake and force them to stop. "You don't. And you don't have to be a part of this anymore."

"I do. I love you." She hesitates, about to say something more, but does not.

This time I manage to reply in kind, though I am awash in a sea of conflicting emotions. My whole body seems about to come undone. To hide it, I embrace Suon, pulling her in close. It feels as though I am hanging on for life.

28

The next morning, Suon and I go together to the citadel. The others are already gathered there, nervous and jittery, no one looking at one another. The streets of the village are empty, the whole place eerily quiet, as if everyone has already left. They have not; they are waiting for what we will do this morning.

Suon and I spent our night together as if it was our last. That feels even more certain this morning as I am faced with not one, but two transfers. When we arrive at the campus, at the moment when I will need to act with speed and precision, I will, in all likelihood, be utterly incapacitated.

I tell Suon this as we wait for Osahi to arrive. "I'll recover. It's just a side effect from what the Acolytes did to me. But it may take a few minutes. You'll need to be in command then."

"I've never been to the campus," she says. "I'm not even from that universe."

"Don't worry," I say, acting with a confidence I do not feel. "I can talk you through it. Osahi and I will give you the lay of the land beforehand, too."

She looks doubtful but doesn't say anything. I hoped

she would gone when I woke up this morning, in spite of what she said. It would make today easier in many ways. She is one more thing for me to worry about. One more thing I can lose to the Watchers.

Osahi arrives with Nicola at his side, both of them appearing not to have slept the night before. Only De Vroes, who was present at our meeting the day before, is absent.

"You've chosen your people?" Osahi says, looking at Suon.

She nods and gestures at two of those gathered, who nod.

"Excellent. We know what you all are risking, and we will not forget it. Nicola has programmed the transfer unit for you. You'll use it for both jumps, just in case there are problems at the way station. Once you are through with them, you can just go on. You don't need to wait for them to secure the outpost. If everything goes accordingly, though, that shouldn't be an issue."

"Where are you putting us?" I say, feeling my voice vibrate with nervousness.

"The physical plant," he says. "You know it?"

"I've been to the campus in my universe," I say, which is a lie. "I imagine it's much the same."

"I'll go over the schematics with all of you once we're ready," he says, and proceeds to walk through the plan to raid the way station again.

When he is finished, Nicola takes the others who will be going with her to one side of the room to go over everything again. Osahi and the two others Suon has chosen gather around us. He pulls up a map of the campus on a screen and sets it in front of us.

"This is the physical plant," he says. "It's the western corner of the campus. There's generators and some other equipment to run water and heat across the buildings, but there won't be many people there. And anyone who is there is unlikely to be a member of the Order or armed.

From there, you'll have a few choices."

He moves his fingers on the screen, shrinking the map so that we can see the entire campus. "You can go aboveground. There are tunnels, but I wouldn't recommend them. The Order will control them and they have locks and codes. We know that Ana is in one of the dormitories. This one here."

He points at the building where I first lived as an Initiate. If Ana is indeed living there, then there must be very few Initiates on campus. Just Order members and those that the Acolytes have performed their procedures on.

"How do you know she's there?" I say. "And how can we be sure she'll be there when we arrive?"

"My sources say she's living in room 612. Sixth floor, two down from the elevator on the right. That is for certain. We can't know whether she'll be there when you arrive. Likely yes, because, according to my agent, she doesn't leave often. But there is the possibility that she's been taken somewhere."

"Who else would be in this building?" Suon says.

"The bottom floor will have a few Order people. They're there to keep watch on the rest. They've all been tamped. Or worse."

"Why keep them here?" I say, feeling a twitch of something. Intuition? Doubt?

"We don't know. I guess these are the ones Molijc doesn't trust out in the world, that he wants an eye kept on. That's why she's likely to be there. The only reason she wouldn't be is if the Acolytes are working on her."

Osahi is looking closely at me as he speaks. The twitch within me becomes more persistent.

"Okay," Suon says, her eyes intent on the screen. "So we get to here through the path of least resistance—"

"Probably along the south side of the campus, along this road," Osahi interjects. "But you'll have to be ready to improvise."

Suon nods. "Right. How many Order people are we dealing with in the building?"

"Two. Four at the absolute most. They're based in the foyer. There are side doors you can use." Osahi indicates where they can be found on the map. "They'll be locked, but I'm sure you can get in. You should be able to get upstairs without them noticing you."

"Alarms?" I say. Osahi nods.

"We can deal with them," one of Suon's chosen says.

It is all so convenient, I want to say.

"Are we set?" Osahi says. We all nod, no one speaking.

It is with increasing trepidation that I watch the lights on the transfer unit approach synchronicity. I am increasingly certain that I am walking into some sort of trap of Osahi's devising. It is too late to escape it, though. I can only hope I will come through these transfers more or less intact.

Others shift nervously beside me, and no one speaks, waiting for the moment when the wall before us will dissolve and reveal another universe. All of us have pulse weapons and the team that Nicola leads is dressed in the same military armor and garb that the extraction team Osahi sent to take Meredith and I from the Order's compound was. My team is dressed normally, weapons concealed. We do not want to attract attention, though we probably will.

I feel the pull of the other universe just before it appears atop the citadel. The light is dim and it is hard to make out where we are going, but there appears to bare concrete walls and a floor. I have a strong feeling of being underground, which gives me a sense of vertigo, given how high up I am currently. There are numbers along the one wall in an ascending sequence, moving from right to left. It is a parking garage, I realize, empty, at least this portion of it.

Someone moves behind me, as if preparing to go

across, but Nicola raises her hand in warning, her eyes still on the transfer equipment. My hands begin to tremble as the wash of the transfer channel settles over me, and I clench my fists tight, staring at Nicola, willing her to secure the channels and send us across. A numb buzzing extends up my legs, as if they are asleep, and I begin to worry that I will fall once it is time to move. I look at Suon, and she tries to smile reassuringly.

"Now," Nicola says, glancing back at the assembled.

She starts forward, stepping across into the other universe, and the rest of us follow after.

I can't see and my mouth is dry. There is a taste of blood in my throat and I cannot seem to swallow. Around me there is talk, alternately loud and quiet, and other sounds I cannot discern. A cacophony rising to a crescendo that drops away, leaving me in a vacuum.

Color returns and then forms, more gradually, still indistinct and blurred together. Nicola is issuing curt orders to her team and Suon is doing the same. Her hand is upon me, keeping me upright.

"What the hell is the matter with him?"

"He's fine. This always happens when he transfers. The Acolytes are not precise."

"Well, he better be good once we get across or you'll be up shit creek."

"You just worry about getting us across. The rest isn't your concern."

The last voice is mine, but it sounds as though it comes from another person standing across the room. I am two or three people at once, all standing in a circle, staring in at me, watchful and waiting.

"Stay with me."

A whisper. I don't know if it is Suon or one of my selves speaking. If I can stay together for a little bit longer, it will all be over. One way or another.

I can do this. You can do this. Stay with me.

"We're ready to move upstairs."

"Good. We'll go in thirty. You wait here until we've secured the site. If you don't hear from us in two minutes, or if we tell you it's gone sideways, enact your device and go across. Good luck."

A pause, and I can feel her eyes upon me, though mine will still not focus on hers. "You're going to need it."

"We'll be fine," Suon says, though she does not sound as though she believes it.

I mutter something to myself and cannot seem to stop once I have started. The words sound as though they are in a foreign language, completely unintelligible. After a moment, I realize it is one of De Gofroy's prayers in the Mayan dialect all Regents in Hierarchy must learn.

"Hold on, just a little longer," Suon whispers, taking me by the arm. Or has she been holding on to me this whole time?

"One minute," someone announces. A male voice, harsh and guttural.

"Get it ready, just in case. We want to enact it as soon as we hit two minutes."

The world sharpens into focus again as Suon speaks. We are in a parking garage, low-lit and empty, the red lights of an exit sign hovering in the periphery of my vision. There is a chill to the air, and I almost expect to see my breath form clouds as I focus on inhaling and exhaling.

"Thirty seconds."

A clatter of sound, very distant, comes from above, echoing down through the concrete. There is a sharp intake of breath from someone, perhaps me. I look at Suon, and she looks at one of the two men with us.

He nods. "On your word."

"Ten seconds."

Inhale. Exhale. My legs are still tingling, but my hands no longer shake. I am afraid to take a step.

"Time."

"Start the channels."

The man busies himself with the device, and I watch as the lights begin to flash with an arrhythmic tempo that slowly begins to resolve. The other agent begins to count forward from the two-minute point, past which we should have heard from Nicola's team.

"Thirty seconds. One minute."

"How much longer, dammit?" Suon says, the stress evident in her voice.

"Any second now," the man says.

As he speaks, I feel the other universe reaching out and the channel forming. I can see the interior of the physical plant, the large generators and other equipment, where once I followed Meredith to a rendezvous with Osahi that never took place. The thought gives me pause, but only for a moment.

"Let's go," I say.

I take Suon's hand and we go across, the others following behind.

29

Lasinha looked at me through low-lidded eyes, touching a finger to his lips and withdrawing it. No smile, not even the ghost of one, was visible. Though he was staring at me, he seemed oblivious to my presence, lost in thought.

His absent study made me uncomfortable, and adding to my unease was the presence of the man to my left. An Acolyte with an ugly, scarred face who had not spoken since our meeting began. It was unclear to me why he was there, though I also had no idea why I was there. Nothing had been said to me, but that was not unusual.

Lasinha appeared to emerge from wherever his thoughts had taken him. "Everyone has their secrets. Everyone. Don't forget that. Even the Grand Regent."

"Even you," I said. An attempt at a joke, though it felt wrong in this somber company and in this tiny windowless room the Order had built beneath Lasinha's house in West Vancouver.

To my surprise, he laughed. "Even me. The important thing is that our secrets not be made to harm the faith. Especially his. You understand, right?"

I shrugged my acquiescence. He was speaking of the Grand Regent, I knew.

"What are his secrets?" I said.

Lasinha flicked his eyes over to the Acolyte's, sharing some unspoken thought with him. I did not follow his gaze, not wanting to see the Acolyte's expression for reasons I could not express.

"We don't know. We just know there are some. We suspect..." He let his words linger in the air.

It could be anything or it could be nothing, in other words. But I knew that was not the case. Lasinha would not be here having this conversation with me if he thought the Grand Regent had nothing to hide. The Acolyte would not be here either. It was still odd that he was here, given that everyone knew the guild was allied with the Grand Regent. Some said they controlled the Church. Those were people usually brought in by the Order for the Acolytes to work on.

"I understand," I said. "You want me to find out what secrets there might be."

"He cannot know about this," Lasinha said. "Under any circumstances."

I shrugged. That did not need saying.

"His weakness is that woman. It always has been."

These words from the Acolyte, abrupt and in a gravelly voice, startled me. I nearly jumped from my seat.

Lasinha smiled and held out his hands. "He loves her, in his way. Even still."

"He doesn't see the threat she is to the faith. The people that she consorts with."

Lasinha leaned back, pursing his lips. "Oh, he understands that. He knows all too well how dangerous Laila is. Rest assured, she will be dealt with."

"On his terms," the Acolyte said.

"Yes. Well, he is the Grand Regent."

They both fell silent, staring at each other, leaving unspoken whatever other thoughts they had. It felt to me as if there were more, as if what they had said was only half the story, and it was left to me to intuit the rest. The silence bothered me, so I spoke, interjecting myself into their contemplation.

"Where would I look for these secrets, exactly?"

"There are files," Lasinha said. "From De Gofroy's time. He had files on all of us. Me, Molijc, Laila. Everyone. If there is a secret that could harm him, it would be there."

"And where are these files?"

"We don't know. Laila has them."

Lasinha put his hand on the tables, his fingers spread wide as he leaned forward. He smiled at me. I knew what that meant.

Suon crouches over me, glancing over her shoulder at something behind us. I blink, the world shifting wildly in focus. She looks back at me, sees I am awake, and puts a hand on my arm.

"We have to go," she says. "We can't wait much longer. Someone will get suspicious."

I try to nod and lever myself up, but my vision spins away and I am overwhelmed by nausea and a coughing fit. The world is black, and a shining point of light pierces the depths of my multitudinous mind.

"We don't have time for this."

"I know. Let's carry him. If we get questioned, we can say that something's gone wrong with his tamp and we're taking him to the Acolytes."

"What if we're going to the wrong way?"

"We shoot. We're on the edge of campus; so long as we head east, we have to be going in the right direction."

I feel hands underneath my arms and the world goes sideways. Soon we are moving, and I hear myself muttering my prayer to De Gofroy.

Please restore this vessel to its true self.

The hum of the generators grows louder and dissipates. Something about the sound brings my vision back to me, though it is jumpy, like a movie skipping from place to place in a scene, leaving blank spots in between. It is impossible to focus on anything as a result, and I am overwhelmed by sensation and have to close my eyes. My head aches and I return to my prayer.

Please restore this vessel to its true self.

I am an apostate. I will not be restored. I will restore myself or lose myself entirely. These are the only choices now.

"Hey. What the hell are you doing? What's happening?"

I flick my eyes and see a Regent standing before us, frowning and suspicious. Hers is an unfamiliar face. I can only hope mine is to her. But of course it will be. This face is not from this universe. Although there is an Aeida here, it is one with a different path, different memories. Not tied to me in any way.

This train of thought only confuses me, and I try to ask this stranger if she knows the other me. The me of this universe. The words come out garbled and incoherent.

"Why is he not talking in the dialect? You better have some answers, or I'm going to have call in the Order."

"Don't bother. We are the Order. This one got loose and went haywire, obviously. We've got to get him back to the Acolytes to look at."

"How the hell did he end up in here? I thought you people were supposed to be watching the realigned?"

Doubt and anger. I manage to focus again, and I can see her asking questions that will lead to trouble.

Please restore this vessel to its true self.

"We are. This one got through, but we managed to contain him. Now, if you'll excuse us, we have to get him to the Acolytes before he breaks down completely. They hate it when they have that much work to do."

"Now wait a minute. He must have come here for some reason. I need to make sure he hasn't done anything. There's important equipment here."

"We really don't have time. The Acolytes—"

"Can wait. I just need to see—"

The odd percussive sound of a pulse weapon discharge echoes through the machinery. I see the woman sprawled upon the ground, her face slack and amused. What does she find so funny?

"Why did you do that? I was talking our way out of it."

"No you weren't. Not fast enough. We were gonna have the whole Order on us by the time she was finished looking around."

An alarm begins to sound, shrill and persistent.

"We may anyway," Suon says, disgusted. "Let's get going."

We start forward again, Suon on my left and one of the others on my right. My vision seems to be stabilizing, my senses returning, enough that I can feel the tremors echoing through my whole body. The buzz of conversations in my head is quieting. Aeida surfaces for a moment here and there, but I hold him at bay. At least I hope.

As we pass down a corridor, I realize where we are, and a thought occurs. Osahi's expression as he told us the plan for this raid looms suddenly in the foreground. He does not expect us to succeed. I blink it away and slump to my left so that my full weight is on Suon. She grunts and her knees buckle, though she manages to keep herself upright.

"Careful."

"The door," I say as we pass it, mumbling into her ear.

"We have to get moving," she says, working with the other to shift my weight so I am evenly distributed between them.

"The door," I say, more insistent this time. I try to plant my feet to stop our forward progress, but I am too feeble to do more than slow our pace.

"It has a passcode," the other says.

"I know it. The door."

Suon pauses, looking at me. "Osahi said."

"Never mind him. The door. I know the code."

After a moment, during which doubt and other

emotions war across her features, she nods. "Okay. Let's try it."

"What the hell are we doing? We need to get going," the other ahead of us says.

"He was in the Order," Suon says. "He knows their codes. He knows his way around the campus."

"He's never been here before," the other on my arm says.

"I have. And I know the code," I say, hoping that somehow that is true. The codes at Lasinha's compound in Aeida's world were not changed. They may not have changed these either.

Suon hesitates again, looking from me to the others and back again. I hold my head steady and meet her gaze, trying to compel her. We will be captured if we stay aboveground. Osahi wants us caught, I want to say, but don't.

"Let's try it."

They carry me over and I study the keypad, trying to get my eyes to focus on the individual numbers. My hands are shaking so badly that I cannot hold them steady enough to press the numbers. I tell them to Suon, who punches them in. The door hisses and unlocks, and we step through to a short corridor that ends in a set of stairs that descends to the tunnels below.

We encounter no one as I guide the others through the tunnels. They are empty, as I suspected they would be. Lasinha will be careful about who can access them, far more careful than we once were. Only he and a few other select from the Order will know the codes. They were also probably alerted to our presence as soon as we unlocked the door, so I can only hope that Nicola's subterfuge with the Society markers on the transfer device is working.

I cannot rely on hope, though, so other precautions will have to be taken. I cast through my mind for what they might be, and find only Aeida staring at me from every corner.

"Are you all right?"

"It's nothing."

"Are you sure? Your voice is…"

"Just the side effects. They'll wear off soon. My legs almost feel good enough to stand on."

Suon looks at me doubtfully.

"Yes," I say. "Let me try walking. I'll need to soon enough if we're going to get anywhere."

One of the others lets me go, but Suon keeps supporting me, and we make our slow way down the dim corridor. The others are ahead, and I call out when they come to a crossroads. We are nearing our destination, and my thoughts are everywhere all at once.

Aeida. It will not be long. No matter what, it will not be long. I don't have enough time.

"This is it," I say, as a black cloud floats across my vision, as depthless as the void that once swallowed me, swallowed us both.

The others go to the door, and I repeat the code. They enter it and the door opens. Above I can see light, an empty stairway. Only for a moment. It dissolves, and time stops for an instant. I am there and then I am not.

When I open my eyes next, I am on the ground. Suon is at my side. "We have to wait," she says. "We can't go on with him like this."

"No," I say. "We can't afford to wait anymore. They may be in the tunnels. You go ahead. We'll be behind you as fast as we can."

The others look at Suon, who reluctantly nods. They turn and go through, the door swinging shut behind them. As soon as I hear it lock, I scramble to my feet and lurch to the door. At the keypad, I enter in the overrides that will allow me to change the codes.

"What are you doing?" Suon says.

She rushes toward me, but I hold her off, surprising her with a brief show of strength. By the time she manages to push me aside, it is too late—I have changed the passcodes for the entire set of tunnels. She turns to where I am leaning against the wall, my eyes opening and closing, fighting the blackness that looms all around, trying to remain for a few moments longer.

"You have to unlock this," she says, taking me by the arms. "We can't leave them to the Order. And what about Ana?"

"It doesn't matter," I say. "She's not there. And I have someone else I need to see."

30

I walk down the corridor as quickly as I am able, though I have to keep a hand against one of the walls for support. Suon watches me go, still standing by the door, paralyzed by indecision. She will not let me get far.

"You can't just leave them there," she yells after me, her voice breaking with strain and emotion.

I ignore her and continue on, stumbling and lurching. My vision comes and goes, blurring and resolving, only to be subsumed by darkness. The light returns for now. My thoughts are the same. Tenuous and incomplete, short-circuited by the others in my brain.

Behind me, I hear Suon start to follow, and I choke back a sob of relief. I cannot do this alone. I need her, even if it means condemning her to whatever fate awaits me should I fail. I will fail. I am out of time. But there is no choice left, not now. I've wrecked the boats upon the shore.

"What the fuck do you think you're doing?"

"Ana is not up there. Osahi was lying."

"How you know that?" Suon steps in front of me, halting my forward progress.

I try to steady my gaze upon her. "You yourself as

much as said you thought this was a setup. It is. Ana is too important to them. And to the Society. They'll have her somewhere where they can watch her constantly."

"And you know where?" Suon swallows, glancing over her shoulder as if she suspects the Order will be upon us at any moment.

"No. I doubt she's even in this universe. Too risky. But that's not who I'm after."

I try to step past her, but she will not let me. I used all my strength in thwarting her earlier. "Who, then?"

"Remember what you said last night about walking away? Leaving the Church, the faith, and all this fighting behind? Come with me and that's what we'll do. I promise. I just need to find someone first."

Suon looks at me, wanting to believe, but not quite able to. "And what about those other two? We leave them to their fate?"

"I didn't know if I could trust them. They're Osahi's people. Besides, they have the transfer device. They can go when they want."

She had forgotten about that. I can see panic swim to the surface of her face. "How the fuck are we supposed to transfer out of here, then?"

"We aren't going to," I say. "We just have to get off campus and stay clear of the Order for a while."

There is little hope of that in my state. But I don't say that to her. It will only worry her more. And now I need her focused on getting us to where I need to go. It will not be long until I am subsumed. What can I do in the time that remains to me? We shall see. First, we must go to the Grand Regent's tower.

After our meeting, Lasinha and the Acolyte stayed together and discussed other matters that were outside of my purview. When they were done, they came to the transfer room, where I set up the channels to send the Acolyte over. Lasinha shook the man's hand and left me to the task. As I worked to set up the channels and match them to a Society transfer from the schedules we had, I could feel the Acolyte's eyes upon me.

"Lasinha does not fear her as much as he should," the Acolyte said. He was talking about Laila, resuming our earlier conversation. "You've seen her?"

I nodded. "Once."

I recalled that day, when the Grand Regent had come to induct me into the Order. She had been difficult to read, more so even that Lasinha in some ways. But I had not thought her a threat, or even particularly dangerous. The Grand Regent had seemed that, with his volatile moods. And I had seen enough of Lasinha to know what lurked behind his smile.

"She is a great danger. Make no mistake. I've long counseled the Grand Regent that we should deal with her. I only hope it is not too late."

I nodded again, not replying. I knew what that meant.

"Do you ever wonder about what we are doing here?"

"The Order, you mean?" I said, taking care not to say anything that would reveal my true thoughts before a man who would, without a second thought, remake my brain.

"The Order. The Church. Us. All of it. We are the only thing that stands between chaos and all the universes. Do not forget that, Aeida."

He paused, his expression suggesting he thought he had said too much.

"Of course," I said, daring to look at him closely for the first time. He met my gaze and I felt a shiver of fear race up my spine.

"Send me across," he said, and I did.

"Where are we?" I manage to say. My throat is so dry. Everything aches.

"We're near the tower. At least, that's what you said." Suon's breath is warm against my lips. I want to kiss her, to draw her into my arms. "We need to stop. You're not well."

"I'll be all right soon enough. We have to keep going."

I pull myself to my feet, using her for support, and look around. We are in a junction I recognize instantly, even with my fractured vision. There are lights blinking in the darkness behind my eyes. I know what they portend. Time is my enemy now. It always has been.

"This way," I say. "Quickly."

We go along the corridor until we come to the door I know leads into the tower. I go to it and punch in the new code while Suon looks on nervously. She is expecting to see Order guards waiting for us on the other side, but I know there won't be.

"Where is everyone?" she says when I pull the door open and my suspicions are confirmed.

"They know where we're going," I say. "They're expecting us."

"Then why don't they stop us?"

"That's not what he wants," I say.

Suon blinks, a look of fear crossing over her face. She knows who I mean. Even so, she follows me to the elevator. A code is required there, but the one I used in the tunnels works here as well. Of course it does. He has been longing for this moment just as much as I have.

We ascend in silence, watching the numbers rise. I pull out my pulse weapon and adjust the settings. Suon glances at me and takes out her own weapon. Her breathing is unsteady. Everything about me is, of course. It is too much to think that I can escape this now; that much is clear. The void looms too near, and Aeida as well. I have one chance to set things right. I hope.

Our arrival is announced by a ping, and the doors slide open.

The corridor leading from the elevators is empty, which does surprise me. Perhaps I am wrong about this. I have been wrong about so much. Suon lingers behind in the periphery of my disjointed vision. Maybe I am wrong about her too. Aeida thinks so, but I am not yet sure. It does not matter; my time is short.

Morris is waiting for us at the door to Molijc's audience chamber. He is standing erect and alert, and looks at us with a blank face.

"Hello, Morris," I say in a gentle voice as we near.

"Who are you?" he says, staring at us.

I hesitate on my name. "Don't you remember?"

A cloud passes over his face. "I don't...I don't remember."

"Will you let us in?" I say, aware that Suon is behind us, her weapon aimed at Morris.

"What is your name?"

I glance at Suon. "Laila."

Morris nods and steps aside, gesturing for me to pass. I go to open the door, and Suon steps forward to follow me. Morris pulls out a pulse weapon of his own and points it at her. Suon raises hers and they face each other, she uneasy and he blank-faced.

"Wait here," I say. "It will be all right."

Suon looks as though she doesn't believe me and wants to argue, but I shake my head. Before she can say anything to dissuade me, I push open the door and stride in.

The chamber is as I remember it: glistening marble floors and walls lined with Mayan artifacts, and at its center on a dais raised above the rest of the room, a throne. Molijc sits upon it, staring down upon me, hatred in his eyes.

"The prodigal child returns," he says in a loud voice that echoes across the room.

It makes us tremble and shake, and it is hard to step forward, even as he beckons us nearer. I clench the pulse weapon tight, its metal digging into my hand. Opposing thoughts war in my mind, clouds drifting across a vast, impenetrable sky. The darkness of night looms at its edges, approaching soon. Are we going toward it, a ship caught inexorably in a current?

"You have your chance now," Molijc says, his voice curdling with black humor. "I'm here, unarmed and unprotected. What are you going to do, Laila?"

I blink at him. What are we going to do? My time is short. I can feel it. And I have failed in what I came here to do, but there is still a chance to do something. To do something that will help set things right. If I can. I look at the pulse weapon in my hand and know what must be done, with a sureness that courses through me and banishes all the other thoughts clattering in my broken head.

Dejian is looking at me curiously, still so certain of himself and all he has orchestrated. We are all things he plays with. I take a step forward, the night drawing ever nearer in my mind. My path is clear and I must take it now, before we are subsumed.

As I take another step, I emerge from behind the throne and stand beside the Grand Regent, putting a hand upon his shoulder. I look down at him and he smiles at me. I smile in turn.

My whole being shatters at the sight. I want to scream, but the darkness is upon the horizon. It is everywhere around us, a seething monstrosity. I take a step forward and nearly fall.

Molijc smiles at my struggles. "What are you here for?"

I blink. The universe goes dark and then there is light. I open my eyes and raise my pulse weapon. Dejian looks uneasy and uncertain. I smile and kneel before him.

"I am your faithful vessel. David Aeida, sub-Regent of the Watchers' Order."

EXCERPT:

THE DOUBLE
VOLUME FOUR OF
THE SOJOURNERS CYCLE

David Aeida now commands his body, having cast Laila aside. He has sworn fealty to the Grand Regent, who wants him by his side and sees that his loyalty is rewarded.

But the Grand Regent is not the man he was. He is paranoid and suspicious of everyone, isolated in his tower, and thirsting for vengeance against those he feels have wronged him. How long until he turns on Aeida as well?

That is only the beginning of Aeida's problems. For he knows the Seeker and the Society of Travelers remain to play their parts. Both desire nothing more than the utter destruction of the Church of Regents and all its works. And though Laila has been defeated, he knows better than anyone not to assume she has been vanquished.

1

The Grand Regent sits upon his throne surveying the audience room atop De Gofroy's tower. I stand at his side, as expressionless as I can manage, though I am suppressing a grin of delight. At long last I have returned to my rightful place. A sub-Regent of the Watcher's Order. A servant to the Grand Regent. A shield against all those who would stand against the faith.

The Grand Regent studies those gathered before him, casting his eyes from one face to the next, as though seeking to penetrate whatever walls they have built up to keep their secrets from the faith. That is against the Protocols, as we all know. What his gaze tells them is that he will see them revealed. And my presence says that, if he is unable to, the Order shall do the work for him.

Everyone here knows what that means, some of us only too well. I see Morris Loverne, that traitor, now rendered compliant, standing alert and stiff at the back of the audience chamber, ready to act should the need arise. It will not. His remaining loyalists within the Church have been arrested and subjected to the Acolyte's m,inistrations. The rest are scattered to the winds. But with what he has already revealed and what I know, we shall find the rest soon enough. Laila Johar, the companion of my mind, and enemy of the faith has been overthrown and banished. I rule this flesh now. She is but a distant voice I barely hear. I have choked the life from her.

It still feels strange to stand here in my own body, to have it respond to my thoughts, to think what I wish to think, and to act as I see fit. I want to luxuriate in the glorious sensation of it all. To be me again, to be truly me. There are the memories the Acolytes stole from me, but that is a nuisance, nothing more. They can be restored, surely, and Laila removed from within me. I will ask the Grand Regent when the time is right.

For now I watch him, savoring my moment of triumph. Our triumph. At length he stands and begins to speak.

"I am here to welcome back a faithful vessel to the Church and the Watchers' Order. David Aeida." He pauses to turn to me and I bow to him. An ironic smile crosses his lips. "David Aeida has been a faithful vessel. More than any of you will ever know. Perhaps more than even he himself is aware.

"He has returned to us after some time abroad." Here he offers a small gesture with his fingers and another ironic smile. "Much has changed since he left and he has learned much about our enemies, as he has told me a little. I will learn more from him in the coming days, I am sure, for David has much to share."

He rewards me with a warm smile. I am unable to stop myself from beaming. Looking out over the assembled I am met by blank, unwavering stares. The grim, expressionless visages of those gathered unsettles me. How many here have been brought before the Acolytes to be returned to the ranks of the faithful? Morris Loverne for one. Myself for another.

I scan the faces, looking for anyone familiar. There are a few of the loyalist High Regents—at least they were High Regents when I was last involved in the Order—and surely they would be left untouched by the Acolytes, or else they would have been removed from their positions. The Grand Regent cannot keep those he does not trust so near and in such influential positions in the Hierarchy. Their unchanging stares and similar expressions all leave me with a sense of deep disquiet.

The Grand Regent pauses, considering his next words. "The last years have been difficult for the faith. De Gofroy's vision was almost vanquished. I have fought to ensure that the quest for the one true universe can continue, and now I feel we are closer than ever to achieving it. Many have fallen in the pursuit of that quest and we should remember them now."

He looks to the ceiling solemnly, intoning a brief prayer, his words so quiet I cannot make them out. When he is finished, he turns back to the assembled. "And make no mistake, we must stay on our guard. The Order has done wonderful work in rooting out the Society agents in our midst, to say nothing of the apostates who would pervert De Gofroy's words. We are so near to triumphing over them both. I can feel it in my soul.

"David Aeida is central to that effort," he says, as if suddenly recalling that I am present, standing beside him. "There will be difficult days that lie ahead, for all of us. But now we are on the path to reuniting our fragmented beings with our true selves—to be Regents no more—I feel certain these sacrifices will all be worth it. We shall save, not only ourselves, but billions across untold universes. Never forget that what we do, all we sacrifice, is for them."

The Grand Regent nods, a dismissal of sorts. Those assembled bow as one being and shuffle out the door under the watchful gaze of Morris Loverne, who resumes his post outside the audience chamber door. The Grand Regent turns to me, the ironic smile returning to his face.

"We have much to discuss, David Aeida. Much to discuss. Where would you have us begin?"

I swallow and try to meet the Grand Regent's gaze, but am unable to. The sharp blue of his eyes seems to cut through my defenses, piercing right to the center of me. Laila was never so intimidated as I am, seeing him for what he is. A leader of the faith, but a man, nonetheless, and fallible in the way all of us are. It is that second I have difficulties reconciling myself with. She loved him and was loved by him and I have seen those memories from a distance when my mind was not my own.

He is not to be trusted, that much I know and need to keep reminding myself. He will use me as he sees fit, casting me aside or sending me to my doom, telling himself it is for the greater good of the faith. He may not even be wrong. I have my own ends to see to, though, and I will need to protect myself. So there are some things that I have seen in Laila's mind that will stay mine, at least for now

The Grand Regent is waiting for me to speak. I hesitate, unsure what tact to use, ultimately deciding to throw caution to the wind and ask for what I truly desire. "Now that I have returned and proven my absolute loyalty to the faith, I would like to have her removed from my mind." I will not say her name.

His expression does not change but his eyes harden at my words. "That is impossible, I'm afraid."

"Grand Regent, I know the Acolytes can do this. And it must be done. So long as she remains within me, I am a danger to you."

He frowns, sitting down upon his throne and resting his chin upon his hand. "You told me you had vanquished her."

"I have," I say. "But can you afford to risk me being wrong? I know what her thoughts about you and the faith are. She will stop at nothing to destroy you."

The Grand Regent's face darkens and I fear I have gone too far. He never did like to hear how Laila truly felt about him, even when she told him herself. It is important for him to believe that, in spite of all that has happened, all that has come between them, she still loves him.

"I think you misjudge her. You do not know her as I do," the Grand Regent says in a wistful voice.

I am unable to stop myself from recalling the moment when I asserted myself completely over Laila, when her own body—and whatever was in its mind—emerged from behind this very throne to derail her sense of herself. What else does the Grand Regent do with that compliant flesh? I suspect the answer is entirely unpleasant, though I am hardly one to cast aspersions in that regard.

"But it doesn't matter, even if you're right," he continues, musing more to himself than to me. "We need access to Laila's memories in a controlled environment, now that we know she has been working with the Seeker for as long as she has."

I want to interrupt and say this was a recent development, that her earlier dalliance with the Society was more a dalliance with Ana than anything else, at least from what I have witnessed. Her current arrangement was a forced one, she was given no choice. But I can sense he does not wish to be interrupted and that such nuances will only make him less likely to accede to my wishes. I need him on my side and believing in me, if I am to convince him that removing Laila is a benefit to us all.

Most importantly of all, I cannot let him know that Laila is gone, vanished from my mind. At least for the moment. I am not fool enough to believe that she is gone for good. That is why I want her removed, so there can be no doubt. This body is mine.

When I banished her it was not like when she wrested control from me and the blank construct the Acolytes built in this body. Throughout all of that I have been more or less aware, though powerless to do anything, unable to take command of my body for more than a few fleeting moments. Now she is gone, utterly, and I cannot see any of her thoughts and memories, as she could see mine and I hers when we were intermingled. All I have is what I can remember of what I have seen, which will have to be enough.

"There are things she knows that we will need to know." He nods, as though to assure himself this is correct. "Besides, I have the perfect guard against her return. Someone who will know beyond any doubt if she is mounting an effort to replace you."

He smiles, an infuriating smile. I do not need to be told who it is to know. Glancing over his shoulder, he calls to someone in the rooms behind the audience chamber.

"You may show yourself now."

I watch, alternating between fury and despair, as Meredith emerges to stand beside the throne.

THE DOUBLE will be available in April 2018.

ABOUT THE AUTHOR

Clint Westgard is the author of The Shadow Men Trilogy and the science fiction epic The Sojourners Cycle. In addition, he has published a work of historical fantasy set in colonial Peru, The Maleficio Chronicles, and a retelling of the Minotaur legend, The Trials of the Minotaur. Clint Westgard lives in Calgary, Alberta.

ALSO BY CLINT WESTGARD

The Double
Volume Four of The Sojourners Cycle

David Aeida now commands his body, having cast Laila
aside. He has sworn fealty to the Grand Regent, who
wants him by his side and sees that his loyalty is rewarded.

But the Grand Regent is not the man he was. He is
paranoid and suspicious of everyone, isolated in his tower,
and thirsting for vengeance against those he feels have
wronged him. How long until he turns on Aeida as well?

That is only the beginning of Aeida's problems. For he
knows the Seeker and the Society of Travelers remain to
play their parts. Both desire nothing more than the utter
destruction of the Church of Regents and all its works.
And though Laila has been defeated, he knows better than
anyone not to assume she has been vanquished.

The epic fourth volume of the Sojourners Cycle centers
upon the many betrayals and lies at the heart of the faith of
the Church of Regents and the devastation upon the lives
of the faithful they have wrought. Desire and guilt, love
and revenge, rage and despair will drive them all, with
consequences for all the universes.

ALSO BY CLINT WESTGARD

The Sojourner
Volume Five of The Sojourners Cycle

Laila's strange and reluctant alliance with the Seeker continues, though she does not know where it will lead her. She fears it will place her in another prison, worse than the one she has just managed to escape.

But her escape is not entirely complete. For though she has been restored to her own flesh, parts of Aeida somehow still remain. Along with some other she does not recognize. Is this some aftereffect of the Acolyte's bizarre procedure? Or the result of the Seeker's meddling?

All this pales in comparison to what Laila soon discovers. That she has an unwanted part to play in an ancient struggle for who will rule the crossings between the universes and all that lies in them.

In the stunning conclusion to the Sojourners Cycle Laila will be faced with a terrible choice, one that will decide her fate and humanity's.

ALSO BY CLINT WESTGARD

Realm of Shadows
Volume One of The Shadow Men
An Alkemya Novel

Craitol and Renuih, two empires a world apart, divided by
the desert that lies between them. A desert ruled by the
Shadow Men.

An uneasy peace holds sway in both realms, hiding
longstanding feuds and bitter rivalries. Until a Shadow
Men raid on Renuih shatters the calm and sets in motion
events no one can control.

Masiph id Ezern, unfavored son of the Imperial Vazeir,
finds himself a hero following the raid. His father remains
unmoved by his exploits and, in his bitterness, Masiph will
find himself a reluctant participant in a plot against the
empire.

As he finds himself drawn deeper and deeper into the
conspiracy, he soon realizes there will be no escaping the
realm of shadows, where intrigue and betrayal abound.
And though the Shadow Men have gone quiet, they will
not stay silent forever…

ALSO BY CLINT WESTGARD

Council of Shadows
Volume Two of The Shadow Men
An Alkemya Novel

Discontent continues to fester within the realms of Craitol and Renuih, fed by intrigues carried out in the shadows. As rivals and apostates struggle for supremacy, a long incubated plan begins to unfold.

Vyissan, a mysterious alkemycal practitioner arrives in Renuih, the latest strike in a long war over who shall control the secrets of alkemya and Craitol itself. He carries with him a secret that, once revealed, will reverberate across all realms. Before he can reveal it though, the conspirators against the emperor will strike their own blow.

But now, a new and more powerful menace looms on the horizon. The Shadow Men have gained the secrets of the Council Adept's alkemya and no one can be certain what they will do with it...

ALSO BY CLINT WESTGARD

Dance of Shadows
Volume Three of The Shadow Men
An Alkemya Novel

War with the Shadow Men looms in both realms as the consequences of the Gvers' Council in Craitol begin to make themselves known. A war that could end in glorious triumph or bitter disaster.

Doubt shadows everyone's steps, for they know there are no certainties in the desert. Especially now the Shadow Men have made the art of alkemya their own.

No one has more questions than Vyissan, for he is working in service to a cause he is no longer sure he believes in. And now he must undertake a journey with those who both loathe and fear him. Before the first sword is drawn, his life will be under threat.

But his will not be the only one, for somewhere in the desert the Shadow Men lie in wait...

ALSO BY CLINT WESTGARD

Unspeakable Rites
An Alkemya Novella

A dead man of no family or account is what Gahryll, Chief
Magister of Tson, sees when the corpse of an Enir youth is
brought to the Magisterium. But Magister Mihuibel sees
something else: a conspiracy involving false adepts
practicing an outlawed form of alkemya.

Against his better instincts Gahryll authorizes an
investigation that draws both Magisters into the seamy
underbelly of Tson where the rich and powerful prey upon
the desperate. When the inquiry implicates one of the most
important families in the Realm of Craitol in forbidden
practices and false alkemya, their positions and ranks will
be threatened.

But that is only the beginning. For the killer will stop at
nothing to ensure his secrets remain hidden and Gahryll is
brought face to face with the unspeakable power of
alkemya that has been unleashed. It forces him to make a
choice. Will he risk everything to fight for justice in a
realm ruled where rank and wealth are all that matter?

Set in the same universe as The Shadow Men Trilogy,
Unspeakable Rites, further explores the nature of alkemya,
its terrible power, and the heavy price paid for its use.

ALSO BY CLINT WESTGARD

The Maleficio Chronicles

Luisa is always more than she appears. Rumor and mystery surround her. And strange events seem to follow wherever she goes.

Born in Lima, City of Kings, to a noble family, her father so fears her true nature that he banishes her to a convent. There she falls under the suspicion of the Inquisition and decides to flee.

Disguised as a man, she embarks upon a series of wild adventures, dueling, carousing, and gambling her way across colonial Peru. But everything changes when someone recognizes her for what she truly is, and soon she finds herself fighting for her very survival.

In a world where she will always stand apart, Luisa undergoes a strange journey, marked by betrayal and murder, terrible powers and mysterious strangers. *The Maleficio Chronicles* is her incredible confession and a story like no other.

ALSO BY CLINT WESTGARD

The Trials of the Minotaur

In the fifth year of the rule of Auten the One Eyed a minotaur is born to one of Colosi's most important families.

Taken from his mother as a newborn, exiled and cast from his family, the minotaur vows to return to the imperial city and take his rightful place as a patrician in the empire. But the patriarch of the family, his grandfather, will stop at nothing to see this blemish to his honor destroyed.

And so begins an epic journey, through lands beyond imagining, marked by despair and exile, triumph and betrayal. At its heart lies a quest to be free.